DAISIES ARE OUR SILVER

To
Morag &
Derek
with lots
of love,

Keep
Smiling!
26.3.02

Daisies Are Our Silver

Annie MacLennan

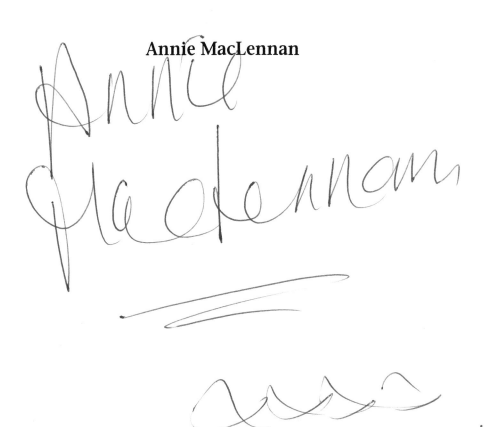

Pentland Books
Durham · Edinburgh · Oxford

© Annie MacLennan 2001

First published in 2001 by
Pentland Books
1 Hutton Close
South Church
Bishop Auckland
Durham

British Library Cataloguing in Publication Data.
A catalogue record for this book is available
from the British Library.

ISBN 1-85821-848-9

Typeset by George Wishart & Associates, Whitley Bay.
Printed and bound by Antony Rowe Ltd., Chippenham.

Dedication

This book is dedicated to all those who thought I couldn't, or wouldn't, finish this work but more especially it is dedicated to my husband John, who not only has read every word at least twice, but believed that I could and would. It was with his constant encouragement and support that this novel was born. I will never be able to express my feelings of thanks.

I hope this dedication will say more than I ever could. So to you, John, my endless love.

Annie MacLennan
August 1998

'Without a past, we have no future'

Origin unknown

Chapter 1

Vera Surridge was sitting on the kitchen steps enjoying the afternoon sunshine as she shelled peas. The long garden rolled out in front of her. The coarse grass which served as a lawn was well trimmed and bordered with a mass of brightly coloured blooms and shrubs. The uniform planting, tallest at the back, shortest at the front, reflected the need for unity and order for the future. At the end of the narrow garden stood a gnarled old apple tree, which still managed to fruit; however, when the eyes took in the surroundings the garden was flanked by a chain link fencing with concrete posts at regular intervals. The obvious lack of interest in disguising the plainness was an underlying need for community spirit and a shared feeling of well being. Across the gardens a continuous stream of conversations could be heard, always conducted from the kitchen doors.

The Surridge family had quite happily left four damp rooms in a dirty back street of Victoria to live on this sprawling south east London estate. Prospective tenants would wait uncomplaining for years, once their name was on the housing list which was always full.

Vera's understanding of anything needing a green finger or two was at best just a misty memory of being jostled through hop fields.

Vera's faded cotton print button through dress was pulled up to her knees, showing a pair of long, tanned, shapely legs that gleamed in the afternoon sun. Occasionally her neat even features twitched nervously over her shoulder listening for the key in the front door. Her nose though long did not detract from her prettiest features, her wide sparkling dark blue eyes that showed a deep seated nervousness.

Her mother, Mabel's, overdue arrival had put her on edge as she hadn't yet finished shelling the peas, and Vera knew her mother would have something to say. She shifted nervously across the step. The newspaper spread across her knees slipped down her legs; she made a grab for it, the heavy enamel pan filled with water and the freshly podded peas caught in the folds of her skirt. As she lunged forward the pan tumbled off the step onto the concrete that now looked like a moving mass of green. The culinary tragedy was endorsed as the large pan rolled helplessly and comically around. Vera was on her feet now. She groaned inwardly as she was not given to verbal outbursts. The full skirt of her dress was soaked and a few peas fell like green raindrops, plopping onto the wet concrete. 'Oh no!'

Behind her she heard her mother's voice. 'Gawd girl, let's be thankful you never went into service. 'Ere, take this!' Mabel thrust a broom into her daughter's helpless hand. 'Don't just stand there, sweep it up!' There was no anger in Mabel's voice, just resignation that her day dreaming daughter had 'done it again'. 'It's about time you learned how to . . .' She didn't finish as she knew it was falling on deaf ears and Vera was, well, just Vera. She watched the distraught figure sweeping away the green wave. Vera took the coal shovel and tipped the peas and pods into the dustbin. As she stepped into the cool of the kitchen her mother always screamed at her. ''Ave you no decency? You 'aven't got no shoes on!'

Vera looked down at her feet; her head dropped to her chest. Her wet feet had made definite footprints on the cardinal red painted floor. She looked up at her mother who had eased her hefty frame into the equally large solid kitchen chair. Mabel sat shaking her head.

'You'd best make some tea. You can do that?' Mabel said sharply. 'Put some shoes on girl,' she urged.

Vera walked out of the kitchen into the even cooler narrow passage. Mabel watched her daughter and tutted and clicked her teeth. She was hot; her feet had swollen as had her ankles. She stood up awkwardly, taking her weight on the swollen knuckles of her clenched fists. Within a couple of steps she reached for her apron from the hook on the back of the kitchen door. She muttered to herself as she wrapped the garment around her bulk. She threaded the ties into the side slits, puffing as she did so. Opening the larder door she noted, 'Mmm, no more peas, just as well it's veg round day.'

Vera's lithesome form appeared in the kitchen. Mabel looked down at her youngest daughter's feet, now clad in navy blue leather sandals. As she raised her head their eyes met. Mabel nodded approval.

What about this tea then?' Wordlessly Vera took the kettle from the gas stove and mechanically filled it from the single tap that sat high above the kitchen sink. She turned to the shelf above her and taking a box of matches, lit the gas ring, firmly setting the kettle down onto the ring which hissed loudly in the uncomfortable silence.

'Where's our Sylvie, then?' Mabel asked.

'Having tea with Doris,' Vera replied.

'Oh, we all know what that means, all bloater paste sandwiches and white tablecloth.' Mabel's tone was derisory.

Vera said gently – she never rose to her mother's baiting or biting comments, 'I don't think so, I think they are having a dollies' tea party in the garden.'

'Dolly daydreaming,' was her mother's response. 'Dolly daydream' was how Mabel always referred to her youngest daughter. It wasn't a term of endearment. Vera was a day dreamer. It was day dreaming over tuppenny novelettes which caused her all her troubles. Vera was the youngest of three daughters; her two brothers had been killed during the war. Her mother had been widowed for more than twenty years. Vera had no memories or strong recollections of her father, other than disjointed family stories and a few faded photographs. All she knew for certain was that he had been more than twenty years Mabel's senior, and that there had been some talk of how they had eloped. If there had been a grain of truth in the stories, no one had the courage of their curiosity ever to challenge Big Mabel. Vera's mother was known to all as Big Mabel; but no one had the guts to call her Big Mabel to her face!

Old Mrs Timms, a family friend, who was the nearest Big Mabel ever got to having a friend, had told Vera, in confidence of course, that 'you're a change of life mistake'. Vera hadn't a notion of what the woman meant, but the word 'mistake' had stayed fixed in her memory. There was no love lost between the sisters. Gladys couldn't stand her sister Rose, but had a genuine affection for her youngest sister, Vera. Vera always felt uncomfortable and distanced from her eldest sister Rose, whose only interest in her youngest sister was to inflict as many cutting remarks as possible about Sylvia, Vera's daughter, who had been born without the benefit of a known father. In Rose's eyes, that was tantamount to eternal damnation, although Vera couldn't understand why. The family wasn't in the least religious, except for weddings, funerals and christenings – and those were sorely lacking in the Surridge family.

Wearily Vera reached for the cups and saucers which were stacked on a shelf above the scrubbed wood table. Placing the cups rim down on the saucers, she then reached into the larder for the blue glass sugar bowl which stood on three large silver lion paws. This simple object had always puzzled her. Why only three? She'd never seen a lion with only three paws. The everyday white enamel tea pot stood on the back of the stove.

Before she could rinse it out, Mabel said, 'It's Ronnie's veg round today, take this,' and from the large pocket of her apron she removed a leather saddle-stitched purse. From it she took a half crown and handed to Vera.

'What about your tea?'

'After all these years I think I can manage a cuppa tea,' Mabel said irritably. The hot afternoon made its presence felt. Vera took the coin and slipped it into the pocket of her skirt.

''Ere, girl, don't go losing that now. And whilst I thinks about it, don't you go forgetting your housekeeping. It's Friday, and food don't grow on trees.'

Vera took no notice of her mother's ludicrous remark.

Mabel continued 'It's just gone three now. If you wait on the green he should be 'ere soon. If 'e gives you the usual in a sack, 'ave a good butcher's, you can't trust 'is kind.'

'The usual', Vera repeated.

Mabel nodded, dismissed her with a wave from her flabby hand and rose unsteadily to make the tea.

Vera hated this job. In fact she hated Ronnie. He was always leering. His teeth were a dirty yellow, short and unevenly spaced. She always kept an arm's length away from him. Stepping from the front step and through the gate, she could see a few of the boys playing cricket on the green. She was pleased to leave the house as she felt restless. The boys waved and a chorus of ''Ello Vera,' rang around the green. She waved back at them, smiling. She sat down on the kerbside, smoothed her skirt over and down her legs, and hugged her knees waiting for the van's arrival.

She didn't have to wait long. Ronnie's arrival was heralded by a loud blast of the van's horn. 'Typical,' Vera thought. Before the vehicle screeched to a halt Ronnie yelled ''Ello our Vera, Usual?'

He had already jumped from the cab and was tugging at the chains holding back the tailboard. Without taking his eyes off Vera, his arm disappeared, searching for the sack. Vera had stood up and with the sun behind her, an extra lecherous gleam arrived his eye as he slowly surveyed her sun-silhouetted shapely curves through her now transparent dress. He smacked his lips loudly, then dragged a grimy hand across his salivating mouth. When Vera didn't move, Ronnie slung the sack over his shoulder and dumped it on the kerb at her feet. Vera rummaged in her pocket for the money. Without thinking she had raised her skirt in search of the seam pocket.

'Very nice,' Ronnie said slowly, his eyes still travelling over her as the front of her dress dropped in sympathy with her search. Relief flooded over her when she found the coin. With an outstretched arm she handed it to Ronnie.

'Just get yer some change then.'

4

His eyes were still on Vera as his fingers fumbled in his money bag. He swaggered towards her. Taking her right hand he pressed the coins into her palm slowly and deliberately, closing each long slender finger over the money. 'There you are, girl. Don't you go spendin' it all at once, eh?' A filthy dirty nicotine stained finger wagged under her nose.

Still silent, Vera lifted the sack onto her shoulder and walked to the gate wordlessly. Ronnie watched her every move and rubbed a hand across his unshaven chin. 'Funny that one,' he muttered. Then, he added quickly, ''spose we'll be seeing you down the dance?' With a leap into the cab, the engine revved and he was gone. Vera struggled to find the key that hung on a length of string behind the letter box. She dragged it through, opening the front door. In the passage she heard her mother call, 'That you, Rose?

Vera sighed. 'No, Mum, it's only me.' As she finished she placed the sack at Mabel's feet, handing the change to her.

'Cor blimey, that much. I didn't wanna buy Covent Garden!' Taking the coins, she replaced them carefully into the large purse.

'Tea?' asked Vera.

''Ad mine,' Mabel said, not realising Vera was asking for herself. Mabel continued, ''Aven't seen your sister Rose?'

Vera's heart sank as she remembered it was Friday. 'Oh no,' she groaned silently.

'I knows,' Mabel said as if she'd read her daughter's mind. 'I also knows she's got me a nice little bit of fish for me tea.'

Vera groaned again. She knew it would be down to her to cook and she just wasn't in the mood. Restlessly her foot traced invisible circles on the floor. 'I think I'll go to the park and then collect Sylvia from Mrs Smithers''.

Her mother looked up, her face creased in bewilderment. 'On yer own?' she said aghast.

'Why not?' Vera said in a defiant tone.

''Ave it yer own way,' and continued consuming what seemed to Vera to be a very cold and insipid looking cup of tea.

Rose Small was looking through the bedroom window that overlooked the small back garden. Her eyebrows arched and her cheeks flushed with rage when she saw her husband, Tom, standing in the garden in just his singlet and loosely belted trousers and plaid slippers. Outraged she rapped hard against the glass to attract his attention. 'How could he?' There was no response 'And for all the neighbours to see.' She rapped harder and hissed, 'Tom,' at the window pane. Tiny speckles of saliva hit the glass, still nothing. Rose snorted.

In the garden below, Tom was more than aware of the scene being acted out above him. He chose, however, to ignore it. It was a lovely day; he had just one more hour of work then the weekend would be his own. That wasn't quite true, not if you had Rose for a wife. He gave a slight shrug and ambled over to the rose bush. He considered the full blooms, then began snapping off the heat shrivelled and dying heads. He reflected for a moment. That's what life's all about. Growing, blooming, then being snuffed out. He let the depressing thought pass and lifted his spirits by remembering that he would have the old Daimler for the weekend, while the Carpenters, his employers for whom he chauffeured, spent a weekend in the country with friends. He heard her knuckles rapping on the window, threw the dead heads under the rambling rose and tucked his thumbs defiantly into the top of his trousers.He made no attempt to placate the noise coming from above.

'Yes,' he said, agreeing with himself, 'this Sunday we'll take, Mum, Sylvie and Vera to the seaside.' He had something few other men had, a mother in law who liked him; or was it only the gin he managed to sneak in for her?

Tom Small was a likeable man. He was, as his name suggested, short. Rose, his wife, stood half a head taller than him, in her stockinged size seven feet. Their only child, Patricia, who was ten years old, was a 'miniature' Rose. She scowled, wailed and generally got her own way, just like her mother.

He gave a quick glance at his wristwatch. 'Umm, nearly three.' Behind him he heard Rose hissing through clenched teeth, 'Tom! Are you going to stand out there half naked all day?'

Tom made no utterance but released his thumbs from his belt and turned towards the open french windows.

'Really,' Rose continued breathlessly, 'don't you know what time it is? You'll never get the Carpenters to the station on time.'

Tom began unbuckling his belt and his trousers began to fall.

'Good God! Tom, what d'you think you're doin'?' Clearly the vision had driven her to forget her usual affected voice.

We are married,' Tom said flatly.

Don't be silly,' Rose rounded on him. 'You can be seen by everybody.'

Her arms were agitating like a windmill in a gale. The sight quite amused Tom but he did not smile. Instead, he took the trousers and shirt with separate collar from the back of the chair and dressed in the scullery. 'I must be mad,' he said flatly.

'Tom. The time!' the unmistakable voice urged.

Standing in the kitchen, Rose grabbed the clothes brush which hung on the end of the mantle shelf and with gusto began to pummel at his jacket. This was too much for him. Turning suddenly, he snatched the brush from her hand. So sudden had his move been that Rose gave a little gasp and took a step back. Calmly Tom replaced the offending item and took his chauffeur's cap from the hook. As he had done for many years, he gripped the end of his jacket sleeve with his finger tips and gently raised his elbow, dusting the shiny black peak. He then placed it under his arm and turned towards the door.

Rose, a little more composed, asked, 'What's wrong?'

Tom turned back to face her. He gave her a long hard penetrating look up and down, saying nothing.

Rose said, 'You know it's Friday. You'll be at Mum's later when you've finished?'

Only his lips moved. 'Ain't I every Friday?'

Rose couldn't hold his look any longer and dropped her eyes and busied her hands on smoothing away invisible creases from her skirt and jacket. When she managed to look up, he had closed the kitchen door silently behind him.

She waited to hear the car pull away, then finally managed to move from the spot where she had been rooted. Feeling somewhat relieved she began to lock up. First the french windows. The back gate. The scullery door. The sitting room with the sideboard which held the gas and electricity money – just in case; you couldn't be too careful. Returning to the kitchen she took the bag the size of a small bucket, withdrew her purse from the drawer and flung it into a bottomless pit. She tugged at her jacket. Neatness and good grooming meant everything to Rose. A quick bob to the mirror assured her that her make-up was fine. On the way to the front door along the shadowy passage she stopped at the hall stand, removed a creation of felt and pheasant feathers and placed it on her head. Running her tongue across her teeth she was ready to open the front door. She gave a quick look over her shoulder and once in the porch banged the door purposefully to. A sigh of satisfaction released itself from her.

Waiting by the bus stop she came over uncomfortably hot as she watched scornfully those ill bred women who went bare legged, sandal footed and, God forbid, with low cut sleeveless blouses with a button or two left undone. 'Mercy me!' exclaimed Rose to herself. She believed it had been a very sad day indeed when women decided no longer to wear hats. As far as Rose was concerned it was nothing less than slovenly. But what Rose didn't know was that she was known as 'all corsets and caustic', even by her mother.

The bus came to a halt in a swirl of dust. Rose had to hitch up her skirt an inch or more to get on to the platform. The conductor tutted with annoyance at the delay. Once she had boarded he pulled at the cord; the bell rang and the driver didn't need telling twice. Rose looked up, having totally misinterpreted the tutting, and gave him a broad, engaging, bright red lipstick coated smile. Rose was convinced it was worth the effort. Just because it was warm, there was no excuse for bad grooming. She tottered along the bus and as she sat down the button on her skirt popped off. Rose was very hot and very uncomfortable, but the smile hadn't left her face, as she offered her fare. She was happy.

Rose was being transported along the south east London roads towards her mother's home, swaying rhythmically if not theatrically as she clung white knuckled to the seat in front, nodding sweetly at the conductor who was oblivious of her strained exaggerated smile; he busily collected his fares. Rose was just another passenger.

Vera had left the small parlour house feeling restless. She decided to take the short cut to the park and welcome the tunnel shaped archways and back alleys that knitted together the endless rows of houses. Reaching the half way point, the coolness of the alley seized her into a feeling of emptiness. She needed some company. Half of her wanted to collect Sylvia from Doris's, knowing too well that she would spoil their fun in the garden. She knew her sisters Rose and Gladys would soon arrive and within seconds would be at each other's throats. Their outright dislike of one another was well known and often Vera would be caught in the middle. It would be her brother in law, Tom, who with his sharp incisive wit would damp down a potential battle of the Boadiceas, particularly when Big Mabel managed to get her two penn'orth in. Vera became altogether aware of the calming effect of the shadowy arch. She was indifferent to weather: rain or shine, she remained the same. She felt she didn't belong anywhere except when working in the comfortable home of Mrs Lownds. Vera rarely went out because the older men thought her 'easy'; the married women thought her 'fast and loose'. Why? Because she'd had a baby at sixteen. The event was always referred to 'that business'. So Vera kept herself to herself. It was July and she'd just celebrated a birthday, but nobody had noticed . . . not even a card, except the one from Sylvia that she kept in her special box in her underwear drawer. The calming effect was wearing off. She could feel the restlessness and urgency charge through her as if waiting for a starting pistol to fire. Deep in her belly there was an ache, a longing, her heart gave a sudden flutter and she felt her stomach tighten. Now decided, she stepped from the blanket of darkness into the bright sunshine and instantly collided with someone.

Her hand rushed to her neck, as she gasped and giggled at the same time, 'Iris!' The female voice, equally amused, laughed loudly and said, 'Vera! I've been lookin' for you.' She linked her arm through Vera's and the two figures stepped out into the lazy afternoon.

'Where you goin'?' demanded Iris, then added, 'Where's Sylvia?' and then without taking a breath and without warning she leapt in front of Vera and began a dance only known to herself. Her beech coloured bobbed curls danced carefree and unrestrained.

Vera watched her with fondness, Iris was the only person who called Sylvia, Sylvia. She never shortened it, neither did she question her arrival or past. Iris was engrossed in a game of singular hopscotch, minus stone, or could it be she was jumping over cracks in the paving stones as 'they're unlucky' according to Iris. Vera smoothed out the crumpled piece of paper Iris had absently thrust into her hand. Holding it at the corners she saw it was a bill poster announcing a dance. She recognized the heavy printed poster as one she had seen stuck on the telegraph pole at the top of the hill.

'Vera, what's a cold buffy? 'Ave I 'ad one and can I 'ave 'n'ot one?'

The sudden outburst expelled in a single breath, went over Vera's head as she read on: Grand Dance Saturday 4th August to be held in the Greenwood Hall 7.30 p.m. to 11 p.m. Cold buffet. Dancing Reg Moore's Starlight Band with vocalist. Entrance by ticket only 1s. 6d.

Aunt Chrissie say I can go, only if you goes 'nall, an' she said she'd get you a ticket . . . ' There was a pause, then in another rush Iris added, 'Thought they was for trains. Will yer, Vera? Oh go on, Vera.'

'To the park,' answered Vera to the only question which really interested Iris. She folded up the notice and popped it in her pocket. She quickened her pace to catch up with Iris who was now swinging on a gate. Vera spoke gently but firmly as she saw net curtains parting and the outline of an angry fist ready to bang on the window.

'Come on, Vera, can I 'ave 'n'ice?' asked Iris jumping off the gate.

'We'll see,' Vera said, smiling back at her, knowing full well that was one promise Iris would not forget.

They turned into Lansdowne Road. Lansdowne Road was just like any other road on the estate, except for the heady fragrance of roses, so strong it almost took your breath away. A few steps along and the eye was immediately drawn to a small paved square set between two houses and bricked on the far side. A cloud of blood red roses filled the small area. The paving slabs covered the foundations of what was once Iris's home. Iris Claygate had been just eight years old when one of the last bombs to drop on the estate destroyed her home and her entire family. This quiet space was a simple memorial kept by friends and neighbours of the well liked Claygate family. Iris dashed off and onto the paving circling one of the bushes, then stopped suddenly, cupping a full bloom in her hand. Gently she lifted it to her face, allowing the petals to stroke her cheek. Vera always felt uneasy when they came this way; she wondered if Iris might remember. Her moist eyes watched the still form in front of her. She swallowed hard, almost not daring to breathe, wondering as she always did what she would do if Iris did remember that dreadful day when she was dragged from this very place barely alive. Vera caught her breath as she watched this attractive, slim young woman. Iris had been taken from this spot an eight year old; she returned an eight year old in the body of a woman in full bloom.

'What's it like 'avin' a baby?' Iris asked, still clutching the rose. This was not an unusual question; it was a question that Iris asked Vera at least once whenever they met. After Iris's long road to recovery she returned to the estate to live with her Aunt Chrissie. At that time Vera had just given birth to Sylvia and Iris was always around cooing and aaahing. Vera always felt that Iris and Sylvia grew up together. Babies had a fascination for this tall good looking woman with high sculptured cheekbones and beautiful dark green eyes. 'Well?' said Iris petulantly.

Vera's eyes were still glistening as she answered as she always did with gentleness and honesty. She said, 'Hard work.'

Turning away, she began walking towards the park gates which were now visible from the bend, and they could hear the rise and fall of children's voices. Iris instantly fell into step with her.

As they walked through the high green painted iron gates Vera's thoughts returned to the dance. How she would like to go. She looked down at her faded cotton dress. She hadn't anything new and neither could she afford anything. Iris rushed away and joined the children. Vera smiled as she rushed off into the direction of the roundabout surrounded by children of various ages. She caught her attention and indicated that she was going into the swings. Iris acknowledged with an enthusiastic nod, as she clearly enjoyed the ride on the roundabout. Vera spotted an empty swing. The motionless swing seemed out of place. Vera lowered herself onto the seat. Her arms circled the chains and with little kicking movements she brought it to life. Swinging gently to and fro she allowed her crowded thoughts to drift.

She caught sight of Iris at the water fountain. 'No, Iris! Use your hands!' and lifted a cupped hand to her lips to show Iris.

Vera considered the possibility of making something new from something she rarely wore. But that wasn't the point; she wore everything she had, and when she couldn't for whatever reason, she always managed to make something for Sylvia. She knew Chris would keep her word about getting her a ticket, if she hadn't already bought it. That would help. But desperation flooded in. For a dance like that a 'real' dress was essential. She shook her head and began swinging.

There had been cries of 'Where's Sylvie' from a few of the children. She knew Iris would soon salve their curiosity. The small park seemed cluttered with children, scooters, tricycles and a stray dog or two which were quickly chased away by the ever vigilant swing park attendant, boldly dressed in brown with the council badge pinned proudly to the front of her brown felt hat. Most of the children were known to this intimidating figure by their first names, so those who were left in her charge were careful not to get in her bad books, because their Mums would be told and spared no detail. This exchange would usually result in the boys getting a thick ear! The gentle breeze and the warm sun lulled Vera into contentment.

'Mrs Chapman,' a voice, said matter of factly. The two words that made up the name brought Vera to a halt. The heels of her sandals scraped on the ground, bewildered with tangible thoughts. She turned towards the voice and said to Iris, 'Of course!'

Iris returned her look, her face crumpled in puzzlement. 'Of course,' Vera said again, meaningfully. 'Of course,' she said once more. Her hand slipped into her pocket. The small purse she always carried nestled in the folds. She clicked it open. Her eyebrows rose; there wasn't a great amount but if she did a little bargaining, perhaps . . . She heard the church clock chime four, and leaping from the swing, she grabbed at Iris's arm, saying, 'If we go now, she'll still be open.'

Reluctantly Iris jumped down too mid swing, her face clouded. 'Where we goin' now then?'

'Mrs Chapman's.' Vera was flushed with excitement. Iris hung back. Vera understood Iris's mood changes; she took no notice and

11

continued to encourage her from the park. 'We 'ave to stop at Mrs Smither's though, just to be sure it's all right for Sylvia to stay a bit longer.' The mass of children's voices chorused their goodbyes; the two older women waved goodbye and in seconds had left the park behind them.

'S. CHAPMAN BOOKS Gold and silver bought and sold.' Thus read the sign written in copper plate in a dirty wine colour, somewhat faded with gold shadowing for maximum effect, which it must have had when it was first painted just after the first world war. Now it looked seedy and had an air of mystery about it. The shop was situated on the outside of the estate on the north road facing the park. It was easy enough to reach when using the cut through and the back alleys. It was most definitely not the place to go by bus, and if you could afford the bus you didn't really need the services Mrs Chapman had to offer. To be fair, it had been known for the 'other' side of the road, the posh parkside as the south side of the estate was known, to view some of the times which sat on the front, close to the pavement. Bookcases, chairs, sofas and even the odd lamp had been known to be purchased by the 'parkside poshies'. It was, however, the inside of the converted front room on the ground floor of the house that served as a shop which interested those who came by. Sybil Chapman was always in attendance. In the winter the front shop interior always gave out a distinct cigarette and paraffin glow. Even in the summer the tall black paraffin heater gave out an even eerier glow.

In the winter Sybil always wore men's socks over the lisle stockings that hid her hideous varicose veins. Her ankle boots were always in sight, zipped up the front and made of suede. The finger mittens were always worn as was the double zipped leather money belt which clung to her pendulous belly. Over her moth eaten cardigan she wore like a second skin, summer and winter, a heavy tweed coat.

The service Sybil Chapman offered was that of a pawnbroker minus the fuss; she did however, count the interest! That is why her swollen fingers were adorned with large diamonds on gold bands and the smell of Turkish cigarettes always consumed the air around her. On Monday mornings, once the washing had been put out on the line, women with large canvas bags would discreetly disappear behind the inner door to reveal their treasures for bargaining. These treasures might have been the good bed linen or the husband's good suit he wouldn't need until the following Sunday. A gold ring would also be offered and the moment the bargain had been struck the brass ring in the bottom of an already open pocket would be slipped on the finger as the woman left the shop looking carefully around her making certain she hadn't been seen. Furtive it was. It has to be said that whatever bargain was struck and with whom, Mrs Chapman never told. She understood it was wisest to keep her counsel.

Vera did as all the other women did who visited this establishment, she looked around and up and down the hill just to be sure. Mrs Chapman could be seen sorting through the vast mounds of clothes. Some she would put on a hanger and put away in the back room. Her dumpy frame and nicotined streaked hair cocked from side to side as she weighed up the value of the garment. Vera and Iris peered through the smaller inside window like excited children on Christmas morning. Vera jerked her head towards the door and gave Iris a playful shove. The three steps leading up into the shop were steep and narrow. Reaching the top like triumphant mountaineers, Vera coughed and Iris sneezed.

Sybil looked up from her newspaper and instantly recognized Big Mabel's daughter. She had shared many a gin with Mabel. Straight up and down was Mabel, hard but fair. Sybil's glasses slid over her pronounced hook nose, giving the girls another look. She licked the end of her indelible pencil before putting it back behind her ear and announcing, 'It's the camphor.' Her mitten covered hands dug into her holey beige cardigan. 'Now what can I do for you, Vera m'dear?'

Vera's mouth went dry, then, having managed a smile, her mouth opened to speak, only to hear Mrs Chapman ask, 'Let me guess, something to do with this 'ere dance thing is it?'

The girls, both silenced into surprise, nodded. Iris sank thankfully into the straight backed chair by the shop door and looked around her. To the left the shop was filled almost to the cobwebbed ceiling with books, jigsaw puzzles, toys of every description, with jars filled to brimming with marbles of every conceivable colour. Vera leaned forward across the counter, showing her need for confidentiality. Mrs Chapman recognised this instantly. She responded in the same way.

'So it is this dance.'

Vera nodded again. She said apologetically, 'I'd really like to 'ave somethin' from . . .' She jerked her head to the door to her left.

'Really. How much you prepared to pay?'

Vera dropped her gaze onto the mountains of dusty garments piled in front of her. She said softly, 'Depends.'

Sybil liked this girl, with her fresh, open, fair good looks. 'Good figure, too,' Sybil pondered. 'Shame to keep those proud shoulders covered.'

Vera found herself feeling more and more awkward and settled her weight on one leg, hooking her foot around her slender ankle.

'We'd better see eh?' Sybil said sharply.

Vera quickly stepped back from the counter to allow the dumpy figure by. On Sybil's belt hung a large bunch of keys. Without hesitation she removed one of the keys and placed it into the dulled brass keyhole. Vera found herself gulping; she had never been in the back room and she didn't know of anyone who had. But all knew of its existence. In there would be clothes on real hangers, some even cushioned. These garments hanging from the high picture rail would have been restored to their former glory.

From the even dustier corner the short figure took a long pole about six feet long with a snap hook which was opened and closed by a grubby forefinger. With the key securely laced back onto her keyring, the chocolate brown door began to open slowly. They stood side by side, the elder sizing up the younger for the dress she had in mind; Vera just blinked expectantly.

At that moment there came a cry from behind them. Both women turned to see Iris, her arms outstretched and with one hand waving frantically above her. Vera followed her gaze. Having settled on the subject causing Iris such excitement, Vera found herself heaving a sigh of relief.

'Oh, Vera,' Her voice was soft with wonderment. 'Just 'ave you ever seen nothin' so . . .' She didn't finish.

Vera's eyes settled on the glass case which held Iris' attention, and knew instantly that she wouldn't be having a new dress. Mrs Chapman had shuffled back to her old battered easy chair and lowered herself carefully into it.

'How much is that?' Vera asked tentatively. 'Is that for sale?' she added quickly.

Iris was standing spellbound. It was a rare occasion indeed to see her so quiet. Had Vera looked again she would have seen tears in Iris's eyes. The crumpled dumpy figure, hands in pockets, looked up.

'What about yer frock then?' Mrs Chapman said, breaking the silence, looking up at the feathered specimen in its glass dome. With a twinkle in her eyes, she added, 'An' 'e don't cost much to feed neither.'

Iris didn't understand but she knew that this woman spoke kindly.

'You, in 'ere.' She ushered Vera into the back room. 'An' you have a good look at . . .' she stopped, turned back facing Iris and asked, 'What is it?'

Iris turned, looking hard at Mrs Chapman, and answered simply, 'It's an owl, a barn owl.'

Mrs Chapman nodded, and with an uncustomary quickness of movement removed the glass domed owl from the cluttered dusty shelf into Iris's waiting hands. Iris was still spellbound; had they disappeared through the wall or up the chimney nothing could have held her imagination as did this delicate creature resplendent in its glass prison.

As the door clicked to they heard Iris say, 'I'm going to call you Barny.' Her eyes searched the bird hungrily. Its bright eyes met hers and she smiled back a smile of understanding and belonging.

Inside the room a curtainless window let in little light. The panes were thick with years of dust on the inside and mud splattered on the outside. A light bulb in the middle of the room hanging from a flex swung perilously above the tall girl. Its dulled beige light matched the rest of the dingy room. It had taken some seconds for Vera's eyes to become accustomed to the light, when from behind her she heard a rustle. Turning towards the sound she gasped with delight at the creation dangling from the long pole.

Well, don't just stand there gawping, girl, try it on!'

The figure was motionless. Vera began to unbutton her dress; she didn't dare take her eyes from this vision for fear it might disappear. She stopped unbuttoning her dress suddenly, blushed, looked down at Sybil and said yet again apologetically, 'I don't 'ave any . . . well umm . . . er . . .' And blushed scarlet again.

'Gawd girl, I'll 'ang it on 'ere. I'll give a knock on me way back in, m'dear.'

She shuffled out leaving Vera open mouthed. Even if I can't buy it, thought Vera, at least I've worn it. She quickly finished undoing her dress and against her better judgement, allowed it to drop onto the dirty cracked linoleum covered floor. Taking up this vision of gossamer cornflower blue grosgrain, in a flash it was unbuttoned and Vera felt it rising up on her flesh. As it slipped over her bare breasts, the shape of the bodice clung to her warm body. The effect was inevitable as she stretched behind her to secure as many buttons as possible. With her shoulders back she stared into the black speckled mirror that hung on the wall and couldn't believe what stood before her. The stitched pleated shawl back flattered her long neck and wide shoulders. The neat sleeves complemented the neat nipped in waist. The skirt with its two soft pleats at the front gave it a perfect bell shape. Its ballet length flattered her long legs and slim ankles. She stood barefoot, aware of the filth beneath her feet, and shuddered. Her breasts were high, full, and her nipples visible and very obvious. Vera stood on tiptoes, not for anything in particular, just because.

Sybil reappeared. ''Ave to get yourself a brassière, you can't go around like that!' she said, giving Vera's middle a hefty slap with a flabby hand.

Vera was more than aware of what she meant and blushed furiously once again.

'And get yourself some stockings.' Sybil stood beside her admiring the reflection of this girl. 'It's the colour what sets it orf, nice fit.' Her tone flat she asked, 'Speak up, do you want it or don't you?'

Don't think I can afford it,' Vera protested meekly.

'We'll see and while I think of it,' she shuffled away to the rear the room, 'Now try these, and oh, these too . . .' Sybil produced satin shoes with high heels in exactly the same colour as the dress and tiny pearl drop earrings. 'Stop this fussing you've friends waiting.'

Without waiting for an answer, she again shuffled off, disappearing behind the door. Vera followed Mrs Chapman into the front of the shop. Sybil asked bluntly, ''Ow much you got?'

Sadly, Vera shook her head. 'Not enough,' she answered honestly, 'I can't afford this . . .'

'Ain't what I asked.' Mrs Chapman eyed the girl warmly. She looked briefly at Iris, then, addressing her words at Vera, said, 'She can 'ave it.' She added with a sniff, 'What about this 'ere frock then?' Knowing that Vera was in no position to offer or to bargain, she said loudly, 'Twelve bob and that's the lot!'

'Everythin'?' Vera gasped.

'Take it or leave it, I'm doin' meself 'ere!'

Sybil had lit yet another of her foul smelling cigarettes and the lighter fell into a seemingly bottomless patch pocket. Vera asked, 'And that?' pointing to the glass case.

'How much?' Her tone was firm and controlled.

Hauling herself to her feet, Sybil said, ''Ere you gets yourself back in there!' She jabbed a thumb at the open back room door. 'An' you m'dear, you gets yourself better acquainted with your new friend.' The old woman looked on as Iris cradled the glass entombed owl in her arms. The silence in the small room was as heavy as the late afternoon. Vera felt her stomach lurch and began chewing her lip. Sybil sniffed. The two women half turned to return to the back room.

'It's dead!' pronounced Iris cheerfully.

With the silence shattered, Vera took a deep breath. Looking at Mrs Chapman she asked 'How much?'

Vera didn't realise just how much this little scene had moved the old woman. Mrs Chapman remained silent, then with a dismissive wave of her hand ushered Vera to the back room. Vera hesitated, then heard Iris say: 'If 'e's dead 'e can't make much of a mess. An' Aunt Chrissie said I could only 'ave one only if it din't make a mess!'

'I said everythin', and I means everythin'. I don't welch on a deal. I'm known around 'ere for that. A deal's a deal.' She unrolled one of her fingerless mittens, spat on the palm of her hand and offered it to Vera.

Although feeling a little confused and flustered, Vera took the offered hand shook it vigorously and said, 'Done!' just like she'd seen on the films.

Handing the blue creation over to the grubby hands somewhat reluctantly, she asked rather timidly, 'Could I borrow your canvas bag to put it in?'

'Go on, then; 'ave a good time at the dance, eh?'

The dress, shoes and earrings disappeared into the bag. 'I'll bring it back Mond'y.' Her honesty was evident. Vera bent over Iris, and gently tried to persuade her to let go.

'NO!' Iris shrieked with horror, 'I'll carry 'im.'

Vera reached into her pocket. She took out a ten-shilling note and one florin and gave them to Mrs Chapman who, satisfied with their safe deposit registered in her palm, dropped them soundlessly into one of her zipped compartments. Sighing, she eased herself into her chair, removed the indelible pencil, licked the end and studied the newspaper that had been wedged down the side of the cushion. She let the girls see themselves out. As they left she heard Iris saying in a singsong voice:

'A wise old owl lived in an oak
The more he saw
The less he spoke
The less he spoke
The more he heard
Why can't we be like that wise old bird?'

Before the lick on the indelible pencil had time to dry, Vera was standing again by the side of the counter.

Sybil looked up. 'Yes?'

Vera said boldly, 'I'd like that.' She pointed to a hanger above Sybil's head.

'Ain't for yourself, then?'

Vera shook her head; she gave a short nod at the window where Iris stood waiting outside.

'Eh, good choice for 'er colouring like.'

Vera said nothing as Mrs Chapman took down the garments.

'Sure?'

Vera nodded again. She blurted out, 'I can't pay you now but I'll bring it first thing Monday!'

'Good,' was all she said.

They exchanged understanding glances. Sybil knew the girl would be true to her word.

Give us yer bag.'

Astonished, Vera watched in stunned silence as Sybil carefully folded the blouse and skirt then just as carefully placed them neatly into the open bag, ''Ere don't run away, there's this too.'

A wide white belt was carefully rolled and placed with her other purchases.

'That's it, then?'

'As I said, I'll bring it in on Mond'y mornin'.' She paused before asking ''ow much?'

Sybil pulled the large zip across her money bag with great deliberation.

'Nothin'! Just be sure to enjoy yourselves. Now, anything else I can do yer for?'

Her show of impatience and mock sarcasm worked. Like a startled rabbit Vera snatched up the bag, called out a hurried, 'Thank you and goodbye,' and ran from the shop.

Sybil relieved her ear of the pencil, settled herself once again and set about the serious task of picking the winners at Newmarket. The smile crossing her face was one of contentment, not anticipation.

The last few yards had left her puffed and the sight of the gate within her reach gave rise to a sigh of relief. She clicked the gate closed behind her. Standing on tiptoes she managed to push her podgy fingers through the letter box in search of the key hanging from a piece of string. Her searching fingers caught on the splintered hole, where the key had been dragged through over the years. She winced out loud. With the key key firmly in her hand, she plunged it into the lock.

'Coo eee. It's only me, Mum.' She added, 'Everything all right?'

Gladys's timid, tremulous voice reached the kitchen. Mabel made a face, tutted, raised her eyebrows and rolled her eyes shaking her head with indifference. This display was witnessed by Rose who said nothing but smiled smugly.

Tom, sitting on the step, slurped at his tea and thought to himself, ''Ere comes Watney's Red Barrel on Tolly bottle legs.'

Gladys took the immaculately pressed handkerchief from her belt and dabbed at her forehead. She thought how unladylike it was. Tucking it back behind the stiffened belt of her dress, she began the four paces to the kitchen. The weather, though glorious, took its toll on her more than generous frame. Taking a deep breath she stepped into the kitchen and was surprised to find Rose and Tom there.

'Oh!' She gasped, managing just to hide her surprise behind a tight lipped smile. 'My, my, what a gathering,' she trilled, looking around, nodding to Rose and Tom, and Mabel who was sitting over a tightly clutched cup.

Rose, sitting straight backed with her legs crossed at the knee, looked at the barrel like figure finding it difficult to believe this woman in thick stockings, laced shoes and hip seams bulging could possibly be her sister. She gave Gladys a long, cool, majestic smile. Gladys acknowledged, 'All caustic and corsets' and smiled as she pushed a strand of prematurely grey hair from her face.

'I'll make some tea then?' And without waiting for an answer she busied herself at the sink filling the kettle.

'Mum?' Gladys asked, in the familiar way that meant, 'Do you want more tea?'

''Ere you are, girl.' Tom had got up from the step and thrown his grouts over the rockery. 'I'm up for another.' Where's our War Wound?' Rose gave Tom a withering look that would have killed a rampaging bull elephant at hundred yards. Rose noticed Gladys's rising colour who continued busying herself without acknowledging his words.

'Arthur is resting . . .'

Tom butted in: 'More like sitting on his arse, or what that where he got his . . .'

'Tom!' Rose said, standing up. 'Really!'

Tom gave a chuckle. 'Oh go on, Glad knows I'm only kidding.' Tom always felt that much bolder when Mabel was about. 'Ain't no one told 'im the war's over, or is he still 'iding down the Dog and Ferret'?'

Unmoved, Gladys had taken the cup and saucer and swished it clean under the running tap. She carefully dried it, and refilled the cup, handing it back to Tom. She knew he was joking for the most part and was well aware of Arthur's nickname. 'I brought some cake. Would you like some?'

Rose gave a brief wave 'No,' indicating to her waist, Mabel said a flat 'No.' It was only Tom who said, 'Yes if it's one of your crunchy ones with the burnt fruit.'

That was too much. Gladys threw down the leather patchwork vegetable bag. 'I didn't come here to be in . . .' She grabbed at her hanky from her rotund waistline and sniffed pathetically into the white expanse.

'Aw, come on, Glad, you knows I'm only joking.' He had stepped into the kitchen and placed an arm around her shoulder. 'Come to the seaside with us Sunday?'

At this Gladys's sobs stopped abruptly. With grave dignity she dabbed at her nose, folded the handkerchief then, tucking it back into her belt, asked, 'Where?'

'What's all this about; the seaside?' Mabel demanded.

'Go on, go on, you up for it too?' he continued enthusiastically. 'It'll do you a power of good.'

'I don't doubt that,' Mabel said sourly. 'Depends where we're goin'!'

Taking the tea offered, Tom announced, 'The Isle of Sheppey.'

The words scarcely aired, Mabel jumped at him. 'I ain't gettin' on no boat!' Her words came out slurred and breathless. ''Ow far is it then, this 'ere island?'

Gladys, caught up in the crossfire, looked down at her mother's cup. There the answer was clear, clear as gin could be. 'Oh Mum, you know this isn't good for you,' Gladys wailed.

Mabel had a vice-like grip on the cup and gave her daughter an icy glare of disapproval. She pulled from the deep pocket of her pinny a half bottle of gin and without a second thought filled her cup. Screwing on the top she gave them all a look of challenge which none of them took up. The bottle was replaced and Mabel continued: 'If this is an island 'ow do yer get on it if yer don't get on a boat?'

Rose had been silent for some while. She pondered on the thought: 'An island'. She was prepared to let it rest. If there was one thing Tom knew it was where to go and how to get there. But truth be known she found it difficult to understand an island without having to get on a boat.

Gladys was taken aback by these revelations. She looked at the stove. 'Oh my, what a nice bit of fish,' she exclaimed as if it been the first bit of fish she'd ever seen. Without drawing breath she continued, 'Thank you, Tom, I know it would be a lovely day but Arthur hasn't been feeling too good so . . .' She stopped for a moment, then with a smile added, 'I'm sure you will enjoy yourselves. I'll go and air the parlour; you do want to listen to the play this evening, Mum?'

Mabel grunted her reply.

Gladys took herself off into the front parlour. It was a small bright room with a single casement window, the top half in equal squares. She lifted the bottom sash window high and the fresh air rushed into the room. She adjusted the curtains, leaving them billowing behind her. She spotted on top of the wind up record player a few records. Dreamily she browsed through them, smiling . . . Billy Eckstein, Nat 'King' Cole and Bing Crosby. She sighed; now, they must have cost a fortune. 'Dolly daydream,' she said wistfully as she replaced their covers, putting them back into the record compartment. She found she had a sudden urge to turn the handle and let the sound drift. Her rotund diminutive stature let out a sigh at the sight of her two late brothers, faces artificially coloured on backgrounds of blue, hung side by side, smiling at each other. And she fled the room like a regal galleon in full sail.

Rose's voice, shrill and dancing attendance on her mother, asked, 'Where's that girl, if she's not back soon you'll have tea late, and that won't be good for your digestion.' She stopped and eyed her mother warily. 'At least let me poach the fish . . .'

Mabel didn't allow her eldest daughter to finish. 'Rosie,' Mabel shouted, 'You wouldn't know how to poach a bit of smoked 'addock, unless the bloody thing stood on its tail and told you 'ow! Her voice reached a crescendo. Tom, sitting quietly on the steps choked noisily on his tea. Rose's mouth gaped wide open, a scarlet outlined hole which, while Mabel's mind was still thinking about seasides, reminded her of moving open mouthed ducks children threw balls at to win prizes . . .

'Mum!' The indignation rose in her face. Refusing to get up she tugged at her too tight, ill fitting jacket. Rose had to have the last word even if it was silent. 'Gin,' she said to herself. 'The bloody gin!'

Tom, recovering from his bout of coughing, took the glare Rose fixed him with. It was he who had given her the bottle. The look said loud and clear, 'Just wait until I get you 'ome.' Tom, now on the defensive, thought, 'What's with a bottle or half a bottle of gin; all the ol' girls do it.'

He was certain he would find out when they got home. Gladys, unaware of this exchange, was delighted when Tom asked her for another piece of cake. She cut him a generous slice and Tom sat unusually silent as he munched, shoulders hunched, deep in his thoughts.

'Very nice,' he managed to say.

Chapter 2

Arthur Edwin Bowles from his height of six feet two inches bent over as he cursed and kicked the deckchair against the chestnut fencing. 'Why?' he asked himself. 'Why does Gladys always have the knack of putting these wretched things not only together properly but,' as he cast his eye over the garden, 'have green fingers as well?' He tugged at the brightly striped canvas. 'Right, you beast . . . ' His tone and volume together with its content stopped instantly as he heard, 'Mr Bowles . . . I wonder . . . ?'

Recognizing the voice he turned with a warm welcoming smile spread across the loose fatty fold of his jowls.

'I wonder, could you?' There was a slight hesitation before she continued.

Daphne Lancaster's white low cut sleeveless blouse left nothing to the imagination. Her generous curves were accentuated by the wide belt that cinched in her waist. Arthur's mouth had gone dry and he started to lick his lips like an overworked St Bernard dog. He took a couple of steps towards her. 'Daphne . . . Mrs Lancaster? Can I be of assistance?' he asked as he rubbed his hands together.

'Well,' she said slowly, her eyes darting at the tangled knot of the deck chair. 'Nasty thing,' she said, smiling up at Arthur. 'It's just that my Bert has just gorn out, and see . . . ' She thrust the small glass milk jug out and turned it upside down. 'Could you oblige?' Her face fell into the hugest smile Arthur had ever seen.

'Oh. Yes. Well now.' He stumbled along. She now rested her ample breasts on the fencing, cleavage spilling out, and asked as her loosely permed blonde locks bounced in reply to the toss of her head, 'I can't stretch no more, you'll 'ave to come and get it.'

Her head down, her eyes locked onto his. The long black spider legs of eyelashes mesmerised him.

'Well?' she drawled, shaking the jug at him.

'Ah yes, well now, let's see. Yes. Right.' He snatched at the jug and rushed into the kitchen, with beads of perspiration appearing as suddenly as morning mushrooms. He didn't know why but he rinsed the jug, dragged the tea cloth from the hook and dried it with vigour. Opening the larder door, the milk was, as he expected it to be, on a marble slab. He thrust his thumb into the neck; the top split and milk slopped onto the tiled floor. Shaking, he filled the jug. Taking a deep breath he took a sprightly leap from the low step into the garden.

'Here we are then.'

Daphne Lancaster gave a knowing smile at the sprightly display. 'Not playin' up then, today, is it?'

Arthur stared back. 'Ah, yes. Depends on the weather, you know. War wound. Not too bad today.'

Daphne looked at the open kitchen door. 'No Glad?'

'Er. No. Visiting her Mum. Thought I'd do a bit of gardening and a bit of this and that. You know . . . ' His head nodded.

'Ooo, my,' Her high pitched laugh echoed around the gardens. 'It's the this 'n' that what I likes.' Another shriek of ear-piercing discordant laughter lingered longer. 'D'you want some, then?'

Again Arthur's face fell into blankness

'Tea!' she said, swaying with the jug as partner. 'What did yah think I meant, then? Ooo, I say.' And another cackle filled the gardens. 'You'd better get yer deck chair out of its knot before you get yourself into one!'

He watched her wiggle up the cement path, step into her kitchen, turn slowly to face him and bend over. Her blouse fell open and she gave a finger wave and asked, 'Sure?'

'Herr humm. Thanks, anyway. Must get on.' He gave the briefest of waves, turned and took a handkerchief from his pocket and mopped his forehead. He then gave the deckchair another hard kick. With, he instantly realised, the wrong leg. It had taken him the best part of an hour to get the deckchair into a safe upright position. Satisfied with the result, Arthur or 'War Wound' as he was better known, went to the brightly gingham curtained kitchen to find the newspaper.

He lowered himself into the canvas as he emitted an affected groan of pain and rubbed his right leg. Once settled into the contraption he scanned the racing pages. It was just wishful thinking. The afternoon had made him thirsty. He smacked his lips and thought of the Ferret. He quenched his thirst by thinking that it wasn't that long until opening time, and anyway Gladys wouldn't be long and a good dinner inside would set him up for the evening. The thoughts gave way to fitful slumber. His stomach was rumbling and, yes, he was thirsty and not for a cup of tea. Although, he mused, peering across the fence, he wouldn't say no to 'french fancy'. He consoled himself and checked his thoughts by putting the newspaper over his face. His generous bulbous nose, sweaty and red, was the ideal shape to hold the newspaper in place. Now, shaded from the sun, he folded his arms and thought on dreamily. Over the gardens the smell of fried onions and liver wafted into Arthur's nostrils. He licked his lips and thought, 'Umm, that'll do nice. Liver,' and it reminded him of the first time he had seen Gladys. The smell of food cooking made him even thirstier. He comforted himself yet again that it wasn't long until opening time and that the Dog and Ferret would have its door open and welcoming. He gave a short involuntary snort. His fleshy lips smacked noisily together. The smell of food and the sound of a man's belly laugh in the distance and the clatter of saucepans evoked memories. 'War Wound's mind was full of part memories: half truths and a lot of wishful thinking.

The Dog and Ferret had played a fundamental, if not instrumental, part in his life as an army conscript. It had been on a summer's day just like this when his call-up papers arrived. While he was half waiting for them he had believed that his job as a boiler man in the general hospital would be a reserved occupation. It was not to be. The war had taken a sudden change of direction. It was 1941. The blitz had worn down everybody. No one admitted it of course: complete solidarity in the face of the enemy. But everybody was tired and bewildered and a feeling of being hunted had begun to show. He was twenty-seven and had no family or relatives so the shift work suited him fine. And he didn't have a girl friend. Why should he need one with the constant whining on about marriage, family and money. He was fine just as he was and his landlady Doreen, when her husband Stan was on nights, was very obliging. He would even take her to the Ferret when he'd overdone it, ply her with port and lemon or a gin or two and the next week's rent would be forgotten. It all suited him fine.

Now had come this. It wasn't that he lacked patriotism, it was just a bloody nuisance. He'd flung the official words, written on official paper with the official buff envelope, onto his bed. There was only one thing for him to do, what all the other men did – go out on a high tide. Drunk! He had stood gloomily staring into the mirror that stared back at him equally blankly. 'Thirty-six hours,' he grunted. He had reached for the packet of Woodbines which lay beside the wash bowl. As he lifted them the morning's water had seeped into the packet. Undeterred he had fingered through the pack and found one that was dry; the rest he put on his bedside table which he knew would catch the remainder of the afternoon sun. He stared down at the forlorn pack, then decided to look upon this misfortune as a form of investment. How many packets of cigarettes would he see after the day after tomorrow? It had now begun. Tomorrow. After tomorrow.

Suddenly there was no today. Realising this, he vowed there would always be today! He then changed that into tonight! He slammed his door shut and descended the threadbare carpet runner whose pattern had long since become indistinguishable. The chocolate coloured gloss paint to waist height with dark green skirting board he had never taken much notice of before. It now struck him as dull in comparison to the bright day outside.

He stopped at the bottom of the stairs to listen for Doreen. No sound came from the kitchen or her sitting room. He was disappointed; he had wanted to tell someone. He resigned himself to the Ferret. They were sure to give him a good send off. He tapped at his pocket, reassuring himself that the documents were still there. In seconds the heavy door had closed behind him and he found the afternoon glare hurting his eyes. He blinked wildly and trod purposefully along the pavement in the direction of the Dog and Ferret. It was just a few minutes easy walking distance away. As he turned into the bit of a dirt road, he was surprised to find the pub still not yet open. He sat down on one of the old benches and pondered on the time. Bert was a stickler for time and routine. He sat hunched forward, his hands clasped loosely together, his elbows digging into his thighs. The sun shone directly on him and its intense glare seemed to intensify the seemingly endless blackness he was being led to by officialdom. He turned his foot and began to toy with the ground of small pebbles and loose earth. He remembered that as a kid he would sit on the very same bench and scrape the dirt with the inside of his shoe and pretend he was at the seaside as he drank his shandy and ate an arrowroot biscuit and scrapped with the other boys. Sometimes in the summer the boys would bring their bats and balls and an impromptu game of cricket would ensue. They seemed a very long way away now. He folded his arms, leaned back against the rickety bench and stared out across the bleached sun and foot-trodden grass far into the middle distance, into nowhere particular.

From inside he heard Bert begin unbolting the doors. As he pinned the far door to the floor he saw Arthur sitting there.

'Eh lad, you got a thirst on then?' His flat Yorkshire vowels were clear as the sunlight. In response Arthur waved his papers at him and stood up.

'Caught up with yer at last, eh?'

'Looks that way,' Arthur said miserably.

The coolness of the pub struck Arthur as cold, very cold. Was it an omen? He shivered a little and stood at the bar. He plunged his hand into his trousers pocket and took out some coins. 'Give us a pint of bitter.'

There was no reply, Bert was having his usual airing. He was standing outside, his enormous girth almost blocking the sun from the doorway. With a deep breath he turned and rocked back through the doors into the cool gloom. Standing with his arms folded over his chest-high trousers with the once white apron tied and folded down over his chest-high waist, he stood as still as a statue.

'Wotcha waitin' for now?' Arthur asked irritably.

'Waiting, lad, for that big 'and to come up to tha twelve. Aye. Right. A pint.' He removed the towel from the pump handles and proceeded to pull a pint. 'So when you off?' he asked indifferently. He'd seen them go and go and not come back. But he didn't ever talk about that. He slid the beer across to Arthur and picked up the coins and with one flourish had them in the dinging till. He watched, interested this time, as Arthur downed the pint. 'Ne'er seen you take it down that way afore.'

'Where is everyone?' It was more of a cry of disappointment from Arthur rather than a question. 'When anybody else goes there's always a send off.' Sounded more like a funeral, thought Arthur. 'Suppose it is an end,' he said, unaware and wearily. He pushed the papers over to Bert. His massive hands took the envelope and took one glance.

'That soon, eh? Still gives you time for a good sup, though.'

'Who with?' he asked forlornly.

'Well, they caught up with you at last then, lad.' And as he laughed his belly jumped up and down in opposite time to his laughing head.

'It's all right for you,' thought Arthur to himself. 'You're not going.' He now felt decidedly miserable.

'They'll be 'ere later. They've just had their dinner. Give ee!'

It was with glee that he took his cloth and began to wipe down the bar top. 'Another, then?'

Arthur nodded. He was going to get drunk as a skunk!

The morning drinking passed uneventfully, other than a few of the boys taking their unreserved unlabelled chairs to chew over the '14-18', to suck on their pipes and narrow darts of old shag. The lack of an audience to Arthur's departure into the tunnels of the unknown didn't deter him from numbing the inevitable. So it was with his arm over the bull neck of Bert that Arthur's scuffed shoes were hauled from the bar into the afternoon sunshine, his feet dragging up the two steps that led into the public bar. Bert lowered Arthur onto the bench, saying, 'This is a private on parade!' Wiping his hands over the even less white of his apron girth, he stepped back down into the public bar, drew up the bolts from the floor and methodically locked the doors on the swish of the plain clock's sweep of a hand on the twelve, indicating three o'clock. Throwing a cloth over the pumps he then, with effort and wheezing, ascended the stairs to the rooms above.

It was the pain in Arthur's neck that awoke him. Hesitatingly he opened one eye to gauge his surroundings. In his mouth he felt something like an acrid sweat swollen sock. He swallowed hard, attempting to find the impossible lost saliva. With the other eye now opened he began slowly to recall the day. There was a sudden sharp pain on the end of his nose. He winced, then his hand rose to the inflamed area. It was his nose; it had burnt in the sun. He groaned and when attempting to stand felt an overwhelming sickness. Turning on uncertain feet he focussed on the steps below him and the open door immediately in front of him. Unsteadily he manoeuvred his way into the public bar.

'Cor blimey, look at that! It's Rudolph.' Charlie's voice continued, 'Talk about your country needs you. Strewth, if we're depending on that we might just as well give up now. So they caught up with you, you bastard!'

'Kitchener!' Bert bellowed from behind the bar. His word was lost.

Charlie started to laugh. 'Bloody state of you. For chrissakes, Bert, pull him a pint.'

Arthur, his elbow balancing his weight, attempted once again to find the clock. Charlie watched him with amusement. 'It's seven thirty.'

The pint he groped for and as he swallowed it was as if his eyes were opened wide and his mind cleared. 'Good grief,' he moaned, 'it's . . . What have I done?'

'Er, if you can't smell the disinfectant . . . '

So that is why he felt so empty and full and also why he was dreaming of hospitals. His mind cleared. He found himself floundering for apologies. But his mouth was still not working in tandem with his thoughts. The smell, the voices, the spinning room, Bert's cash till with every trill sounding and feeling like bullets in Arthur's head. It wasn't long before what should have been 'a bit of a do' whirled into the incomprehensible tones of 'Time gentlemen please!'

Even now Arthur couldn't be sure if he hit the floor, or the floor hit him or if Bert floored him. Floored he most certainly was. He was hauled unceremoniously to his feet. Feeling that he had suffered enough, he had insisted on going home. All was fine until he remembered, too late, the steps outside the bar. He found himself floating. The accompanying bright lights seemed fitting for a hero off to war, or was he back from the front or was he dead? The heat of pain was unmistakable. He tried opening his eyes. The bright lights were swiftly extinguished and Arthur fell, this time down into oblivion.

And that was the end of 'Arthur's War'. The next six months he spent in various hospitals having the broken bones of his lower leg set, broken and reset.

Leaving the hospitals behind him, he returned to work at the Woolwich Arsenal. The work wasn't hard and it was here that he was nick-named 'War Wound' for, however, all the wrong reasons.

It was in the late spring of '43 that because of an oversight of Doreen, his landlady still, he found himself without sandwiches for his break. Vocalising this, he headed for the canteen. The limp he bore with courage, when he remembered to limp, that is. And it had been known for him even to forget which leg. He did indeed have a most pronounced limp on leaving hospital but exercise had cured, well, most of it. The 'limp' was in War Wound's mind. On this spring day however his mind was overworked with the injustice of having to pay what he considered inflated prices in the subsidised canteen. His large hand groped through the cutlery for knife, fork, spoon. The large white plate he tucked into his chest like an oversized schoolboy.

It was then he saw her. A tiny girl of maybe eighteen, nineteen or maybe very early twenties. She had dark hair trapped in the white netting from her white cap. Her overall showed off her tiny waist. She didn't look like the other women in the canteen, who were loud and sometimes vulgar, Arthur had thought. He knew about these things, being a ladies' man. Her quiet presence was cool, like a nurse; she gave everyone a short shy smile and she spoke softly. Standing in front of her, Arthur asked, ''Ave you got puddings?'

The diminutive figure stepped back at the request. Her eyes widened with alarm at what Gladys considered a little overwhelming. Regaining her exterior composure, she replied, looking up into this tall man's crystal blue eyes, full lower lip and firm square jaw, 'Custard tart, or bread pudding.' Still a little alarmed, she was surprised to find herself saying in a confidential tone. 'I'd have the custard tart; there isn't much fruit in the bread pudding,' then added conspiratorially, 'And that's burnt.'

Arthur hadn't heard a word. He watched her face, glowing; the white cap began to resemble an angel. 'Did you make it?'

She shook her head, picked up the pudding dish with custard tart in it and solemnly handed it to him. With liver and onions on a place in one hand and cutlery in his breast pocket, the dish he held between his thumb and forefinger. Juggling with the two he turned without taking his eyes from her. The generous portion of liver onions with gravy suffered a bout of inertia as he stopped suddenly and shouted, 'Melanie! That's it. You're just like her, that one in that flick, *Gone with the Wind*.' Stepping out triumphantly, he slid on the gravy. Most of the liver and onions found its way into his pocket. The fork stabbed him on the nose. Lying prostrate on the floor, he managed to utter, as his finger curled into a mouth full of custard, 'Very nice.' Gladys had blushed to her roots; her hands rushed to her fire hot cheeks. But how good it felt.

They had married the following July and Arthur moved in with her, her mother and her baby sister Vera, and he lived cossetted ever after.

The sudden surge of pain on his face was eased as he heard his name floating over him.

'Arthur, Arthur! Oh, Arthur,' said Gladys. 'Oh Arthur, you haven't done a thing.' Gladys removed the scorching newspaper from his face. 'Oh Arthur.' She folded the newspapers in half and threw it at him. Sadly, but resigned, she turned back to the kitchen, her barrel frame rolling from side to side to prepare yet another meal.

Chapter 3

Vera hurried along. She had safely returned Iris into the care of her Auntie Chrissie and collected Sylvia. With the canvas bag clutched firmly in her hand, Sylvia dangling on the other, knowing she was late she made mental notes of what not to say. The canvas bag worried her. How could she get it into the house without questions? How was she going to make up the housekeeping? Mabel never took kindly to excuses; she didn't ever have to make any. How could she explain where she had been? She knew Mrs Chapman would keep silent, and she had promised to return the bag on Monday. The sun, now quite low, still startled her into momentary blindness as she turned the corner. She was still frantic with worry.

Sylvia pulled on her mother's finger. 'Give us the bag, Mummy. If I go in first I'll tell Gran it's got me dollies in it. We swop 'em like the boys do cigarette cards.'

The childish words with the adult insight pulled Vera up short. She looked down into the fair haired beribboned round face which returned her gaze, silently and innocently.

As if reading her mother's thoughts, Sylvia quickly added, 'I'll come downstairs quick. I won't look.'

At this Vera bent down and pulled her to her, whispering, 'Thanks.'

'Shan't tell Gran, neither,' Sylvia said with a gleam in her eye.

'A little too wise,' Vera thought, smiling down.

At the gate she handed over the soft canvas bag, battered and rather the worse for its numerous journeys. As she searched for the key through the letterbox she raised her finger to her lips and issued a 'Shhh' to Sylvia, who nodded, enjoying every moment of the adventure. She could have been one of the Secret Seven, she beamed to herself. Once inside Vera dispatched her daughter to the stairs with a quick tap on the child's rump. Without a sound she scampered up the stairs and as Vera stood leaning against the bannisters listening, she heard Tom's voice from the kitchen. She took a deep breath, shook herself and stepped into the kitchen, smiling but knowing also that the worst was to come. It wasn't Tom that greeted her; it was Gladys's warm, sincere tones.

'Vera, how lovely. I'm pleased I've seen you before I leave. I really

31

must go now.' Gladys hurried on, 'Arthur promised to do just a little in the garden. Still,' she sighed wistfully, 'You know just how much I like my garden. It's not the same as here.'

Mabel found a small hand patting her on the shoulder, looked up and said, 'No, it's a bloody sight bigger.'

'Mother!'

Gladys continued, 'Did you find your little friend?' She was of course referring to Iris.

Vera nodded.

'Good.' Gladys settled her arms across her wide belly, feeling a tinge of sadness and also happiness. Vera seemed to bring such pleasure to Iris and by return Iris seemed to fill Vera with a purpose. Gladys, however, kept her thoughts to herself, knowing that Rose would raise more than an objection.

Rose looked up at her baby sister. 'Well?' she demanded, taking advantage of her mother's incapacity. 'Where 'ave you been?'

Before Vera had time to swallow, Sylvia rushed in. On her arrival, Tom instantly turned into the kitchen as if from nowhere saying, 'Sylvie! What about a game of ball?'

Sylvia didn't need to be asked again; she was out in the garden with her uncle before anyone could ask any questions. Vera stood relaxed, then she wondered to herself, where did he get that ball from? Her relaxation was shortlived as her mother asked, 'Well, where 'ave yer bin?'

Vera seemed to stare at each of them in turn. First to Rose's frosty demeanour which seemed impossible in this weather. To Gladys's warm, welcoming, trusting look of interesting news, to her mother's florid, sweaty face with her red chafed knuckles fixed hard on the scrubbed wooden table. Hearing the laughter from the garden, she gave a long smile, turned to look out into the garden and replied, 'Just in the park.' She hadn't wanted to lie. She felt she hadn't.

'Now I really must go.' Gladys picked up her belongings, kissed her mother, nodded to Rose, took her youngest sister's shoulder and placed a warm kiss on her cheek. Then added, as was her greatest fault, 'Don't you forget about this dance now, it'll do you good.'

Vera found that the swallow she was half way managing stopped short at a hiccup in her throat. She said nothing and smiled.

'And Oh! before I forget, have a lovely time at the seaside on Sunday; Tom's got it all planned. Cheerio!' she called out, and left the house, stepping down onto the tarmacadam path. Vera seized the opportunity. 'Seaside? Who's going to the seaside?'

Mabel relaxed against the back of her chair. Rose, still sitting poker straight backed, gave a sniff.

'Tom?' Vera called into the garden.

Rose said stiffly, 'You'll get no sense out of him now.' She craned her neck to see what was going on in the garden. She saw nothing but felt a pang of jealousy at the child's squeals of laughter. Patricia never did that. Looking up, she found Vera looking quizzingly down at her. 'O, nothing very special like. Tom's got the car. The Carpenters have gone visiting friends and . . . ' Rose wittered on in what she considered a formal guide of the plane ride back. In the chair Mabel dozed loudly, her head half lolling on her shoulder and one of her chins resting on her chest. Vera gave an irritated glance but, not wishing to break the opportunity, encouraged Rose to continue with an encouraging and interested smile.

'Isle of Sheppey.' It was Tom's voice behind her.

Vera turned and gave him a puzzled look.

He added, 'It's in Kent. Not far, only take an hour.'

Vera's eyes widened. 'An island?' she gasped, her imagination running away with her. Sylvia tugged at her mother. 'Can we, Mum, can we? Gran's goin' an all, but Patricia's not goin', she's goin' on the Sunday School trip.'

That puzzled Vera. 'On a Sunday, they usually go on a Saturday.'

'Yeah that's right. One of the teacher's not been well, so they are 'avin' early prayers, or somethink like that and goin' on the Sunday. Shame to waste the day. Up for it then? Mum's rarin' to go. Ain't that right?'

Mabel stirred slowly, opened one bleary red bloodshot eye and nodded sagely.

'Well,' said Rose. 'I can tell you it's not Ramsgate!' Her tone was withering and scornful. To make her point she gave yet another tug at her ill fitting jacket, followed by a meaningful sniff. Tom, standing in front of Vera, asked 'Well?' Vera nodded and Sylvia dashed back out into the garden.

Rose tutted. Mabel roused herself. 'Sandwiches,' she pronounced. 'I've got a nice bit of brawn ready for slicin'. That all right?'

Tom swallowed hard, his stomach reaching his throat. 'No, you keep that for yourself. Rose'll do us a few. Won't you, luv?'

The intimacy implied by the last word surprised Rose. 'I'll do what's needed. I don't think we'll go hungry.'

The surprise did nothing to remove her frostiness. Giving another elaborate sniff she said, 'Ham and mustard, that'll do. What d' you think?' She directed the question at Mabel, who had begun to loll once again. 'Mum! Ham and mustard?'

Vera had thrown open the larder door. 'Oh, I think I'll do some egg and cress, cheese and tomato. We've got a few crackers too.'

'Hold up.' Tom's voice drifted in from the garden. 'It ain't a bloody banquet. But it sounds good to me!'

Rose looked up and shook her head disapprovingly. 'Your language,' she said sharply.

Mabel rose slowly to her feet. 'Lawd, I'd best get me 'at out the wardrobe.'

Vera froze on the spot. The excited flush that once filled her face had suddenly drained. The wardrobe referred to was in her bedroom as was the canvas bag that contained her 'housekeeping'. Flustered into action, Vera managed to say calmly, 'No it's all right, Mum, I'll pop up and get it in a mo'. I'll just make a cuppa for us all, eh?'

Rose shot a suspicious glance at her sister. Sylvia, with a quick understanding of the situation once again beyond her years, piped up, 'Want me to get yer 'at, Gran?' The offer was made direct and innocent sounding.

Mabel became a little confused by the sudden rush of offers and retired back into her flat and hardened cushioned chair. 'Think I got a bit of the sun when I went out.'

Vera gave a silent sigh of relief as she lit the gas and Sylvia gave her mother a knowing pixie smile which Vera did not acknowledge for fear of giving their game away, and began to wonder at the impish smile if Sylvia knew what was in the canvas bag. She wasn't going to think about it now.

'Well if we're up for another cuppa,' Rose said, standing, tugging for the umpteenth time at her ill fitting jacket, 'we'd better go in the parlour; it's getting a bit crowded out 'ere.' She eyed her sister again.

Vera gave a brief smile of agreement. Rose added, 'It's the play you'll be wanting then tonight?'

Rose wondered if her mother was nodding in agreement or whether she was nodding at something in her half dozing state.

Rose was gone. Sylvia in a flash went upstairs. Vera held her breath. Tom lumbered in, spinning the ball from one hand to the other. Mabel got to her feet and begun to totter towards the door.

Rose bustling in her usual imperious fashion into the parlour, plumping up cushions on the small solid two seater settee, was beginning to feel something in the way of elation. She felt she had no reason for such a feeling; maybe it was, she mused about her self imposed duties, that it was the thought of a visit to the seaside. She stopped abruptly with a cushion held close to her. It wasn't Ramsgate. Ramsgate had class. It had a harbour and Eastcliffe and Westcliffe and a Marina. What did this island have? 'Mud flats, probably,' she said out loud. Taking command of Mabel's chinz winged armchair, the large flock cushions were as usual flat. She raised them, punched at them. The reversible seat cushion she on the spur of the moment decided to turn; lifting it and running her fingers around the inner edge she found a familiar shape.

'Gin!' Rose rasped, then hearing the door open she quickly returned it to its hiding place.

Mabel stepped laboriously to her chair. 'Think I'll have a bit of a doze, then it'll be all right for me to play. There's a good girl,' Mabel puffed as she lowered her bulk into the large armchair.

'Good grief, she must be tiddly,' Rose registered silently.

Sylvia burst in and said breathlessly as she waved a straw hat decorated with faded flowers, ''Ere Gran, it's a bit dusty.' Her excited and breathless tones were wasted; Mabel was asleep.

'Put it on the back of the door, near the bags,' Rose ordered. 'And ask your Mum where this tea is.'

Sylvia nodded, only too pleased to leave the room.

In the quiet of the kitchen Tom was still throwing the ball absentmindedly from hand to hand. He resumed his seat on the kitchen step and stared into space. Vera, waiting for the kettle to boil, had placed the cups and saucers on the tray ready. On the opposite wall beneath the shelf hung a calendar that Sylvia had made for her Gran. The traditional season snowscene seemed out of place on such a lovely day. She lifted the small brown covered calendar and searched for the present month. With one hand on the table, the other holding back the small pages, she stared intently, trying to make some sense of the days and dates. So engrossed had she become she was startled to find Tom at her side at the stove, beginning to pour the water into the pot. Carefully he studied her face. So far as he knew there was only one reason a woman would need to study a calendar that closely. Having emptied the kettle he gave a small nervous cough and scratched his cheek. After some time of mental deliberation he ventured an indifferent, light, 'What's up, then?'

Vera was even more startled at the question and blushed. She bit the inside of her lip, opened her mouth to speak, then shook her head slowly and remained silent.

'Oh gawd, no.' Tom groaned inwardly. Putting on a bright smile, he said, 'Oh go on, it can't be that bad. Can it?'

Judging by the look on Vera's face he thought the worst. Still smiling, he put the teapot on the cork mat and covered it with its woolly tea cosy.

'Want one?' he asked, indicating the pot. Vera shook her head. 'Be back in a minute.'

Vera watched him as he took the tray into the parlour. She could trust Tom and she had to tell somebody, so it had to be him. Sylvia dashed in. 'Can I 'ave the ball?' Vera nodded a reply. Sylvia scooped up the ball from the chair and scooted into the garden and within seconds the ball's gentle thudding on the outside wall could be clearly heard.

Tom was saying, 'Now what is it? You can tell me.'

Vera put the door to without fully closing it. Her hands behind her back, she held onto the round door knob for support.

'Well?' he said with a small shake of his head and an outstretched hand. He watched as her face drained once again. 'What 'ave you b'en up to?'

Vera's mouth opened. This time words rushed out in an audible whisper. He listened to every syllable of the even hoarser whisperings. Relief swept over him. He gave a hearty laugh and said 'Is that all?'

Vera nodded.

'How much?'

'I've got to give Mum seventeen and six for me housekeeping but,' she looked out into the passage, 'I've got me china pig upstairs, but I 'aven't been able to get up there yet. You know what Mum's like.'

It sounded almost like an apology. This made Tom laugh even louder. Vera raised a forefinger to her lips. Tom thrust his hand into his back pocket and pulled out a pound note. He knew about the dance. 'Here, take this.'

She stared at the note as though it was something from another planet. 'I couldn't,' she finally managed to gasp.

'Go on, a night out'll do you good. Dare say Iris'll enjoy it too. It ain't a crime. 'Ere,' he said slapping the note into her palm, 'just between you and me, eh?'

Vera nodded thankfully.

Reading her thoughts, he said quickly, 'Old Carpenter gave that to me. Him and the missus have gone away for the weekend. Not a bad sort.'

Vera put the note safely into her pocket. 'I don't know 'ow to thank you.'

Tom smiled. 'You can thank me by not thanking me and put a bit of a smile on.'

Rose pushed against the door. 'What's goin' on here?'

Tom quickly cut in. 'Been telling our Vera how Mum nearly didn't 'ave her nice little bit of fish.'

Rose gave a violent snort, another tug of her jacket for emphasis and said, 'If she thought I was going to put it in me bag, then she'd better think again! Smelly things.' Her nose wrinkled.

'What you mean is, you forgot!'

Rose glared, Tom laughed; Vera gave a weak smile of puzzlement.

'I jumped in the old jallopy and fetched it. Couldn't be 'avin our Mabel without her grub.'

'I came in for the biscuit tin; she's moved out the corner cupboard again.' She pushed Vera away from the larder door. 'There it is.'

Tom, goading Rose, added, 'You wouldn't be talking like that if she was bright eyed and bushy tailed.'

'Tom Small,' Rose said, her voice lowering in anger. 'She wouldn't be like this if you didn't keep giving her gin!' She glared, then turning to Vera, said, 'And what 'ave you been up to? I know that look.' Without waiting for an answer she asked, 'Will that child ever stop that infernal banging? It's giving me a headache. I wouldn't let our Patricia get away with it. Anyway, she'd know better.' Then, as was Rose's way, she was gone.

'Who won that one?' Tom asked with a shrug and a wry smile.

The dulled yellow straw hat with its equally dulled posy of flowers, petals of the nondescript blooms having obviously been lost, had for many summers hung forlornly on the hook on the door that led to the under stairs cupboard. It oversaw the cutting and filling of sandwiches, the nimbleness of the fingers placing them in various coloured tin sandwich boxes. The Thermos flasks filled with tea were at last ready. The hat was perched phantom like on the acorn of the bannisters, awaiting its owner. The bags that were once beneath this creation were filled, together with the boxes and flasks.

The hat was snatched from its place and dusted down and wiped clean, but the floral display remained jaded and lacking.

Sunday morning rose. The sun, already hot, heightened with each waiting moment. The waiting was well rewarded. Tom brought the limousine whispering to a halt in front of the gate. He emerged, relaxed in a short-sleeved white open-neck shirt. Dark beige twill trousers held firmly with a leather belt completed his outfit as he approached the front door. Behind, great excitement by way of orders came from Mabel, dressed in a light cotton edge to edge jacket of blue; the hat was now after great discussion firmly on her head. The vegetable dyed flowers hung a little more loosely and the colours had run into the straw, but with a little imagination this small catastrophe had been remedied with a new home found on the outer brim.

Vera called from the kitchen as she tidied up, 'Come on, now, Sylvia, Uncle Tom's here!'

Sylvia had heard her Gran in the passage giving orders. She took the bucket and spade that lived in the bottom of their wardrobe downstairs and waited on the turn for her mother.

'Do bring them bags, Vera,' urged Mabel 'And you get down them stairs, or we'll go without you.'

'Oh Mum, really,' Vera said sharply. 'Oh, come on, luv.' Her face smiled up at her daughter's flushed excited face. If Vera was truthful, she too was beginning to feel a little more than excitement. Obediently Sylvia stood at the foot of the stairs with her grandmother. Mabel eyed the rusting bucket and splintered spade. 'Sandcastles, then?' she said with a nod. The child looked up at this large woman from whom she often withdrew into herself when in her company. Mabel always took it that she was a bit soft like her mum. In fact the child was not only in awe of this mountain of a woman but a little afraid.

The door opened. Tom's voice was welcomed into the small passage with the three females standing there 'All ready for the *Sky Lark*?' he asked with a broad grin and with a rubbing of his hands gave a cheerful chuckle.

Rose was sitting in the front passenger seat. The shoes she had chosen were a mistake. Her feet, already hot, were beginning to swell over the high front, and high stacked heel. Her only concession to this day of relaxation was a linen jacket with matching tight skirt, which should have been left to those with a less full figure, or of less broadness of the beam. She sat, resolutely refusing to have the window opened through it would inevitably become stuffy. Her chosen headgear was cream, frothy and lightly veiled with an obligatory feather of uncertain beginnings.

Vera, standing at the rear of the passage with two leather bags filled to brimming, was almost staggering forward with their weight. 'C'mon girl, shake a leg.' Mabel's voice grew lighter as she stepped through and out onto the asphalt front, making sure all neighbours were aware of this day out.

'You look nice,' Tom heard himself say. 'Give me them.' Reaching for the bags, he took them from her, then noticed just how soft and feminine Vera was dressed. She wore a soft yellow sundress, with a square neck, and the matching belt sat comfortably around her neat waist. He noticed before it really registered, as she closed the kitchen door, how the skirt of the garment hung softly from her hips and with the sun behind her how it showed to her advantage her long and shapely legs. The bags still hung from his hands. Vera looked at Tom. ''Ave I forgotten something?' Tom shook his head, glanced over his shoulder and looked at Rose. 'Ready then?'

Mable, duchess-like, gave a regal wave to Rose. Opening the door, Mabel settled herself into the comfortable soft leather seat. The two women did not exchange a word.

Tom stepped down and walked quickly to the boot. Unlocking it, he carefully settled the bags with the small basket of food Rose had prepared. He raised an eyebrow.

Looking up, he saw Sylvia. 'C'mon, luv, the tide'll be out by the time we get there,' he said, laughing with the excited child. He opened the offside rear door and Sylvia humped in beside her Gran. Vera followed, enjoying every moment of this morning. Lifting her skirt carefully, her lithesome form slid effortlessly into the rear seat. She unwound the window, allowing the fresh morning air in. Rose groaned, 'We're not goin' to suffer a gale from here to there, are we?' she demanded.

Vera took no notice. She took the small coloured bucket with the small spade placed inside and put it on the floor of the car beside her. 'Now,' she said, looking at her daughter, 'you can have a good look about.' Another moan emitted from Rose. Vera smiled to herself.

Mabel was getting a little restless. 'We orf then?'

Tom glanced into the rear mirror. Catching her look, he smiled and said, 'Ready when you are, Ma'am.'

As Mabel laughed her body shook. With another regal wave of her hand, she said, 'Forward, James.'

Everyone laughed except Rose. Her feet hurt and the button had just popped off her skirt, and she could smell fish. Rose said to herself, it's like taking coals to Newcastle! Then with an excited giggle from Sylvia, the car pulled silently away from the kerb and purred contentedly on its gentle journey.

It was just after ten thirty. The car purred, Rose sniffed, Mabel snored spasmodically, Tom hummed to himself, Vera smiled and Sylvia's eyes missed nothing as the gleaming black car took them to the seaside. She was the first to spot 'the sea'. It was at this point that

Mabel, hearing the word 'sea', asked, 'Where?' It was a false alarm; what Sylvia had spotted was the river. A few hundred yards further along the scene changed dramatically. They were surrounded by sheep. 'Look Mum, herds of sheep!'

Vera watched the pastoral symphony that was painted in moving canvas. 'No,' she said softly, 'flock.'

Sylvia's once excited face now looked troubled and she asked, 'That's what's in pillows?'

Vera smiled and shook her head. 'Not that kind of flock.'

Sylvia was happy. Not only she had learnt something new, she had never been this close to sheeps before. A very good job it was her mother had not heard her use 'sheeps'. That would have ended as a different story.

'Filthy things,' Rose remarked. 'Just look at them, all mud an' blood!'

Vera gave a sigh. 'Rose, it's their mark. The red. It's a kind of ink. And they are living . . . '

She didn't finish. 'Still filthy creatures,' Rose said, unconvinced.

'Boats!' squealed Sylvia.

'Really, Vera, don't you take your child nowhere?'

Again Vera smiled. Nothing but nothing was going to spoil this day. Her mind was made up. And Sylvia was right. There were boats, lots of them. It was a river they were approaching, with a high, wide bridge.

Mabel snored and roused herself from her own half sleep. 'Eh. What?'

Vera touched her mother's arm. 'We're going onto the island.' Her tone was reassuring.

'Gawd!' was Mabel's only response.

Rose sniffed once again.

Halfway across the wooden rickety bridge, Tom said, ''Ere, Mum, you're abroad now. Isle of Sheppey, here we come. Island of sheep, that's what it means, you know.'

'What country we in, then?' Sylvia's face puckered in puzzlement.

'Uncle Tom's only joking. We're in Kent.' Vera didn't admit that she'd looked it up in one of Tom's road atlases, the night before.

Mabel, reassured of terra firma, fell soundly back to sleep. As she wedged herself into the upholstered corner, her sunhat slipped. Vera made a quick grab for it over Sylvia's head. It sat in her lap looking just as forlorn if not lonely. The small bunch of what Vera remembered were once red rosebuds, or were they African violets, she still couldn't be sure. She picked at the petals and stared at the back of Rose's head. Vera reflected that in the hour or more of travelling few words of conversation had been made by Rose. Vera wondered if perhaps Mabel had noticed how over the years the petals had been 'lifted'. The hat been always packed away in a large brown paper bag, except for when Rose would use the petals, dipping them in warm water and using them for rouge and lipstick, until she discovered red food colouring. The leaves were used as eyeshadow even into the later years before she married Tom. Vaseline mixed with just a touch of fine soot from the fireplace, often bottled and hidden away, served as both eyebrow and eyelash colouring, not forgetting the crease of the eye. There was no doubting that Rose was, and some might think still was, a dramatic looking woman. If only she wasn't so ... what was she? inflexible. Vera wondered if Rose could still remember the evenings they had sat on their shared double bed in candle light, a scarf thrown onto the floor at the foot of the door so as not to attract attention, holding a small hand mirror applying what Rose called 'doing my face', or 'putting my face on'. Quite suddenly Rose turned and glared first at Vera, then the hat. Looking straight at Vera, she gave a look which clearly said, 'I dare you!' It was such a lovely day Vera had to control herself from poking out her tongue at Rose. So she gave a half smile of understanding.

Sylvia tugged at her mother. 'Look, it's the sea! We're at the seaside.' She leaned over her mother and grabbed at her bucket and spade.

''Ere we are. Front row view.'

Rose sprang up, her nose on the windscreen. 'It's deserted,' she said in disgust. 'There's not even a ... a ...' she faltered. Then she added boldly, 'A toilet.'

'Don't worry about that, Rose,' Mabel's tired voice cut in. 'There's three of us, we'll find somewhere. Behind a bush maybe,' she added, goading a response from Rose.

'There's none of them either!' Rose folded her arms and sat back in her seat, staring blankly out of the window. Tom parked the car high above the shore. Cliffs and paths ran higgledy piggledy at random down the grassy eroded front. Even though the weather was glorious, the wind could be heard whipping around and across the vehicle. Mabel had a good look about. 'Nice place for our dinner. Nice to see a bit of grass.'

'That's not grass,' Rose moaned. 'That's mud!'

Mabel ignored her. 'C'mon, boy, give a lady a hand out.'

Tom, already out of the car, was unlocking the boot. 'Hang on a mo', Mum, I'll be right there. Got a surprise for you.'

Sylvia, the bucket swinging from her hand, the other firmly held by Vera, waited to see what this surprise could be. On seeing it, she smiled and said, 'Oooo cor!' Judging the wind direction he took from the boot a tassled brown plaid car rug. Placing it on the grass he then took a gaily striped canvas cross shaped deck chair and pulled it open, hoping it would accommodate Mabel's bulk. On top of one of the large bags rested a tea towel. He took this, folded it over his arm, and approached Mabel, who was unaware of anything. He offered his arm to her and said, 'Follow me, M'lady. Luncheon awaits.' He spread his arm in a sweeping gesture towards the 'banquet'. Mabel, spotting the upright canvas chair, roared with laughter. 'You are a one. Hope that,' she said, pointing at the chair, 'will hold all this!' Mabel slapped her thigh. Taking Tom's arm she swayed regally towards the 'table'. Wedging herself into the chair, she rocked it from side to side purely in the search for safety, and satisfied herself that it would hold. Her hands clasped the wooden arms. Looking up at Tom and eyeing him suspiciously, she asked, 'Where d' you get it?'

A huge grin fell across Tom's face. 'I borrowed it, just for you.'

'You,' Mabel answered, wagging a sausage like finger at him, '. . . make sure they get it back tomorrow.'

'M'lady,' he said attentively and bowed from the waist. He said solemnly, 'Luncheon is served, ladies.' Another sweeping gesture made towards Vera and Sylvia who were giggling at this impromptu pantomime.

Smiling, Vera shook her head. 'Not just yet. We want to have a look around. Coming, Rose?'

Silence was her only reward. Rose sat stiffly, staring out to sea. No one knew that she was a little fearful about moving in case her skirt dropped. And, she comforted herself, there was nothing to see anyway. Silently she shook her head, then wondered if it would be wise to take off her shoes. She pondered on the problem whilst Vera and her daughter, swinging hands, climbed the rolling leas. After a few yards they heard Mabel say, 'You gonna sit there all bloody day? Oh, please yourself!'

Mabel, suitably enthroned, tea cloth on her lap for a napkin, took charge of the bulging bags. 'What yer got in 'ere?' Sylvia looked up and smiled. Vera looked down and giggled.

Tom was sitting on the travel rug. Rose, still unmoved from her perch, looked on.

'For a queen on the throne now, won't be the same, you know,' Mabel informed them.

Tom looked up and wondered, has she been on the gin yet? She was talking as if this enthronement had taken place just that morning. Or maybe it was the upright thronelike canvas chair. 'And . . . Einstein's dead.' Her announcement surprised him. The fresh air's got to her. He still couldn't find the connection. But that was Mabel. He looked up and watched as the large heavy face chomped at a sandwich, her large mouth still clearly not big enough for the amount of sandwich she wanted it to consume.

Tom erred on the side of caution. 'Quite right. Another sandwich. I know, a cup of tea, that always sees us right.'

Mabel nodded, incapable of answering as her mouth was stuffed full and her jaws were grinding at the food unmercifully, even as she found another sandwich to her liking. Tom sat in silence listening to the chewing as he rested his forearm on his knees sipping his tea.

Vera and her daughter had reached to the top of the leas where it turned into an almost blind bend. On reaching this, Vera pointed towards the other side of the road. 'Look, Sylvia, there's a shop and a pub. There 'as to be a ladies in there,' she said, thinking of her mother.

Sylvia nodded and added, 'Uncle Tom'll like that too.'

Vera stood puzzled for a second. 'Oh, you mean the pub?'

Sylvia nodded.

As they walked the few yards to have a look in the shop, Sylvia asked unexpectedly, 'What's in the bag?'

Vera raised a finger to her lips. 'I'll show you when we get home. You really haven't looked?'

Sylvia solemnly shook her head. 'Said I wouldn't.'

Relenting, Vera said in a whisper as if someone could overhear, 'It's a dress. For the dance.'

The child's face lit up. 'What, a posh frock?' Her eyes filled with dream-like wonderment.

'Yes.' It was Vera's turn to sound dreamy. 'It's . . . ' she stopped abruptly. 'I will show you when we get 'ome tonight.'

They both stood in silence, staring into the window. It was full of animals made from cockle shells. Seaside rock, buckets and spades. Toys and a few dead flies, not forgetting the single bee or was it a wasp? In the corner of the window there stood a kite. It was yellow and blue and it had a long tail with feathery knots. Vera watched as her daughter's eyes fell on it. Wordlessly, she looked at her mother. Vera read the look, but did not acknowledge her silent wish. It would be cruel, and Vera had begun to feel a little guilty at her frivolous overspending.

'Let's go and get some food before your Gran eats it all.'

Taking her daughter's hand she began to sprint down the hill towards the black speck of the car that glinted in the sunlight. 'Last one's a cissy!' She let go and Sylvia flashed past her. Seconds later they both collapsed in a heap on the rug at Mabel's feet sturdily clad in high fronted lace up shoes. Breathlessly they grabbed sandwiches and devoured them hungrily.

Mabel, taking yet another sandwich, parted the slices and with thumb and forefinger removed the filling. 'What'yer call this, Rose?' Her voice was disbelieving. Dangling the food in mid air, Rose took a look and said flatly, 'Ham.'

'Ham?' Mabel exclaimed in a bellow. 'I've seen your father roll fags with thicker fag papers.' The memory gave way to a throaty sarcastic chuckle. 'It's not yer 'am cooked and cut off the bone.'

'That,' Rose said, weary of her mother's derogatory remarks, 'what you're talking about is boiled bacon.'

Unperturbed, Mabel continued, 'It's that ready sliced packed stuff, that costs a fortune, *and*,' she added, just to have the final word, 'Where's the mustard?'

'I don't eat mustard.'

'Yeah, but you're not eating 'em!' Mabel was triumphant. She put the slice back into the bread, filled her mouth and chomped away once again.

Rose was sitting half in the car, her spreading beam end on the side of the seat and her feet firmly on the running board. 'If you don't like them, you don't 'ave to eat 'em.' She watched as her mother chewed noisely, which Rose found repulsive.

Sylvia broke the tension which the child was unaware of and asked, 'Can I go and make some sandcastles?'

Vera took a look over the cliff into the bay far below. 'It's all pebbles.'

Tom broke in. 'No, I've found a bit of a sandy spot over there.' He pointed towards the nearest waterbreak.

Vera nodded. 'But not on your own.'

'I've finished me grub, just for the minute, mind; I'll come with you.'

In a flash they were both on their feet and running towards the wooden steps that led onto the beach below.

''E'll never grow up, that one,' Mabel said, her sandwich flapping at them, underlining her point.

'Sandwich, Rose?'

Rose turned towards her sister and gave her a steely look that asked if she was about to pull her sandwiches to bits.

44

'Egg and cress.'

Vera rummaged around the various coloured tins, found the sandwiches and offered them to Rose. 'If you think I'm getting out of this car...'

Vera raised a hand in defence. 'I'll come to you, and it isn't muddy. It's not even damp.'

With the red lidded tin in her hand she settled on the running board beside her sister. Giving the tin to Rose, she noticed her sister's swollen feet. 'Why don't you take 'em off?'

Rose picked at the sandwich, eating mouthfuls that befitted a bird. Her back was lowered, her elbows resting on her knees. Vera continued in the absence of reply, 'You can't sit here all day.' Vera's voice was sympathetic; she couldn't understand why anybody would want to sit half in a car on such a beautiful day dressed as Rose was. 'Go on, take off yer jacket,' she urged with a smile.

Rose tossed her head towards Mabel. 'Never, if I ever look like that!'

Vera looked at her mother, watching the jaws grind up and down from side to side. 'Mum's enjoyin' herself. She don't get out much, and...' she hesitated, choosing her words carefully, 'She's not as young as...'

Rose's voice rose, sharp edged: 'And what do you mean by that? I'm in the prime of life!' The words exploded like mini bombs of indignation. Her face was crimson with fury. She finished showing her disgust by throwing the sandwich at Vera.

'Rose was damned cussed,' Vera thought to herself. Usually given to unfathomable depths of patience, she had lost it with this demanding woman, 'truculent, or was it petulant?' Vera no longer cared. As she rescued the sandwich from the running board, something caught her eye. She looked up into the wispy cotton wool clouds and there saw a seagull circling. It appeared to get lower with each decreasing circle. She stared at the snowy wonder, then Rose's veiled trivial hat. 'Just once,' thought Vera, willing the seagull to drop an almighty plop onto her hat. She sat wishing and staring at the gull, willing it with every fibre of her body to... just this once. With a sudden leap to her feet she threw the sandwich over the cliff on to the beach below. In a second the gull had dived out of sight to search out its bounty.

'No need for that kind of thing.' Mabel glowered between mouthfuls. 'Throwing good food away, and it's about time you two stopped this bickering. I would have eaten it!'

Rose said under her breath, 'I bet you would.'

Vera felt a surge of overwhelming sympathy for Rose. She was always alone, she didn't mix much. To Vera's thinking she believed Rose 'cried inside'. She was nevertheless a difficult woman to get to know. She was her sister but there the similarity finished.

Vera leaned back against the car stretching out her legs and crossing them at the ankles. She looked up at Rose sitting straight and starched and said enquiringly, 'Rose?'

Rose instantly recognized this tone. Sharply she asked. 'What?'

Vera began, 'Why didn't you and Tom 'ave more children? Well, I mean . . . you've been married for ten years. What I mean is,' she continued falteringly, 'did you decide not to 'ave any more, or don't you do "it" any more?'

Rose, face still flushed with the earlier indignation, couldn't believe her ears. Scarlet faced she turned onto her younger sister and hissed, 'What did you say?' Rose's eyes flashed like lightning within their dark tunnels.

Vera, unperturbed, continued. She was used to Rose's rages and whilst she knew her patience towards her sister had recently begun to grow thin, she continued, 'Or, is that you just don't want to?'

The emphasised word 'you', savaged Rose. Her teeth clenched, her jaw fixed, she gave a withering glare at Vera, having noted that Mabel was life's double of a beached walrus stuffed into a chair with facial hair to match. The words dripped from her lips, not wanting to arouse Mabel's insatiable interference with anything she wasn't directly involved in.

Rose, now enraged, kicked out at the sandwich box. 'You' – the word whipped at Vera's face – 'You,' she hissed even more ardently, 'are nothing but a hussy, a Jezebel, a fallen woman. It's thinking like that, what got you in trouble. Her,' she jerked her dark head in Mabel's direction, 'should have thrown you out. If Dad'd been alive he would 'ave.' She took a breath. 'Look at you, no stockings, and no brassière, showing everything you got. Pregnant at sixteen. You disgust me. Things like that are not talked about. What did you do, get jealous when Patricia was born? Thought you'd like a real dolly too?'

It was Rose's remark about Patricia that fired Vera. Whatever kind thoughts and patience she had once held for Rose had just left her. Looking up into Rose's crimson face sealed her thoughts. Rose hadn't finished. 'And as for her – her hand flicked over the cliff, presumably indicating Sylvia – 'Sylvia indeed. What kind of name is that? A bloody American one, I s'pose! A tart, nothing other than a tart!' She took another breath. 'Talk like that . . . fast and loose, and that's what most people think!' She folded her arms punctuating her full stop.

Calmly, Vera picked up the dented sandwich box, squeezed on the lid and looked at her sister, who had not realised that her outburst, though not answering her question directly, had in fact told Vera everything she wanted to know. She stood up slowly and looked down at her sister, which gave her an advantage. She answered coolly, 'Sylvia is named after the song, an English folk song, "Who is Sylvia".'

Before she could turn to make her point, Rose bellowed, 'Who is Sylvia? Huh? Should have been who is Sylvia's father?' Rose gave a snort of delight at the kill. 'Now that is something we know would make our day!' With arms still folded defiantly across her, she sat even more boardlike against an invisible chair back.

Vera put the box back on the rug, and asked her mother if she would like some tea, as the woman was unable to move forward or sideways to lift the flasks from the ground. Mabel grunted a reply. 'Then,' said Vera, 'I'm going down onto the beach.'

With eyes half closed, awaiting fitful sleep, Mabel said, 'You'd better get our Sylvie up 'ere for some food.'

Vera nodded, a feeling of desolation reaching deep within her. She spotted the steps that Tom and Sylvia had used and made towards them. It was still windy, and the sudden gusts caught her skirt as she walked. It wasn't cold. As she started down the wooden steps she could see Tom and Sylvia racing up and down the shingle beach with a kite. Like the kite, she felt her thoughts and spirits rise. Unhesitatingly, she too raced down the steps onto the beach and began like them to tug at the string, watching the kite soar higher and higher. Elation flooded through her; she was soaring too. She was that kite . . . she was free.

The three of them raced up and down the shingle beach, the shiny pebbles under their footsteps creating crunching waves. Eventually, they fell exhausted onto the sand. Tom took the kite and tied it securely to the bottom of the handrail. Patting it in a reassuring fashion, he then sat down heavily on the patch of sand. Taking a handful, he watched intently as it fell through his fingers as it was caught by the soft offshore breeze. The beach was a bay accessed only by the rickety old stairs. The wind that whipped across the leas on the cliff top was not a problem; here the sun shone high and hot, the breeze from the sea soft and gentle.

Sylvie asked, 'Can we make some sandcastles?'

Vera shook her head 'No. Not just now, you go up to Gran and get yourself somethin' to eat; I'll be up in a bit.'

'When I come back?' the child asked plaintively.

'Course we will,' broke in Tom. 'Mind you, we'll 'ave to wet this sand.' He raised a handful and let it fall to the breeze 'See?' She nodded and gave him her bucket. 'Right, thanks. I'll get to it now. Strewth,' he laughed to himself under his breath.

'Go on,' Vera encouraged, 'don't make a noise. She might be 'avin' a bit of a nod.'

Sylvia ran up the steps as Vera looked on. With a slight wave of the hand the child had disappeared out of sight.

Vera looked up at the kite fluttering high above, her eyes screwed up against the sun and with a frown of puzzlement across her face asked, 'Will it stay up, then?' She shielded her eyes with her hand across her brow, waiting for Tom to answer. Tom was still toying with the sand. Handfuls drained through his fingers as he stared through each sparkling grain. Vera gave him a playful shove. 'Well?' she demanded.

Tom looked up at her. 'Eh?'

Vera shook her head. 'Tom Small. The kite . . . will it stay up all right?'

'Should do, there are more thermals up there than down 'ere.'

Well, Vera thought, he should know, he was in the RAF.

Her gaze was still fixed on the kite as she lay back on the sand, her shoulders resting on a grassy hummock. Her long legs she crossed in her customary fashion at the ankles and raising her hands above her head she began searching for a juicy grass to chew. Tom watched her. Her head was tilted backwards as her fingers searched through the rough grass. With her arms above her head her dress had risen above her knees. Tom looked on longingly. They seemed to go on forever. Sun tanned and shiny, they gleamed under the afternoon sun. His eyes followed her long limbs up to her waist. It was neat, small and tidily trimmed with the narrow belt. Her breasts were high and with her arms above her head had slipped from the restraining gathers of her bodice. Tom began to bend towards her. His hand was hovering, shaking almost above her belly. She gave a squeal of delight, kicked off her white canvas shoes and dug her toes into the sand. 'Found some!'

Tom remained statue-like. Her head was still tilted at an angle. He leaned into her, bent over the curve of her neck and brushed his lips against her skin below her ear. He gently put his hand on her waist and found his fingers hard into her, raising her up into him. He felt her body quiver, then just as unexpectedly relax in his grip. He waited. His breath was coming in short hard silent gasps. Slowly Vera's eyes opened, her long lashes swept upwards and her bright clear eyes fixed onto his. It was all he could do to stop himself from shouting out loud, 'Vera!' He stayed silent. Vera's eyes still held his as she lowered her arms. One arm fell lightly on his shoulder; the other fell to her side and with the hand she began to unbutton her bodice. Her belt was also swiftly unhooked and Tom instantly felt the warmth of her nakedness as her dress fell open onto the sand. He nuzzled his face between her breasts. He brushed her lips with nothing more than the lightness of a butterfly, then his mouth searched hard into hers. His bit and nipped at her full bottom lip.

He heard her whisper his name: 'Tom,' she whispered in his ear. She felt the cool steel of his belt drop onto her bare middle. The gentle shock made her breasts full, her nipples raised and spread erect. Tom's shoulders had cut off the sun from her body. She could feel him kneeling closely beside her. Then with his shirt swinging free from his torso, she clung to him. Her hands felt his muscles in his back moving slowly and rhythmically. In seconds he had moved across her body to gather her up to him. Her head fell onto his shoulder and as she opened her eyes the sun's stabbing heat seared through her.

They lay on their backs, side by side in complete silence. Without turning towards her, Tom said, 'Vera. I'm s . . . ' He stopped. He wasn't sorry and he knew she wasn't. He remembered so much. Vera was still buttoning up her dress and she bent over him. 'Shhh,' she said it like a lullaby. Then to add weight to her utterance she put two fingers on his lips to erase his response. Vera sat back against the hummock once again and began sifting the sand through her fingers. She had wanted to ask if he and Rose ever did 'it' any more. She now knew the answer.

Tom, his shirt still free from his trousers but buttoned in its usual way, raised himself on one elbow and he too began playing with the sand again. Then they caught sight of each other, grinned and laughed at themselves.

Vera said shyly, 'We saw the kite in that shop up by the dirt track.'

Tom nodded. 'I know, Sylvie gave me the exact directions.'

'Oh, I thought that was it. You didn't get the dead wasp either, did you?' she teased.

'No,' he said, giving her a heave to her feet. 'It was a bee, see, clever dick!'

'C'mon, let's get something to eat. I feel quite 'ungry now.' He looked at her over his shoulder and gave her one of his impish smiles and a slow steady wink.

Tom tugged at the kite string, and began to pull in the flight. Vera was brushing down her dress when from above they heard, 'Oi, 'urry up. I've got to go to the lav.'

Vera looked up and there standing on the top of the steps stood

Mabel teetering. Vera gave up a look of grave concern. ''S' all right, Mum, don't move, I'll be right there.'

Mabel was unmoved. 'If you thought for one minute,' her voice thundered down at her daughter, 'I was gonna get down them steps, you'd better think again!'

As Vera dashed past Tom, he managed to give her a smile and say, 'No peace for the wicked eh?' The look she gave him in return made him wish he had cut out his tongue. He made a grab for her but she was gone. At the top Vera took her mother's arm. As she led her along the cliffs she wondered how on earth she had managed to get out of the deck chair; the last time she looked Mabel had been well and truly wedged. 'Where's Rose?' Vera's voice tried to disguise her irritability.

'She won't get out of that car!' Mabel gasped, her breath coming in laboured gasps.

'Take it easy, Mum, there's a ladies over in that little shop.'

As they passed the car, Vera hissed at Rose, 'Give us a hand.' Rose turned away, choosing to stare back at the sea. 'Well, don't you need to . . . go?' Vera asked in hushed tones.

'Silly cow,' Mabel muttered under her breath. 'She'll do 'erself a mischief.'

Sylvia joined them, asking where Uncle Tom was. 'Just behind.' He's brought the kite along, and Sylvia, you musn't ask like that ever again. It's rude.'

'Uncle Tom didn't mind.'

Vera gave an exasperated sigh. 'You go in with your Gran now, all right.' She took two pennies from her pocket, knowing that Sylvia would not use the same toilet as her Gran.

'No need for that, luv, we'll share.'

Vera shook her head and thrust the penny into her daughter's hand. 'I'll wait here.'

She stood with her arms folded. In the distance she could see Tom, with the kite safely tucked under his arm. She felt a flash of anger, then indignation, then a warm feeling enveloped her and she just stood and watched. She knew. She just knew . . .

'Well, come on, girl,' Tom said to Rose. 'Don't you want to go to the . . . well, you know.' He jerked his head quickly towards the hill.

Rose gave him one of her long withering looks. She could have asked the same, but by the sight of him she'd guessed he'd gone already. Ignoring him, she turned back to the sea. He shook his head and began to tidy up. He carefully folded the rug, and within a few minutes the boot had been loaded.

'What about these?' He waved a sandwich box at Rose.

'Feed to them!' she said tossing her head towards the circling gulls, 'they've had everythin' else.' She swung her legs into the car, slammed the door beside her and locked it.

'Oh gawd, it's goin' to be a long way home,' he groaned.

As he waited for the rest he decided that a detour to the Bunch of Grapes at Cudham would be called for; a pint was definitely called for, and a gin or two for Mum would keep her sweet. Rose could sweat; she usually did.

Chapter 4

The following Monday morning found Vera ringing the front doorbell of Mrs Lownds. She searched the stained glass door for movement behind. There was none. In earnest Vera pressed the bell again. The sound would have been enough to raise the dead. Vera took a step back and searched for any signs of life at the bedroom windows. All seemed in order. The curtains were open and the milk was conspicuous by its absence. Vera always took it in when she 'did'. Her basket heavy on her arm, she took another step back, searching every inch of the front of the house. Vera thought it might be different had she not arrived early as Mabel had had one of her 'turns' last night, and she'd left early to be sure she would be home early. She knew Mrs Lownds wouldn't mind in the least. But where was she? Vera leaned wearily on the gate post, last night's events catching up with her. Sighing, Vera stepped backwards onto the pavement, and called out softly to catch the very deaf Mrs Lownds' attention. She couldn't too loudly as it was only just eight in the morning and this was Bromley.

She had started out early, to keep her promise to Sybil Chapman, and had returned the canvas bag. Mrs Chapman hadn't even been in the shop when she arrived. She had opened the side door and had received the bag back as a matter of course. Vera had taken the quickest way, through the park, across the main road and swiftly along Acacia Avenue. But now, where was Mrs Lownds? The milkman rattled past Vera, giving a cursory glance, knowing that at that time of the morning it was the 'early' milkman that everyone used. Sighing heavily yet again, Vera took another step back and 'Cooo eed', all to no avail.

Tom Small had risen early too. He was troubled. Sunday had been a good day. If only he could have . . . still, that was yesterday. He drove along, the engine purring, the car responding to his lightest touch. He lit a cigarette and with his elbow resting on the open window felt content. The early morning was still hazy but the high cloud would soon burn off giving way to a clear blue day. The journey home yesterday afternoon had proved difficult; still he cut his tongue out, fancy saying 'No peace for the wicked' after doing *that*. He consoled himself with a thought that was ungenerous: 'Well, she didn't say no!' The amber indicator clicked out. In addition he punched his arm through the open window indicating to turn right. In the crown of the road he swung the car into Acacia Avenue, and as he did so a thought sprang to mind. His hand slipped into his immaculately pressed trousers pocket to find some coppers for the telephone. A box, he knew, was on the next corner. Suddenly, there was something in the road. He caught a glimpse of it out of the corner of his eye. He stopped the car by literally standing on the brakes; the car was heavy and what would he expect to find in this side road at this time of the morning? He leapt from the car shaking, terrified of what he might find beneath the wheels.

He kicked open the door so violently that it swung back on his leg, but oblivious of the pain he knelt in front of the newly waxed and polished radiator and bumper. 'Vera!' Trembling he knelt down beside her. The contents of her basket were still rolling into the gutter. 'Vera,' her name formed on his lips and fell from his mouth like a strangulated whisper. Her eyes were closed; she was dazed and dusty. He lifted her head and gently rested it on his knee. Gratefully he saw her eyes slowly open. A look of puzzled astonishment showed in her face. 'Tom.'

'Thank God,' Tom managed to say. Still trembling, he lifted her shoulders onto his knee. Then in an over zealous manner he brushed down her clothes. 'Oh Vera, I'm so sorry. What y'doin' around here this time of the morning?'

Vera suddenly started to life and began pushing away his searching hands. 'Will you stop, Tom Small, I was looking for Mrs Lownds.'

'Well, you won't find her in the road,' Tom replied, offended. He hauled her to her feet 'So, you're all right then?'

'Of course, I just slipped, that's all.' Vera regained her composure, basket hanging from her elbow, and packed back the contents with every bob and curtsey. Flushed, she looked at Tom's forlorn face.

Tom stopped mid curtsey by gently touching her wrist. 'Vera . . . '

Vera instantly recognized this tone and waited. His face was contorted, attempting to put into words the thoughts in his mind. Eventually he said, 'I'm sorry, you know, about what I said. Yesterday; you know, about being, well, you know, about no peace for the wick . . . ' He couldn't finish the word.

'S' all right Tom,' Vera said gently, putting him out of his misery.

'Blimey, Vera, you didn't half give me a turn.'

'Don't talk to me about turns. I was up half the night with Mum. She had one of her breathy turns. I'm sure it's her 'eart.'

Vera was walking onto the path of the neat colourful front garden. Tom followed demurely behind.

'How d'you mean?'

Vera pushed the bell hard. 'She can't get her breath and she goes a funny colour like. Sylvia gets frightened. I 'ave asked her to see the doctor, but,' here she sighed heavily, 'you know Mum.'

Tom nodded sympathetically. You didn't argue with Big Mabel. 'What about old Doc Thomas? I mean, if she's gotta undo her clothes, like, she might feel a bit happier with an old un.'

Vera returned a nod of acknowledged exasperation. 'Where is Mrs Lownds?' Vera peered through the letter box, her upbringing giving way to worry. Without a chance to haul him back Tom had thrust himself between the dividing privet hedge and the wall and was banging on next door's knocker. Wide eyed and open mouthed, Vera looked on in open mouthed horror. You just didn't do that sort of thing in Bromley, she lamented.

The door opened and an elderly woman looked enquiringly at Tom. 'Sorry to trouble you, luv,' he said cheerily. 'You wouldn't 'appen to know if the old girl next door's all right?'

The elderly woman gave Tom a look of disdain, said, 'No hawkers,' and promptly slapped the door shut.

'Charming,' Tom said, turning to Vera. 'Natives ain't so friendly round 'ere then.'

At this Vera managed a smile. Tom was always good at being able to do that. Tom was beginning to brush himself down with the back of his hand when the door swung silently open. The hallway was empty.

'*Mrs Lownds!*' Vera screamed.

Within seconds the sound of shuffling feet emerged from behind the heavy stained glass door. A frail genteel figure stood quietly on a coconut mat that was so deep Tom was sure it would devour her. She stood no taller than four feet eight inches tall and with her hands placed on the small of her back, accentuating her rounded back and jutting neck reminded Tom of a dulled decrepit 'Silver Lady' from the bonnet of a very ancient Rolls Royce.

Gathering his senses, Tom asked, 'You all right, Ma'am?' (he always pronounced it 'Mum'.)

Clear crystal grey eyes looked up into his. 'They are, aren't they?'

Vera interrupted. 'Where have you bin?' I've been worried out my mind.'

The elderly face replied, 'They are lovely, aren't they?' She smiled benignly. 'Is this your young man, Vera?'

54

'Er no, he's my brother in law, Tom.'

'Very nice too, would you like a cup of tea, young man?'

'Very kind of you to offer, M'am, but . . . '

Mrs Lownds, her hands now resting on her small rounded middle, sighed. 'They are a little early, but we're all the more grateful for them.'

Tom gave Vera a helpless look. Suddenly it dawned on her.

'Mum,' she whispered, although she didn't know why; Mrs Lownds was as deaf as a post. 'Chrysanthemums, that's what they're called, mums.'

Tom was none the wiser.

'Where 'ave you been?'

Mrs Lownds made a gesture. 'It's Bessie, she was locked in the coal bunker.'

Tom couldn't stand any more, 'Who was and what do you want with coal this time of the year?'

Mrs Lownds smiled up at him. 'It's cheap rate.'

Tom shook his head. 'Who's Bessie?'

At this point Vera kicked his ankle to catch his wandering attention, lowered her eyes for Tom to follow and there, purring around their ankles, was Bessie the ginger cat.

'Oh, Bessie,' Tom said, as if he had known all along.

'After the queen, you know,' The frail figure continued undeterred. 'She was a red head too, you know.'

Vera felt that this exchange had gone as far as it could.

'I'd better come in now.'

Vera stepped into the hall, and as she was closing the door, Tom suddenly said, ''Ave you got any coppers for the telephone?'

Vera dug deep into her pocket. 'Here,' she said, counting out a few coppers into his open palm.

'Ooo, I don't need all that.' He took it and hearing the door close behind him tossed the coins into his hand then shook his head and asked himself, 'What did I want these for?'

Behind him he heard Vera's voice,' And don't forget to bring Mum a nice little bit of fish on Friday.'

Tom slid into the driver's seat, lit another cigarette and sat quietly thinking over the last few minutes' events. Then asked out loud, 'Who did I want to telephone?' He could see the telephone box from where he sat but he still couldn't remember who or why he wanted to use the telephone.

Vera removed the cornflower blue creation she had hidden beneath a heavy greatcoat, placing it carefully on the knitted patchwork cover. She watched as Sylvia's eyes opened and squeals of delighted approval fell in 'Ooos' and Ah's' and 'OO, Mummy!' Her eyes lit up as she fingered the garment. 'Put it on, oh, go on, put it on, Now!'

Vera raised a warning finger to her lips. 'Not too loud, Gran'll hear.'

Sylvia sat on the edge of the bed. She was not usually allowed to do this but she knew that this time she might get away with it. Taking the wooden hanger from the heavy dark oak wardrobe she hung the dress up and put it on the back of the door beneath her dressing gown.

'I'll put it on later, after I have pressed it. I'll make sure your Gran's listening to her play or having a snooze. I'll slip downstairs now and make some tea.' She put a finger under her daughter's chin and asked fondly, 'You want some?'

Sylvia's eyes were alight. 'Up 'ere?'

Vera nodded.

Vera took that as a yes and padded downstairs, stopping momentarily on the half landing to listen for, she hoped, Mabel's unmistakable snoring. There was not a sound. Vera continued and in the kitchen she could hear the wireless. She filled the kettle, popped it on the stove, then put her head into the parlour and asked brightly, 'Like some tea, Mum? I'll make us some then I've got a bit of ironing to do.'

At this, Mabel stirred and asked, 'What, on a Wednesday?'

Vera felt herself getting hot, but she only nodded and smiled.

'Sure, I don't know what you find to iron these days. It runs up the electric, you know?'

Vera nodded again. 'It won't take long.'

She removed her head and shoulders from the room and waited for the kettle to boil, tapping her foot impatiently and folding her arms to keep calm. The back door was still open; there were signs of dusk gathering. The sun was low and orange over the grey blue slate roofs. With the tea made, she put one on Mabel's small side table, and took hers and Sylvia's upstairs. Seconds later she returned, removed iron and ironing board from beneath the stairs and tiptoed back to the delight of Sylvia, who liked to see her Mum get one over her Gran. To make the evening perfect, Vera produced a half pound of broken biscuits and Vera, sitting with her daughter, felt as elated, and more schoolgirlish than she had felt in years. Together dunking biscuits each exchanged nervous glances at the blue gap that showed beneath the open dressing gown hanging on the back of the door.

Vera slid to the floor, saying, 'Look, there's these too.' On her knees in front of the wardrobe she hunted inside for a battered shoe box. Pulling it free, Sylvia heard the rustle of tissue paper. This thrilled her; rustling tissue always meant something special. From the yellowing box Vera removed blue satin shoes and a smaller tissue packet.

The blue shoes looked out of place on the worn, dull and cracked lino floor covering. Realising this, she placed them on the rag mat at the side of the bed. Sylvia stared unblinkingly at them. She had never seen such shoes before. For fear of them being a dream she dared not touch them, and stared even harder. The tissue continued to rustle. Vera leaned back on her heels and undid the small packet. Inside a delicate silver filigree watch with marcasite shoulder and face felt heavy in her hand. She wound the small bracelet of the watch around her fingers. Her face hardened and her smile fell. Looking at the entwined initials, hastily she replaced the item into a rustle of tissue and then just as swiftly opened the smaller packet. As she twisted towards her daughter a broad smile cut her face in half. The smaller package she put in the pocket of the greatcoat which she pushed into the back of the wardrobe. She knew that it would be safe from prying eyes there as the greatcoat was used only in the winter when the weather turned icy.

Sylvia's eyes dropped onto the tiny drop earrings. 'They're beautiful,' the child gasped. 'Oh go on, Mum, put them on.'

Vera shook her head. 'No, they're for the night time. And it will be past your bedtime soon. So hop into that bed now, madam.'

Sylvia wailed, 'Oh no, not now, Mum. Please . . . '

Vera shook her head. Collecting the cups and saucers, again she raised her fingers to her lips. 'If you get yourself into bed, I'll do this.' Her hand gestured to the dress. 'And then, if you're still awake I'll put it on. No, just hush, you'll 'ave your Gran up 'ere. I want you in that bed by the time I get back. All right?'

The child nodded willingly. 'You'll look a princess,' she added sleepily as Vera left the small bedroom.

Vera did as she always did. She stood silently on the half landing and listened for Mabel's snoring. Once again she was disappointed. Reaching the passage, her footsteps had been heard. 'You make sure that back door's shut and the front door is locked and bolted!' The thick voice added, 'I'm off to me bed.' Vera stood and rinsed the cups. Taking the rubber nozzle, she idly circled it around the sink. The even thicker voice continued, 'An' don't you go forgetting to bring that board and iron down.' Vera squeezed the end of the nozzle, and childlike, grinned.

Vera once again padded back upstairs. Sylvia was sleeping. Taking the dress gently from its home on the back of the door she placed it on the ironing board and with sensitivity pressed the garment into its original form. Satisfied with her work, she drew it up from the board and held it against her. The only mirror they had in their room hung from a heavy chain; momentarily it reminded her of the corner of the wardrobe. She stood on tiptoes, just catching a glimpse of her shoulders. The moon had begun to rise; without a second thought she took off her dress and slipped into the newly pressed gown. With the moon rising behind her, Sylvia stirred. Opening her eyes she looked at her mother. How beautiful she looked. She wanted to look as beautiful as her one day. Through her daughter's sleepy gaze she slipped on the blue satin shoes, looking down at her bare legs. Vera asked absently, 'I wonder if Rose would lend me some stockings?'

Hearing this, Sylvia laughed. 'Mummy, you don't wear them.'

Vera replied without thinking, 'With this dress you have to.' The child slept with images of her mother's simple beauty.

Tom Small sitting in his threadbare armchair looked up at Rose and asked, ''Ave you any coppers?'

Looking down at him across the table, she asked, 'What for?' Tom didn't move, then said, 'For the telephone.' Rose's face screwed up questioningly. It was at times such as these that Rose didn't ask what for. His expression was forged in granite. Rose remained questionless and silent. Reaching into the drawer behind her she lifted the small metal savings box, unlocking it with a tiny key that hung from a double thread of cotton. She said, 'How many?' Without waiting for an answer she put six pennies on the oilcloth table top, allowing them to run a little. Tom looked at the spewed pennies, stood up and scooped them into his palm. Rose closed the drawer without looking up then returned to making herself appear busy clearing the table of the cups and saucers. Rose heard Patricia call from her bedroom. Leaving the tray on the side she began to mount the stairs. Tom, barely noticing as he walked past by to the front door, threw a 'Won't be a minute.' Rose paid no attention and had reached the top of the stairs.

Tom reached the telephone box at the corner of the road. Heaving open the heavy door he put two pennies in the box, dialled the number and waited. Hearing a voice, he quickly pushed button 'A' and said, 'It's Tom, 'Ow y're fixed for Friday again?'

A titter of a laugh came through the line, followed by, 'Ooo, you are a one. Let's see, how about two?'

Tom nodded and agreed. 'You're sure then?'

'Course,' the female voice shrieked, causing Tom to pull the receiver away from his ear.

'You'll be ready?' he asked nervously, not quite sure whether he was being fair.

'Always ready for you, lover boy.' She gave another long titter of a laugh.

'Friday then.' Tom replaced the receiver, and as an afterthought pushed button 'B', just in case.

He sauntered back to the house. The sun was all but gone. All that remained was a distant dark orange glow clinging to the roofs of the houses lining the bottom of the road. He didn't go directly in, but took the side gate and went into the garden, standing alone chain-smoking until the lighted end hovered around like a firefly. Reluctantly he turned to go into the house, knowing that his every movement had been observed by the ever present Rose. As the moon rose, he clicked the back door shut and shoved in the bolt.

Vera, finished with her pressing, had returned the board and iron to its home beneath the stairs. She'd locked up, and standing at the sink had a quick wash and cleaned her teeth. Switching off the light she moved silently through the house up into the bedroom. She undressed slowly and reflectively. She couldn't switch on the light, the bulb had been taken out from the ceiling light so she could use the iron. She listened to Sylvia sleeping soundly. Vera couldn't resist touching the blue material that shone in the moonlight in the small room. She opened the window wide and stared out. The delicate earrings on the tallboy sparkled in the dimness. She toyed with them; the small drops swung to and fro. The silver hoops caught the moonlight. They reminded her of the wristwatch. She went to the wardrobe and her nimble fingers sought the small tissue package. Kneeling down on the cold floor, she undid the tissue without a sound. There in her hand the elegant piece of jewellery sat. Turning it over she could clearly see the entwined initials. Staring into the darkness and sighing, she once again wrapped it up and tucked it firmly into the greatcoat pocket. She knew she couldn't leave her dress on the back of the door, as Mabel would be in there at the earliest opportunity to see what she had been doing. She also knew that Mabel had no interest in the old wardrobe and there the secret would be safe. With the dress safely at the back of the wardrobe the greatcoat was pulled forward so as not to crush her neat work.

She slipped into her nightdress and, welcoming sleep, slid between the sheets of the double bed beside Sylvia who stirred slightly. Before closing her heavy lids ready for sleep, she allowed a small smile to curl her lips. On the top of the tallboy, 'Porky' the china pig eyed her, glinting clearly in the moonlight. In him was her salvation for the remainder of things. In the morning she would take the palette knife and slide out a few coins, and hopefully one or two of them would be a half-crown, 'Or at least a shilling or two,' she moaned inwardly. Then the heavy lids fringed with long lashes fell onto her cheeks and sleep came.

He heard the church clock strike one as he rounded the corner and began walking beside the row of terraced cottages. He felt conspicuous even though he knew that the car outside would have drawn a great deal more attention to his presence. He stuffed his hands into his trouser pockets. The day was humid; maybe a thunderstorm was in the air. He had left his cap and light jacket in the back of the car and was grateful for the open neck shirt and he had rolled up his sleeves. The terraced cottages lay on the main road side of the estate between the cut and the shops. They were small, with low brick front walls. Few had gates and those that existed were wooden. All the fronts had been concreted over. The paths were short and tiled in white and black squares. He was sure some of the net curtains twitched as he passed by. He stopped outside and surveyed the two up, two down dwelling, pulled his hands from his pocket and in two strides had tapped on the door with the gleaming bright brass knocker. For Tom it seemed an age had passed before the door opened silently before him. The silence and tranquillity of the net curtained narrow road was instantly shattered as Lil said,' Oooo, it's you, didn't think you'd come, like.' Her voice was high, shrill and thin and echoed up and down the road.

Tom sighed.

She stepped back, opening the door for Tom to step into the narrow passage. 'Well don't just stand there, come in.' Her back flat against the wall, she let Tom pass. 'Go on, down there,' she said with a wave of her hand towards the back of the house.

The door clicked to and Tom was aware of her close behind him. He stepped down into the small room which overlooked the tiny back. The room was comfortable, threadbare in its upholstery and like every house in this area was dingy. A scrubbed wooden draining board hung precariously from the side of the deep sink and the high mantle shelf that Lil was standing in front of framed the old black leaded hob and oven; the black flue pointed endlessly skywards. A small line was strung from one side of the mantle to the other, and he noted a number of items of underwear hanging from it, none of them for a man. The silence was broken only by the steady tick of the clock that took centre place on the mantle. His thoughts were displaced on hearing her say, 'You ain't never done this before 'ave you?'

She was right but there was no way Tom was going to admit it. He returned a look of blank indifference. Slowly he folded his arms across his chest. He looked at the figure standing directly in front of him. 'Why?' he asked himself strangling a groan of perplexity, 'Why, do women dye their hair that corn yellow colour?' It seemed to Tom that every woman had given her natural hair up to the peroxide bottle.

'Well, what d'ya think?' Lil demanded, her finger tapping the table, impatiently waiting for him to answer.

Tom followed her lowered eyelids to the table. He viewed the table in silence with a lingering steady gaze. Lil, overcome with impatience, put her hands on her hips, drummed her fingers furiously, then to draw his attention she thrust out her full heaving landscape, thinly embraced by her low front cotton dress, the buttons straining against its contents.

Tom stared down into the heaving bosom, and the full hips swaying as she tapped her foot. He watched the fall and rise of the trapped globes in silence then, making a slight clicking noise with his tongue against his teeth, said slowly, 'They're a bit small, ain't they?'

The ample flesh shook alarmingly as Lil, her eyes narrowed, asked, 'What did ya expect? I goes out of me way for you men.' Her head wagged from side to side in disbelief. The once heaving landscape had now returned into its prison and had fallen either side of her broad frame.

Unmoved by this display, Tom said enquiringly, 'How much?'

The look that crossed Lil's face was thunderous. Her mouth gaped open, her eyes widened with indignation. Her mouth was still speechless as Tom dug into his pocket and produced four half crowns which he tossed onto the table. The sound and then the sight of them closed Lil's mouth. Her jaw softened, her eyes fixed on the coins on the table. Tom turned and moved to the door.

''Ere,' she cried after him. 'You've come this far, you might just as well 'ave...' There was a rustling behind him then a packet was shoved into his shoulder. Turning back, he reached out for it and tucked it under his arm. 'And,' Lil screeched at him, 'Don't you come back 'ere. What I got on offer, you can't buy nowhere.' Then, in a highly threatening tone, 'I bet your Rose don't know nuffin about this. Mark my words . . . ' The words were coming fast and furious. 'An' don't you think your Rose don't know. Rose is like 'er mum.' Lil tapped the side of her nose knowingly, then gave a nod of finality.

Tom ambled comfortably along the passage and once more out into the sunshine. He whistled softly as he gave the package a reassuring pat as he reached the corner, then said to himself, 'Wasn't as bad as I thought.' Relaxed behind the steering wheel, he put the car into gear and it whispered in response. He then thought, 'I'll catch Arthur at the Dog and Ferret.' The thought pleased him. He pulled away; the indicator clicked breaking his thoughts bringing him back to the afternoon in all its sultry glory. It was then he laughed out loud.

Mr Carpenter had given him another Friday afternoon off. He wondered whether the gin-slinging Missus had something to do with his generosity. He hadn't told Rose of his freedom and neither did he intend to. Stopping at the traffic lights, he gave a quick look over his shoulder at the package on the back seat. Another quick glance at his watch confirmed that he had the time . . .

Tom made a hasty detour; the traffic lights were in his favour and within minutes he was pulling up outside. Cautiously, before leaving the cover of the car, he looked around the front garden and pavement for any sign of Rose. Secure in his mind that he had timed it right, he nimbly leapt from the car and strode boldly up the garden path. Once inside the front door, the chill of the north-facing house enveloped him, but instead of feeling refreshed it spurred him on. Slowly, burglarlike, he opened the coloured glass panelled kitchen door. A huge sigh of relief left him as here in front of him was further confirmation that Rose was nowhere around. The french windows were firmly shut. Then he laughed at himself; all he had to do was to stop by the hall stand, and if one of Rose's stuffed feathered or veiled parrots was missing or on its wrong perch, Rose would most certainly be out! Nothing could be clearer than a green light.

In the top drawer of the dresser he fumbled for a pencil. He scribbled a few words on the back of the rates envelope, and put the parcel and the note on top in the middle of the oil clothed table. Giving another furtive look around him, he was once again standing in the sunshine in the middle of the road. He rubbed his hands together, and car and man as one drove away in conspiratorial pleasure.

It was shortly after two when Rose arrived home. Petulant Patricia was dragged unceremoniously through the front door.

'Now,' Rose said, her voice rising, 'I'm not going to tell you again, me girl, we are goin' to your Gran's an' that's final!'

Patricia sulked and scowled and with her hands tightly gripped together behind her, began bouncing off the wall. She watched as Rose removed her hat and smoothed down her hair and her heavily contoured skirt, and looking down she couldn't but give a crooked smile as she watched her mother's rapidly swelling ankles beginning to set over the high heeled shoes. Her dark seamed stockings ran a wavy disappearing route under the broad feet.

Sighing, Rose turned to her daughter and with an exaggerated sweep of her arm, asked, 'Why don't you want to go to your Gran's?'

Patricia knew that if she mentioned Sylvia there would be another argument, and her mother would force her to go. On the other hand she knew her father would be home late as it was Friday, and her mother would not take her to the park, and she would most certainly not go with that Sylvia! She knew the wisdom of silence and by choosing that she might just get her own way. She leaned back against the wall. 'I'm hot,' she gasped breathlessly, holding a white knuckled fist to her head, every movement a carbon copy of a matinee heroine. Still, she did have the best tutor. Her mother.

'Oh baby!' Rose's voice dissolved into sympathy. 'What's the matter?'

'Don't know,' replied the now sobbing child.

Rose swept away a few wayward hairs from her forehead. Taking the child's hand she steered her towards the bright kitchen. Inside she pulled a chair from the table and sat Patricia down. The afternoon sun was streaming through the french windows. Rose quickly unbolted the doors and with a swift kick pushed them wide open. It was only when she turned back into the room that she perceived through flared nostrils an unwholesome odour. She sniffed at the air loudly, her nose wrinkled and creased to find the source. She eyed the centre of the table, grabbed the wrapped deposit, and clutching the brown envelope to her myopic vision, read out loud:

> 'Rose
> Can't stop. Hope these are OK.
> I'll see you about 7 o'clock.
> Tom'

Patricia began to grizzle.

'Shut up!' Rose shouted at the sobbing child. She used her fingers as though they were somehow detached from her hands, the little fingers raised in obvious distress. Her fingers, Rose believed, were made for the finer things in life, not soggy indescribable packages!

Patricia threw her head down onto her folded arms and her shoulders shuddered with every sob. Rose's fingers probed the damp deposit and from it came a faint but familiar sound; undeterred Rose began to tackle the parcel with agitated diligence. Bending low over the table to expedite the task in hand, Rose, finally finding a loose end, stripped it away energetically; finally, it was open!

Patricia, her curiosity aroused by her mother's deft fingerwork, had curled her unshod feet around the rung of the chair. She perched her head on interlocked fingers on raised elbows, and waited for the scene to unfold. The piercing scream that emitted from Rose's strangulated vocal chords chilled the still afternoon. Whether it was that or the dull thud of Patricia's stout frame hitting the floor, or the thwack which connected as Rose's hands flew to her horror struck open mouth . . . Only the giant bluebottle that emerged exhausted from its feast of sweating smoked haddock will ever know the truth. The bluebottle died. Petulant Patricia posed for days with her bruised pride.

And Rose roared at Tom.

Mabel said, 'It's a nice little bit of fish.'

And Tom? He laughed. The afternoon's entertainment had been well worth his ten bob!

Chapter 5

The remainder of the week flashed by, much to Vera's delight. On her way home from Mrs Lownds with her week's money, she knew it was time to tackle 'Porky'. She'd been putting it off, but now she knew the time had come: 'Porky' would have to cough up. She was angry for thinking that she could save silver, she should've kept it to coppers but maybe now he'd save her bacon as she knew that the money in her purse wouldn't last the week.

Rose had made her obligatory Friday visit with the familiar smelly, newspaper swathed parcel, and even as Vera strolled along she could still smell the poaching fish that heralded Friday tea. Oh, how the smell wafted through the house! Vera groaned. 'Has it stuck to me dress?' She paused to look in a shop window, and as she caught sight of her reflection in the painted glass she cocked her head to one side and asked, 'What can I do with my hair?' Without thinking she swept the short fine hair behind her ears and struck a pose. The heavy basket fell into the crook of her arm. She jumped back startled when a face appeared from behind the glass. Feeling the blood rush to her cheeks, she relied on her long legs to escape around the nearest corner.

The day was sticky and her dress clung to her. Her long, even strides took her quickly home and on reaching the gate, she stopped short before easing it open, to check the shopping. Sure that she had forgotten nothing she turned towards the green where the boys usually played as it seemed oddly quiet. Mabel would be out, which meant she could give her dress another quick rub over with the iron. Her fingers searched for the key and finding the string she tugged it through the letterbox. Before she'd time to put it in the lock, the door was snatched open and she tumbled from the glare into the gloom. Looking up as she steadied herself her eyes were met with fiery yellow flames dancing wildly in hollows of pitch. From within the blanket of blackness came a grunt. Vera stood transfixed, then a blast of hot breath rushed across her cheek. The smell of stale gin hung in the small passage. It was 'Big Mabel' and it was her bulk preventing Vera from moving. Vera felt the basket slip into her palm. She curled her fingers around the handle and gripped it tightly. The glassy eyes still held hers.

'So,' Mabel's voice bellowed at her daughter's startled frame, 'this is where our housekeeping money goes.'

Vera gasped, her mouth dropped in horror and then closed tight. There in front of her, hanging limply from Mabel's rough hand like a child's punctured balloon, was her crumpled blue creation. Vera resisted the urge to clutch at her throat. Taking a deep breath she drew herself up to her full height. Her heart banged hard against her chest with fear and anger, overtaking her feelings of confusion. Mabel continued. A large swollen sausage-shaped digit prodded and jabbed violently at the skirt. 'Well? I'm right 'n I?'

Vera couldn't think. All she could see was her dress. Her mind raced and it was anger that replaced confusion. She curbed it and returned her mother's accusing look with a defiant toss of her head. Vera knew better than to say anything until her thoughts cleared.

Then standing tall, she towered over 'Big Mabel', saying, 'It belongs to Mrs Lownds' niece.' With her thoughts collected, she added convincingly, 'She let me borrow it.' How did she find it? Her thoughts started to race once again. Why would she need to go into the wardrobe? Still, Vera knew that her mother was nosey, malicious and jealous. A slight sigh of satisfaction over her quick thinking emitted slowly from her tight lips and her head remained erect and her jaw set.

At this unexpected revelation Mabel's mouth opened; her jaw fell, her chins swung as her head jerked down and back just like a strutting turkey.

Vera wanted to swallow hard as she wasn't given to lying.

'Mrs Lownds' niece?' Mabels voice was choked with disbelief.

Vera tossed her head in an act of defiance. Then gave a curt nod in silent answer.

At this, Mabel threw down the dress in disgust, leaving it in a twisted heap on the floor behind her. Then she strode sweating along the passage towards the kitchen, shouting over her shoulder, 'It's a tart's frock.' Levelling with the kitchen door she turned, drew in a long breath, let it out slowly, with a raised eyebrow for maximum theatrical effect and added, 'Then look who's wearing it.' Her words ended on a triumphant note as did the yellowing uneven and broken toothed sneer that followed.

Before Mabel turned away, Vera noticed the sweat pouring from her. Her fatty throat glistened and her dark grey hair looked black, drenched in sweat.

In the kitchen, Mabel, still shouting, added, 'I'm goin' over to see ol'

Mrs Tibbs, we'll 'ave tea when I gets back. An' I don't want to see that bloody frock again! Understand me, girl?'

Vera's eyes, springing hot, allowed the tears behind to flow silently. She stemmed the desire to sob and was thankful that Sylvia was with Doris. Mabel's voice was still screaming even as Vera went upstairs. Once inside she dropped onto the old bed, clasped the dress to her and sobbed softly. Its brilliance looked out of place. Vera knew that hiding it away would only fuel Mabel's wrath.

It was only seconds before she heard the front door bang shut: just another few seconds and then she would be free. Standing in front of the bedroom she waited just in case her mother returned just to catch her unawares. Vera had been holding her breath; gradually she allowed it to escape slowly. There were no more sounds. Cautiously she tiptoed down the stairs. With the parlour door wide open she narrowed her eyes to scan across the green. Yes! she had gone. Vera could see just a glimpse of her mother's waddling form on the far side. 'Now,' Vera said spontaneously, 'I can press me dress.'

In the kitchen she sliced the bread ready for sandwiches, filled the kettle, lighted the gas, turned it low and put the kettle half on the ring, then leaning against the sink one quick look at the early setting sun confirmed that she didn't have much time. She hoped that Iris wouldn't have one of her unpredictable mood changes. She allowed the dulling thought to evaporate. 'Now,' she asked out loud, 'What to put in the bread?' Hunting through the larder she came across a small tin of pilchards. She laughed. 'At least these don't stink out the house.' Quickly she put them in a dish and shook in vinegar and pepper. Taking a fork she mashed them together, then carefully spread the mixture on the bread to make sandwiches quickly finished. She took a tea towel, damped it under the tap, wrung it out and draped it over the tea tray. 'Now I can iron my dress.'

The dress that had minutes earlier lain limp and crumpled on her bed now, newly pressed, hung proudly from a hanger on the back of the door. Only now it was radiating pride. It wasn't covered nor was it hidden. Vera kicked the legs from the board and stood it flat; leaning on it observing her work, she smiled. The iron and board were put back under the stairs and as Vera reached the top of the staircase the front door opened. Mabel had returned. Confidently she leaned over the top bannister. One look at her mother's face told her: 'Gin!'

Her mother's staggering steps stopped suddenly as she fell into the parlour. Seconds later standing on the half landing heard Mabel snoring. Vera grinned broadly and with great satisfaction: 'I'm off to the dance,' she said out loud, without fear of being heard. Back in her bedroom she couldn't remember what triggered off her anger. Was it the dress, her mother, the weather, the gin? Whatever it was, her pink china pig 'Porky' lay in pale pink silvers on the floor, his contents spread over the floor. Vera could just recall the splintering but she wasn't sure. She was certain of the carpet of silver that spread itself in front of her. Methodically she counted up the half crowns and shillings. God, she had no idea just how rich she was. 'Porky' certainly had 'saved her bacon'. She stood staring at the silver towers. 'There's more than five pounds there!' A joyous tearful gasp struggled free. Now she could give Tom back his pound, and she would still have more than enough not only for the coming week but also enough for another week's housekeeping, without having to break into Mrs Lownds' money.

She pushed the window up and called softly across the gardens to Sylvia, 'It's time to come in now, you can see Doris tomorrow.' In the distance Vera heard a groan of protest, but Sylvia was a good girl, she wouldn't be long, and Vera knew she would take the short cut through the shrubs at the bottom of the garden behind the old apple tree.

While she waited she slipped silently downstairs into the kitchen. Standing by the back door she watched as the shrubs swayed until a fair head popped through. Vera raised her hand and as she always did put a cautionary finger to her lips, indicating a need for silence. The child stood up, brushed down her knees and pulled her dress into order, then disappeared behind the tree only to appear seconds later at the back door. Vera gave her the dustpan and brush. 'Be a good girl, and run upstairs and brush up the bits on the floor for me.'

Cheerfully Sylvia took the pan and scampered up the stairs. 'Cor, Mum,' Sylvia exclaimed as she emptied the pieces into the dustbin. 'What 'appened to "Porky"?'

Vera laughed. 'Let's just say he saved my bacon.'

Sylvia wasn't sure what she meant, but she did see piles of silver money. She shrugged and said nothing further.

'Before I take these in for your Gran, would you like some?'

Sylvia eyed the plate of sandwiches. Next to bloater she loathed pilchards. 'They're all gritty, like.'

Vera frowned a look of disapproval.

'I thought I was 'avin' me tea at Auntie Chris's?'

Vera gave a quick nod of agreement. 'Wash your hands and face whilst I take these into the parlour.' She stopped at the closed kitchen door and before opening it said, 'Don't make a sound; I don't want to wake up your Gran. All right?'

Vera had already put some warm water into the shallow sink and watched as the child reluctantly took the face cloth and the block of yellow soap and smiled as the child played with the water before rubbing the soap over the flannel.

Her hand grasped at the brass knob parlour door. It turned slowly then, opening the door just enough to put her head around, she was relieved to see that Mabel was still in a deep sleep interrupted only by an occasional snore. Mabel's sturdy laced shoes encasing her overfilled stockinged legs were splayed, and just a hint of the pink knee length bloomers could be seen. She was propped up in the corner of the solid armchair. A few strands of hair were straggled across her perspiring brow and the buttons at her neck were askew. A handkerchief was clenched tight in her fist. Her fleshy upper arms spread over the high back of the chair like splattered butter pats.

All that could be heard was the whisper of Vera's skirt as she moved into the room as she set down the plate of sandwiches on Mabel's side table. Vera considered for a moment whether or not to bring in the cake and a cup and saucer. One glance through the window told her that the dusk was quickly gathering. She took the tea towel she had dangling from her arm and threw it over the plate, and left the room just as swiftly and as silently as she entered. She set the catch back into place, and gave a heavy sigh of relief.

Back in the kitchen Vera sat the unusually impatient child on a chair and told her that she wouldn't be long. This was the moment Vera had been longing for. She slipped into the bathroom. She took from the glass fronted cabinet a small bar of scented soap that Mrs Lownds had given to her for Christmas. She ran the water and allowed the creamy foam to run over her. It wasn't the same as having a bath, and there really was no time, and she couldn't afford to have the old water heater blasting its use around the house. That would raise Mabel. Hot water like everything else had to be paid for. The creamy foaming fragrant soap rushed over her body as she stood on the towel. Soon she had washed down and the fragrance lingered. She stepped back into her dress. Now, when she returned to the foot of the stairs she would be dressed. Her heart began to race at the sheer indulgence. 'Please,' she pleaded to one in particular, 'Don't let Mum wake up until we've gone.'

Having offered her prayer she took the stairs in twos and threes. It was an early dusk but as Vera stood in the blue dress it was as if she'd stepped into a Mediterranean summer, not that she had been, or knew exactly where it was. She just knew how to spell it.

She snatched a few coins from the tallboy then from the wardrobe dragged off a hanger a light coat. She was just about to open the door when she spotted the ear-rings. Quickly she unscrewed the backs and standing in front of the small mirror took time to put them on. Finished, she shook her head gently. How much she longed for a long mirror! Again she tossed her head, just to catch a glimpse of the delicate shapes that hung from her fleshy lobes.

Then as a finishing touch, she wetted her finger and thumb. Teasing her hair away from her face, she gave another flick to her hair and with another flick of her finger and thumb eased her short hair around her ears, showing the small earrings to their full advantage. She spat once again on her fingers and thumbs just to make sure her new style would stay in place.

On the bottom stair Sylvia waited as she watched her mother descend. Her eyes widened and she squealed with delight. Vera raised a finger to her lips then with a quick wave of her hand indicated to Sylvia to open the front door. The child instantly understood. The cool of the evening rushed in, and taking her daughter's hand, blushing, Vera sprang from the doorstep into the shaded front.

Vera, hand on hip, her white cotton duster coat draped through her arm, looked every inch the professional model as she slowly twirled for Chris in the cool of the passage waiting for Iris. The day had been long and hot and now the evening had a welcoming freshness about it. She continued to twirl as she heard Chris say almost enviously, 'My, my, don't you look the business.' She stopped abruptly, wondering if Vera had taken offence at her ill chosen words. Vera had not. Chris added swiftly, 'Only you could do justice to that frock. One thing's for sure, you won't be short of dances. 'Ere, you got your dance card ready?' she finished with a nervous laugh. The truth of the matter was that never had she seen Vera look so elegant. Without thinking she exclaimed, 'Stockings too!'

At this Vera swept up her coat and swung it across her shoulders. 'Umm, I had to twist Rose's arm,' she confided, looking down at her stockinged legs. 'D'you know, I'd forgotten just how uncomfortable they are,' she confessed.

'Cor, I should be lucky to afford them posh ones,' Chris said, pointing at her heel. 'Fully fashioned eh?' She noted the high patterned turn of the ankle.

Vera threw an absent unselfconscious look over her shoulder down to her ankle. 'Mmmm,' she mused. The truth be known, Vera hadn't noticed.

Chris stood looking admiringly at the younger woman. Yes, she was envious. Yes, she too wanted to go but she had Iris and once Iris was in her mind it altered her thinking from a woman with unfulfilled needs to a carer. She wiped her hand nervously on her brightly coloured and frilled half apron. Realising what she was doing, she began undoing the bow and removed it. She flung it over the bannisters, leaned into Vera confidentially and began, 'You will keep an eye on 'er?' She followed this through with a slight toss of her head to the stairs. 'You know what she's like when she gets excited. I know it's light refreshments.' Then she added as an afterthought, 'That does mean no drink, don't it? She'd drink it like water.' She smiled as if she had betrayed her niece.

'Chris, stop worrying.'

Chris cut her short. 'Sorry, luv, you know her as well as I do. You've got the patience other people don't.' She said it firmly but sadly.

Sylvia popped out from the kitchen and was disappointed to find her mother with the coat back on. 'Just one more look, Mum, please.'

Vera flushed slightly, held open the coat and felt as if she had just revealed herself to be naked.

The child stood in front of her mother, between the two women.

'They twinkle even in the dark.' Sylvia gave a giggle.

'Now,' said Vera, assuming her parental tone, 'you be good, and do as Auntie Chris tells you and . . . '

At this point Iris emerged from the half landing. 'Look.'

All three turned their gaze on Iris. 'Oooo, Iris, you do look nice,' Sylvia piped up.

The two older women exchanged warm glances. Chris touched Vera's arm. 'I had to take up the hem, but that's all. It was a lovely thought. Looks a picture, don't she?'

Vera smiled warmly and nodded.

Iris stepped onto the last stair and stared vaguely at Vera. 'Oh no, thought Chris. The excitement's got to 'er, she's goin' to have one of her turns.

To Vera's astonishment, she watched helplessly as a solitary tear rolled down Iris's cheek. Vera's throat tightened even more when Iris said, 'Oh Vera, you look like the little fairy we puts on the Christmas tree.'

Vera was touched, Drawing herself up she took Iris by the hand and said, smiling into her face, 'Thank you. But remember I haven't got a magic wand and neither do we have pumpkin for a coach!'

Chris snatched the apron from the bannisters and dabbed her eyes.

'So, we'd best hurry up, or we'll be late.'

Chris handed Iris a white cardigan. 'Just in case it gets chilly on the way home. And you make sure you come home the main road, eh.' Iris nodded enthusiastically.

Chris gave a slow shake of her head, then taking Sylvia's hand said, 'C'mon, it's time you had something to eat.'

Vera bent to kiss her daughter. Gently she stroked her face and whispered, 'I'll try and bring you something back, and we'll have a midnight feast.' Vera raised her eyebrows conspiratorially.

Sylvia flung her arms around her mother's neck, kissed her cheek, then playfully flicked the little crystal drops of her mother's earrings.

Vera wagged a mock warning finger.

''Ave a lovely time!' Chris called after them as she watched them stroll side by side down the narrow road.

It didn't take them long to reach the main road. Standing on the top of the hill Iris announced, 'Eight, and that's counting that one,' and she pointed at a telegraph pole on the other side of the road. She gave a sideways glance at Vera for her confirmation. Vera, much more concerned with crossing the main road to reach the hall, returned a look of blankness. 'Eight. Eight what?' Then she realised, Iris had finished counting. Often she would count lamp posts; it was more often the telegraph poles that took her attention. Whether or not she was correct didn't come into this 'game' of Iris's. Vera replied with a smile, 'That's right. Eight.'

Iris beamed.

Vera took Iris's wrist, tucked her clutch bag firmly under her arm and waited for the traffic to ease up. In a jiffy they were across the road, Vera not listening to Iris's chatter, until she heard her say, 'We're here. I can hear music. Listen.'

Vera looked up at the hall from where the music came. Together they climbed the two flights of concrete steps that led up to the short path into the hall. At the swing doors, they stopped. Eyeing one another, Vera began to wonder who was the more nervous. And if it was her, why? Resolutely Vera pushed her shoulder against the door and the pair tumbled in. Regaining their composure, Vera was amazed to find herself facing a wall of backs, fronts, bodies of all kinds. The music they heard had been drowned now by voices of high, low and laughing tones. Bobbing up and down between a wave of shoulders they began searching for the ladies' cloakroom. Grabbing Iris's arm she managed to shout above the babble, 'Over here!'

As Vera removed her coat she found herself trembling. She put her coat on a pile on a low table behind her. Taking her small clutchbag she searched for her powder puff and lipstick. Iris watched her, fascinated. Vera became aware of Iris's gaze. 'Give me your cardigan, I'll hang it on this hook.' She placed the garment carefully on the coat hook on the back of a door that appeared to lead nowhere. 'Probably the attendant's room,' she thought. She had been here only once before and that was a really rather posh wedding, and so far as Vera could remember there hadn't been as many people, although at the time it seemed like a banquet. She turned back to the small shelf that sat beneath the mirror and watched amused as Iris took the powder puff and pulled it across her cheeks.

Vera took her lipstick and showed it to Iris. 'Here.' She indicated to Iris how to put her lips. Vera pouted her lips and Iris copied. The lipstick applied, Vera took her powder puff and dabbed at Iris's lips. 'Now, don't you go telling your Auntie Chrissie,' she said, smiling broadly. Taking the puff and lipstick she applied the soft pink colour to her lips and patted them, then taking the other side of the puff, she applied some powder to her cheeks. Then to Iris's delight Vera brought out from her bag a small bottle of perfume. It was a small bottle, so Iris thought it had to be real. There was a picture on the bottle, but she couldn't quite see it. Vera tipped up the bottle and the liquid dropped onto her finger, she invited Iris to smell it. Iris nodded. 'It's lovely,' and sniffed. Vera put a dot behind Iris's ears and another couple of dots on her wrists. Iris stood still sniffing at her wrists.

'Right,' said Vera, 'Let's find that buffy.'

Opening the door, the band suddenly struck up a quickstep. The two girls looked at one another, simultaneously they flushed. Vera, not wishing to make a fuss crossing the path of the dancers, decided to skirt the hall, Halfway to where the cold buffet sat, a finger stabbed into her back. Turning, she looked at a very large man dressed in black with a black bow tic. 'Tickets,' he demanded.

Vera, somewhat taken aback at this enormous form, delved into her bag. Finding the tickets she offered to him cautiously. He smiled, then tearing them in half, said, 'Thanks. It's a bit loud now. If you take these over to there,' he waved an arm in the direction of the food, 'with these take what you want and they'll take them in exchange. Okay?'

Vera looked at the halves in her hand, smiled, turned and, placing her hand in the small of Iris's back, piloted her to the buffet. Looking over her shoulder she mouthed the words, 'Thank you.'

The enormous frame smiled. Vera felt a rush of relief.

Iris had said very little but when she gave a quick look, Iris's face was full of nothing less than sheer wonderment. Her eyes were wide and sparkling; it was as though she was absorbing every sight and sound around her. Vera scanned the faces about her, none of whom she recognized. The band swung into another quickstep and the dancers continued their intricate footwork. Standing at the buffet table Vera was taken aback with the choice. 'There aren't any bloater paste sandwiches here,' she thought. Almost as if Iris had read her mind looking at the sandwiches she remarked, 'Them bloater?' Vera shook her head. 'No, not here.'

Iris studied the plates of sandwiches, the bridge rolls with mustard and cress peeking through the halves. A few dusty trifles lay on the end white clothed table. Vera shook her head, just a little disappointed, 'It was free though,' she silently reminded herself. A grey haired, bespectacled woman offered Vera a plate with a paper napkin and pointed to each of the plates, speaking in such a rush that it reminded her of a railway station announcer. Vera raised her hand slightly just to slow her down, then added, 'Not just now, thank you. We would like a drink.'

The woman eyed her and pointing with the plate to another table at the far end of the hall, said, 'Over there,' her tone acid.

'I'll 'ave a buffy,' Iris chimed in cheerily.

Before Vera could make a reply, the grey head thrust itself across the table, glared, then announced with another sweep of the plate, 'This *is* the buffet.'

Iris gave a quick shrug and looked puzzled at the empty plate. Quickly Vera nudged Iris and indicated with a nod of her head towards the end table. 'We'll get ourselves a drink.' The music lulled momentarily as they weaved their way through the swaying forms. In the surprisingly calm seclusion of the drinks table, Vera offered the torn tickets to the tall thin figure behind the table and asked for 'Two sparkling oranges,' then shyly added, 'With straws please.' She watched him flip off the bottle caps. ''Elp yourselves to straws,' and pushed a box towards them. 'Them's is for food,' he added with a flickering of his eyes over the crumpled ticket halves. Vera tucked the tickets in her bag and they stood silently watching the dancers, and sipped contentedly on their drinks. The band was playing a slow foxtrot. Vera envied the couples dancing; she had never mastered the foxtrot, although to be fair she could manage the basic steps, but it was the funny odd lack of rhythm in the steps used to make a reverse turn that left her as confused as a column of figures did. All the women were dressed in their summer finery. There were the odd flashes of diamond rings and heavy necklaces cutting into fleshy necks; the rhinestone settings caught the evening light gleaming like rivulets of perspiration. Vera wedged her bag into the angled window ledge and as she twisted around felt the gentle swing of the small drop earrings. Self consciously she flicked one with her little finger and smiled reflectively.

The hall sat high on the brow of the hill and nestled lengthwise into the common ground at the rear. It was built in the style of a cricket pavilion with a verandah on three sides. Through the high windows, the lower half of which were frosted, Vera could clearly see the sun dipping behind the hill. The common was known by the locals as 'the short cut', but was often shortened to just 'the cut'. Everyone used it to cut through the estate without having to use the bus; also there was a small parade of shops on the other side. Children played on it from dawn to dusk in the summer, and schools used it for their playing fields and sports days. It was open and very often windy. This, however, did not deter the courting couples even in the winter.

The back of the hall had been concreted and there were plans for showers or some such thing. Vera had noticed a number of the men using the door behind her, although it was clearly marked: IN CASE OF FIRE PUSH BAR TO OPEN'. Vera was well aware there was no fire, so why? It wasn't the gents'. She shook her head and had her attention drawn back to the band as they struck a third and final quickstep of the set. She almost jumped out of her skin when a voice from the side of her asked, 'May I have this dance?'

She found herself staring open mouthed at the young man who was now standing in front of her, extending his hand.

'Oh go on, Vera,' urged Iris, 'I 'aven't never seen you dance before.'

Vera glanced from one to the other, then said, 'Now don't move, and if anyone asks you to dance . . . ' She took a deep breath, 'wait until I get back. Right?' she said firmly.

Iris giggled. 'Oh go on, I won't move from this spot.' Then she gave Vera a gentle shove, smiling broadly at her.

As his arm went around her waist her mind went completely blank. Was it a foxtrot? A waltz? She listened earnestly to the band. 'A quickstep.' She gave an inward sigh. He lifted her arm, and her fingers fell into the palm of his hand. She gave a shy sidelong glance at him and also managed a weak smile, then on the next third beat they glided away. Vera knew she wasn't telling her feet what to do, but they were doing quite well, she thought, because she hadn't tripped him up ... yet! He was tall, elegant and very well turned out and Vera noticed just how nice he smelt. No Sunlight soap for him, she thought. He wasn't sweating either and the suit he was wearing was very good quality. 'Oh God, he's talking to me!'

The mellow rounded voice asked again, 'It is Vera. Your name?' Vera wondered how he could talk and dance and concentrate and not sweat. The pressure on the small of her back signalled her to pace time to allow other couples to pass. 'I'll be doing double reverse turn chassis next,' she said, her heart fluttering. As they turned, over his shoulder Vera could see Iris standing with her hands clasped together. Vera found herself smiling, then she gave a short laugh because only her eyes could be seen over his shoulder. Vera's mind was going wild. 'A side lock, or was it a chassis, or was it a half side lock?' And she still hadn't fallen over!

'My name's Harry,' the mellow tones continued.

'Vera,' she said breathlessly.

'Yes, I thought so. Your friend ... '

She didn't realise she hadn't allowed him to finish and cut in, 'Her name's Iris.'

'Very pretty.'

Vera frowned and asked herself 'Her name or her looks?' Just then Iris came into view. Yes, Vera agreed, Iris was very pretty and the pink two-piece looked simply stunning. Vera could do nothing as Iris gave a little wave. Then thinking quickly, she raised her fingers from his shoulders and returned the wave. Suddenly, the music stopped and he said, 'Thank you. May I?' He indicated that he would walk her back to where they had been standing. He asked Vera, 'May I have another dance?' Vera, mute, nodded.

'Well!' declared Iris, as he left them with an engaging smile, 'who's that?'

'Harry,' Vera said, staring at her shoes.

'Can we 'ave another one?' Iris dug Vera in the ribs with her empty bottle. Vera danced with Harry twice more; she even managed a foxtrot. Standing once again beside Iris he said, 'Perhaps I should get some chairs.' He looked about him. The chairs were mostly in clusters around the small square tables. Shaking his head he said apologetically, 'I'm sorry.'

Vera smiled and shook her head. 'We're just fine here.' Then she added, glancing at the side of the stage, 'We can always sit there.'

Iris had nodded enthusiastically at this proposal.

'Some food then, I think.'

Vera stretched across to the window ledge and he followed, looking puzzled. Vera produced the creased halves. He stared down at them blankly. Then, looking up he smiled at her and raising his hand in a wave of dismissal said quickly, 'Oh, no, that really isn't necessary. Allow me, please.'

Vera looked even more puzzled as he walked towards the buffet. As she turned back from replacing her bag, he had disappeared completely from sight. Vera craned her neck to view the faces over the table. Where was he? Resigned that had disappeared forever, she and Iris sat on the edge of the stage, waiting for the band to begin again.

The band started up and within a minute of the music commencing, Harry appeared from behind the stage with a tray full of food. Iris stared at Vera and Vera stared at Harry.

'Here,' he said at last, having followed their stares. 'I hope you will enjoy this.'

He handed the tray to Vera and as she took it another tray appeared like magic from beneath. 'There,' Harry said with satisfaction, 'Now you have more room.'

They each sat with a tray on their knees and as Vera looked at the choice of food she knew it couldn't possibly have come from the buffet tables.

The over laden tray held two large plates of savoury pie with egg salad . . . chunks in a white runny sauce, and tomatoes that were as red as the lettuce was green. He was saying, 'If there is anything else you would like . . . ?'

Vera didn't give him time to finish. 'No,' she gasped.

He said almost apologetically, 'The rolls aren't as fresh as they should be.' He raised his palms. 'It's the weather.'

Vera gave a nod of mutual understanding.

He disappeared to the front of the stage.

Before he was out of earshot, Vera called after him, 'You don't work for Lyon's, do you?'

He swiftly turned to face her and answer good humouredly, 'No, and I don't work for ABC either.'

Vera gulped.

As he disappeared, Vera turned to Iris and said, 'You know what this means?'

Iris shook her head.

'It means,' Vera said in a low voice, 'we can save the tickets for,' she looked around her as a forkful of lettuce filled her mouth, 'some food for your Auntie Chrissie and Sylvia.'

Iris nodded.

A voice above Vera's bowed head over the tray said, 'Tea or coffee?'

Alarmed Vera looked up into Harry's face. Before she had a chance to answer she heard Iris say, 'Coffee?'

His mellow voice replied, 'Black or white?'

Iris said, 'Yes.'

'Good, one white and one black. Yes?' he finished.

As Vera nodded compliance, she became aware of the lettuce leaf that was wagging to and fro. As swiftly as a frog she snatched the offending green tongue into her mouth, then turned as red as the tomatoes.

Harry hesitated, then directing his question to Iris asked, 'May I have the pleasure of the next dance?'

Iris took a little time to take herself away from her lap banquet. Before answering she looked at Vera then with honesty said, 'I can only do the "Gay Gordons". We learned it at school.'

Harry gave a quick look at Vera, who had still not recovered. Softly, he replied, 'Good, then when the band plays a "Gay Gordons" I hope you will join me.'

With a mouthful of food being chewed, Iris nodded a promise. This time they waited a few more seconds just in case he re-emerged from the front stage. Then after some length Iris said, 'I ain't never 'ad me dinner out before, 'ave you?'

Vera shook her head and allowed her colour to fall.

Just minutes later, true to his word Harry arrived with two cups of coffee. He set them down on the edge of the stage beside Iris.

'Everything all right?'

Vera and Iris nodded in unison.

He smiled at them. 'Good.' Then he added somewhat enigmatically, 'I must get back.' Then he was gone.

Vera and Iris sat side by side, enjoying every morsel; satisfied, they leaned back. Vera drew in a breath of complete contentment. She hadn't during her repast taken much notice of the band, until a voice, a male voice, could be heard singing a ballad. For a moment she was puzzled; she knew the voice and the song, but it wasn't from one of her records. Springing to her feet she twisted her body around the corner of the stage. She looked up and his eyes caught her gaze of total astonishment. It was Harry. 'Good grief, it's Harry!' she gasped. 'He's a Bing Crosby.'

Vera sat down beside Iris who had begun to eat Vera's scraps. Iris gave a look of half interest in the subject and asked 'Bing who?' Then she frowned as she tackled an awkward lettuce leaf.

'What I mean,' Vera said, still breathless, 'is he's a crooner with the band.'

Iris, still chewing on the lettuce leaf, asked, 'What's that?'

A dazed Vera shook her head. The hair she had carefully flicked behind her ears fell forward with exasperation. 'No, No! It's not a what it's a him, *Him*.' She gesticulated. 'Harry,' she gasped at last.

Iris was still unimpressed and asked for another orange. In an uncharacteristic moment of irritability, Vera snatched at her hair and forced it behind her ears and pointed a finger at their coffees. It was now dark, and Vera had become increasingly aware of the scrappy trail of Sunday suited men using the fire exit. The doors were open just enough to allow the now chill air through the minute gap. She shuddered.

A pair of black scuffed shoes stopped in front of her. She started to look when she recognized the voice. She felt her heart freeze.

'Well, well, what 'ave we 'ere then? Don't we look pretty little girls then?'

A veil of blue smoke settled around her.

Vera looked directly at him, not attempting to disguise her displeasure. A cigarette was pinched between his nicotine stained fingertips and dirty finger nails hidden in the palm of his closed hand and the other hand was firmly dug into his ill fitting jacket pocket. His hair was greasy and unwashed and the curls had been slicked down with brilliantine and forced into an unruly knot at the base of his head. She felt Iris edging into her. Before she had a chance to say 'Ronnie', Harry had appeared. Seeing another man, he said sociably, 'Good evening.'

Ronnie glared back at this neat presentable man. Harry repeated his greeting. 'Good evening.'

Vera stifled a gasp. Iris hid behind her. Ronnie leered at the two women then taking a long draw of his cigarette gave a nod to Harry and asked, 'Which one's yours, then?' His glowing cigarette pointed at each woman in turn.

Harry didn't answer him immediately and the hand of greeting was slowly and deliberately lowered. He gave a quick look at Vera who was struggling to find audible words. Eventually she managed, 'Harry, this is Ronnie. Ronnie, this is Harry.' She stumbled for a second as she didn't know his surname. Once again Harry raised his hand ready to grasp a handshake in greeting. Vera hurriedly added, 'He delivers our vegetables.'

Harry smiled. 'Oh, you're a greengrocer.'

'Yeah,' Ronnie said as he stamped on his dog end. 'Amongst other things, if you follows me?' He spewed out another blue grey cloud, adding, 'A little bit of this and a little bit of that, eh?'

Harry did follow him and listened. He saw more than one of his sort at these functions. His thought was interrupted as Ronnie asked, 'What 'ya'do?

Harry answered simply, 'I sing.'

'Nah,' Ronnie said with a snarl, 'for a real job I means.'

Harry squared to this obnoxious individual and looking down on him answered unswervingly, 'I sing.'

Ronnie, staring at the flattened butt, stuffed his other hand in his pocket and turned slightly towards the fire doors. Harry watched him as Ronnie swaggered off and was surprised that he didn't bang the doors. He had witnessed first hand what he often saw at these dances. Iris was still cowering behind Vera, Harry was staring hard after Ronnie and Vera was rooted to the floor. Once again the band struck up a tune. The wooden floor reverberated to the pounding feet and the walls seemed to echo their silent thoughts.

Vera followed Harry's gaze, looking long and hard after Ronnie. She took a deep breath to steady her nerves – how she loathed that man – then she heard Harry say, 'Good evening, sir.' His tone was welcoming and respectful, then over the stomping feet and the soaring trombone solo Father Brennan's voice could be distinctly heard. Vera turned towards the friendly brogue, and heard him say, 'Come along, me boy, it's too nice an evening to be letting yourself getting hot about the collar over the likes of that . . . ' He saw Vera listening and moderated his tone. Smiling at her he said, 'My word, what a picture you look.' And towards Iris, he lifted his arms. 'Won't you not give me the next dance, lass?' Without waiting for an answer he gave a comical backward kick, flaring out his cassock and waltzed Iris away, who was looking bemused but smiling.

Father Brennan called over his shoulder, 'Now you two go away with you and have a chat, or whatever it is you young folks do these days.' Facing them in the middle of what could only be described as a one legged polka, his friendly chubby face crumpled into an enormous wink then shouting at them, he said, 'Don't go worrying about me, I'm in good hands with Iris, here.' They watched the tubby little man, his silvery grey head bobbing about. He released an arm and shook it at them, vigorously shouting, 'Shoo! I'll be waiting on a lemonade, for when you get back.'

Harry smiled. Shaking his head he said quietly, 'Quite a character.'

Vera relaxed. 'Yes, he's a lovely man. We all know him, what I mean is all of us on the estate like . . . '

Harry took Vera's arm and led her to the door. 'Your family are Catholic, then?'

'Oh no!' Vera didn't know why she had replied so defensively. Then she added softly 'Father Brennan just seems to be there, and he knows everything' It was an insipid response to a weighty question, Vera considered. Then thinking again she decided to add nothing further.

At the door they paused and looked back at them both. Father Brennan's attempts were now more of an Irish jig with a touch of the flamboyant highland fling. Looking at each other they stifled a giggle. Harry drew close into Vera and whispered in her ear. 'He's not been drinking the altar wine. What do you think?'

Vera shook her head laughing; her short fair hair fell down onto her face.

Outside she was surprised to find it warmer then she had imagined. They both leaned on the rail, resting their heads in their hands, staring into the distance. Vera gave a whisper of a sigh. 'Why does everything look so, so,' her face screwed up searching for the right word, 'gentle,' she said finally.

He said nothing but watched her.

She continued, 'In the night, I mean.'

He looked down on the hill winding out before him 'Most people would think the night frightening.' He watched smiling as she shook her head.

'No. Never frightening, it's quiet. It's peaceful. It's,' she gave a shrug, 'restful.'

'So,' he asked, changing the subject, 'What do you do when you're not out dancing?'

She considered before answering, then answered him honestly, 'I listen to the wireless. I like music and I have some gramophone records. I don't get to play them often. Mum's not keen, you know.'

He nodded sympathetically. He had a feeling about her. 'What records do you have?'

Vera suddenly realised she was in conversation. She started back; she wasn't used to this. Flustered, she said, 'Oh, just the usual Billy Eckstein and the croo . . . ' She stopped abruptly, not wishing to offend him, 'ballads, that sort of thing, I read too and I belong to the library and I have a rockery.' She found herself babbling; she was telling him everything except what he wanted to know. She gave a heavy sigh and fell silent.

His voice was thoughtful and ponderous as he said apologetically, 'I'm sorry, I didn't mean to cross-question you,' He spread his arms, his palms raised skywards. 'I'm just plain nosey. I'm sorry,' he said again.

He turned towards her and she looked deep into his doleful face. His eyes were laughing, not at her but at himself. Yes, she decided, he was mischievous. Without looking away, she fixed her gaze even more firmly and asked, 'I suppose you meet a lot of . . .' How she hated the coming word, she did not consider herself one, 'girls,' she at last managed to gasp.

He turned and folded his arms, his back leaning against the rail now.

'No, not really. They find me.' He sensed her unease. 'Perhaps I can get you a drink?'

She turned around and gave a brief shake of her fair head. 'No, no, thank you. I'll have to get back soon.'

She wasn't sure what he meant about girls finding him but she knew he was very attractive, and she knew she would never see him again after this night. But what a night she would have to remember. Dancing with a handsome stranger. Standing under the stars. Being waited on. The sheer luxury! 'Trouble is', she thought wistfully, 'I haven't got anybody to tell.' Then she thought again. 'I'll tell Mrs Lownds, even though she is as deaf as a post.' She laughed out loud at the thought. Surprised at her boldness she reddened instantly.

Then, as if by magic – had he been reading her thoughts? – he asked, 'What work do you do? Sorry, I'm being nosey again.' He touched her arm and Vera shivered involuntarily. Resigned as she always was to her honesty, although she had lied unashamedly to her mother, she said, 'I . . .'

Before she had a chance to finish, Harry's fluid voice asked, 'Your friend, Iris, isn't it?' His thoughts now in full flow followed with, 'She isn't . . .' He hesitated and, not wishing to hurt her feelings, looking directly at Vera finished with, 'not well.' He was now looking through the open doors into the hall. Vera's eyes followed his. Together they spotted Iris with Father Brennan, still in high spirits, their heads bobbing about like corks free on an ocean of colours.

Vera sighed and thought of Iris's bobbing body, her face flushed with enjoyment. She said without any prompting, 'The, her family . . . a bomb, direct hit. The house was flattened. No one expected Iris to be found alive. She was under the stairs.' Her words came out staggered and laboured. 'They did find her. There wasn't a mark on her.' She looked out over the hill. 'That's not quite right.' Once again she stopped. 'Head injuries.' She felt him move closer. 'She was in hospital for a very long time. She lives with her Aunt Chris. When Chris was told that Iris would be put in an institution, she gave up everything to look after her.' Vera looked up into the face searching hers. 'Iris was only eight.' She heard him sigh in understanding. Still she continued, 'When she came back to live with her aunt,' she looked appealingly at him, 'she was still just eight years old.'

Harry slid closer to her. 'Can't anything be done?'

Vera's head dropped.

'My daughter is eight.' Her tone was firm and resolute. 'When Iris went back to live with her aunt, my daughter was just . . .'

Once again he interrupted her train of thought. She ignored him and turned away, even though he had slipped sideways into her. She concentrated her gaze on the hill below and continued with a determined flourish, almost as if she wanted to shock him. Out of the corner of her eye she saw he was leaning contentedly on his elbow, resting on the rail, staring intently in a relaxed manner at her.

She rounded on him, her usually gentle features pinched and jagged. Her voice was sharp; her eyes first narrowed as if gauging his intention, then widened as she blurted out: 'You don't understand. It's difficult to talk about. No one understands 'cept me and Chris. Iris is, is, is,' she began to falter. She took a deep breath and as she did so Harry took a step back. 'There are times when Iris is, clear like. She doesn't – she's quick and,' shaking her head she asked herself, 'What is that word?' Remembering she said quickly, 'Spontaneous, that's it. Spontaneous. It's not that she doesn't know, she can't, no, that's wrong, she doesn't think. It isn't her fault. My daughter's eight. Iris is more like my daughter than my daughter. Oh,' she groaned. What had got into her? Her face fell into her waiting palms.

Harry remained silent as he watched this touching display of friendship, sincerity and loyalty. He knew she had finished and stood perfectly still, not wanting to stop or startle her. He was relieved to see that her face, although flushed, was calm and once more soft to the eye.

Shaking her head slowly she said soberly, 'I'm sorry.' She watched him shake his head in what she knew was sympathetic understanding. She turned from him and rested her head in her hands, her elbows angled on the rail. She heard herself release a heavy sigh and without looking at him continued, 'She, Iris, doesn't . . . well, can't remember what happened. The house was never rebuilt; it was turned into a garden. We, that's us, look after it. It's got two garden seats; her family's names are carved into the back rests and there are rose bushes.' She interrupted herself. 'We walk past, that's me and Iris, like, nearly every day and I get so frightened that one day when I'm with her . . . she stands tracing her fingers over their names, you know, she might remember and I'll be the only one there . . . ' she sobbed softly. Raising her head, she added slowly, 'So frightened, what would I do, what could I say? There are times I think to myself that she has . . . ' she considered the word carefully. Once again she slowly shook her head. 'I'm not sure, I just have a feeling that she knows something. Oh, I don't know anything, it's just a feeling. Sylvia was only weeks old when Iris came to live with Chris and they sort of grew up together. I've never talked to anyone like this before, about anything. I love Iris like a sister, like a daughter, oh, I don't know. Sometimes I think that people, them that don't understand, just how . . . how . . . just how . . . ' She stopped again and her hands held her head. 'It's so bloody . . . ' she couldn't use the word.

Harry watched as her small fist dropped onto the rail making the lightest of thuds. Feeling helpless but warm to her vulnerability he took her shoulders into his hands and turned her gently towards him. Slowly his arms encircled her, then drawing her into him he gently rested his hand on her head and finished her sentence for her. He said simply, 'Exhausting.' The simple word brought Vera into convulsions of sobs, low and muffled into his chest.

He let her sob; he caressed her soft freshly fragrant hair and patiently waited.

Vera's sobs began to subside and between bouts of blinking and sniffing she saw behind the tears something white fluttering in front of her. She blinked several times and then saw the immaculately pressed handkerchief being offered. Gratefully she took it and when she looked up at him he was smiling and she heard him say before taking it, 'Truce?'

She smiled, nodded, dabbed her eyes and gave a loud sniff. He released her as she started toward the verandah rail and listened to what she was saying. 'I don't often get out, Chris bought the tickets. Me bringing Iris with me gave Chris a break, even though I had to leave Sylvia with her, I know that Chris wouldn't let her off with . . . ' Once again she interrupted herself, 'Oh, you don't want to hear this.'

He was staring blankly but he was thinking as he looked down at the neat perfectly formed jigsaws of houses connected together by a bland ribbon of grey tarmac. Even the soft moonlight falling on the grey slated roofs inspired him only to wonder why or how anyone could build such a sprawling mass. Behind the identical doors and roughcast walls, how many other Veras and Irises were there? It was a long way from his home in Gloucestershire. He was taken by surprise when he heard Vera ask, 'Do you live local?' She swept her arm over the rail. He could have told her that his mother lived in the house in Gloucestershire and his father had rooms in town and they only met occasionally.

'No,' he said, shaking his head, 'I live in a small flat in Islington.'

Vera wrinkled her nose and wondered how such a nice person like him would want to live there. He answered her silent question. 'It's central for my work, and it's cheap,' he finished cheerfully. And then he added as if he had just reminded himself of something, 'Please,' he said as he opened his jacket and searched in his inside pocket. He found his pen and an odd scrap of paper. He put them into her hands. 'Do let me have your address and telephone number. Please.'

Vera quickly wrote her name in her very neat hand, then thinking that Mabel always opened the letters, wrote down Mrs Lownds' address. And as she did so she found her hand trembling. 'Thank you.'

'We don't have the 'phone, not yet anyway.' She had lied again. They would never have one of those things in their house, her mother had said.

Then another thought struck him. He took her left hand and stared at her fingers. Vera found herself staring down at her hand. 'No wedding ring, are you married?'

What a question, thought Vera. I wouldn't be standing here if I was, and then she allowed the thought to be aired. He smiled down at her indignation.

'Sorry. Sometimes it's easy to make a mistake.'

'I have a daughter of eight. I have no husband and I have never been married.' Her tone was severe but also very amusing. She tossed her head defiantly, daring him to make fun of her. Then without warning she found herself saying, 'Sylvia's father was an American soldier. GI,' she added for effect. 'He went back home without knowing and I didn't bother to try and find him.' To her astonishment she heard Harry singing the refrain from 'Who is Sylvia?'.

'Where,' she asked incredulously, 'did you learn that?'

'School,' was all he said.

It was then that Vera knew he didn't care who was Sylvia's father, or whether she was married, or unmarried, widowed, or even worse divorced, he liked her because, just because. She watched as he hastily replaced his pen and the scrap of paper with her name and address on it. He patted his breast pocket. 'I will write and that's a promise.'

He seemed in a hurry, so she asked, 'Are you going?'

'Yes, well not just yet. I have one more number, then I have a private party in town to attend. Sing for my supper, you might say.'

Vera felt her disappointment showing on her face.

Harry brushed her hair from her face and cupped her head in his hands. He lifted her lips to his, kissed her softly then he was gone.

All that remained was his voice drifting out across the verandah where she stood alone.

Behind her she heard the sound of a car spluttering up the hill and a sudden clash of gears. Her taut nerves gave way to a fleeting moment of lonely despair. Tears welled but she held back the sobs. Harry's handkerchief was still screwed up in a tight ball. She unravelled it, then folded it in half and tucked it safely under the sleeve of her dress. She brushed her skirt with the back of her hand. It was an empty gesture. Then she took a deep breath, drew herself up to her full height and straightened her shoulders. She was now ready to go back into the hall. As she moved towards the open door behind her, to the left where the laurels had overgrown into the verandah she heard a sound. Someone, she was sure, was behind them. There was no wind or breeze to talk about; she strained her eyes through the dark blanket about her just as a cloud obliterated the moonlight. 'Courting couple,' she said to herself and stepped into the hall. The glare unsettled her then she became used to the lights and smokey atmosphere and the deafening music.

A familiar moist hand pulled at her arm and she looked into Iris's flushed face and excited eyes. Father Brennan's dumpy figure stood in front of her, his face covered with the largest white handkerchief Vera had ever seen. He was mopping his heavily sweating forehead. As he pushed the voluminous whiteness back into his pocket he said, 'My my, this one sure can dance!' His leather belted tubby girth rose and fell as he gave a laugh and a gentle squeeze of Iris's arm by way of compliment. 'This jitterbugging thing is quite beyond me. A nice slow waltz is more me. I'll be pleased to leave this jazzy nonsense to the youngsters, like yourselves,' he said laughing, patting his oversized middle.

Looking directly at Vera with more than a twinkle in his eye he asked, 'Where's the young fella, then?'

Before she had time to answer, the band had struck up loudly.

'C'mon, me pretties, 'tis a Paul Jones, me favourite!' Delighted at the prospect, he hooked his arms around their unsuspecting waists and with a hop and a skip propelled them across the floor. Taking charge, he stood them side by side in the inner circle. Iris gave Vera a nervous look, a frown not far away. 'Just follow me.' She gripped Iris's hand. They bounced along to the music waiting for it to stop. The men were almost running in the opposite direction each with their eye on their girl, willing the music to stop as she came in sight. Their feet thundered to the cheerful beat then at last the music stopped abruptly. Iris was opposite Father Brennan. Vera stood in front of a young imply-faced lanky individual. The couples glided away to a waltz, and those without partners wended their way back to their seats.

Vera's next partner was a large man of local dignatory status. She allowed her now more confident feet to lead her into the intricate steps of the foxtrot. Over her shoulder she saw Iris with an elderly, white haired tall elegant man, who was obviously an accomplished ballroom dancer. He was however gallant enough to realise that dancing was not one of Iris's strongest points and gently manoeuvred her into a swaying rhythm. Vera smiled broadly. Yes, she was enjoying herself immensely. She felt herself relax and allowed the music to flow over her.

The large rotund and very heavily puffing dignatory excused himself from the dance and with Iris by her side Vera rejoined the dance now almost at its conclusion. The end of the music found them both with partners still. Vera, laughing, fell into the hands of Father Brennan, determined not to give up on his pursuit of his favourite dance. The quickstep proved far too much and they stopped at the drinks table. 'What's you be havin', then, me girl?'

Vera looked at Father Brennan's smiling wrinkled face. 'One of those sparkling orange drinks.' Then she added '. . . with a straw please.'

The band began the haunting melody of 'In the still of the night'. Standing with her back to the dancers, Vera too began to sway to the inviting tone. Father Brennan watched her, lost in thoughts. From behind her a gentle tap on her arm brought her back to the present. Still languid in thought she turned dreamily toward the voice that followed the tap. 'Would you care to dance?' There followed a light nervous cough. 'It is an excuse me, and if you don't mind, Father?'

'Go on, away with you lad,' Father Brennan replied with a flap of his hands like an oversized butterfly in motion. Vera felt as though she was floating. Floating through time. Floating away all her troubles. 'Dancing on air' was the line from another song that came to mind.

Her feet obeyed her simplest wish. Even the thud of heavy feet on wooden floor and the blue grey layers of cigarette smoke that filled the hall did not detract from the exquisite feeling of freedom that ran full and relentless from the top of her head to the tip of her neatly shod toes.

Without any warning, Vera stopped stock still. Her partner, the suddenness taking him by surprise, found himself instantly recovering his balance only to pitch forward into Vera's shoulders and outstretched arms. With her firm footed stance Vera thrust him upright. The force staggered him backwards. Without a second glance she strode across the floor to the door, leaving a domino wave of couples unlocking intertwined lost and confused feet.

The icy finger of fear was stabbing her still in the small of her back. She walked, her head high, her expression stoney, her eyes fixed on the fire exit. She pleaded inwardly, 'I didn't really see it, I only imagined . . . ' She bit into her lip. The taste confirmed her fear. Blood!

Her eyes widened: the doors were shut. She grabbed at the bar, shaking it, then pulling at it furiously. Why was it closed? She'd seen it open. A trail of men had used it. Why now was it shut? Deep inside she knew. She wrestled with the bar, and above her silent cursings a calm voice said, 'Let me.'

She glared into the enquiring countenance. 'Open it, *now*!' she screamed at him.

Silently the figure obeyed. With a single clunk the doors opened. As Vera stepped out into the silence, behind her she heard a shrill female voice call out, 'Close the door, George, otherwise Mum'll get a chill, dear.'

The doors creaked slowly to, leaving a shaft of yellow behind her.

She looked up. Over the door the metal scouts' shaped hat shade was empty. Her fingers, flicking at the light switch, were to no avail. The yellow light and a soft lilting melody were her only companions. The recently laid concrete felt uneven beneath her feet. Her soft shoes padded silently. She paused for a moment to get her bearings.

She stopped. Listening hard, something caught her sharpened senses. Turning from the concrete she cautiously, with a hand on the corner of the wooden building, followed her instinct. Letting go, she stepped up onto the verandah. The wooden struts had rotted away at the base. The dry wooden boards creaked softly under her ponderous footsteps. The hand rail wavered to the touch of her trembling grasp. The high moon picked out the glossy leaves. She scanned the overgrown jungle. There came a rustling. Was it in front or beneath her? A dead leaf caught up in a night breeze? She stopped and listened once again. This unused rear of the building was dusty; from the common ground all manner of deposits fell. The building nestled into its side; it was inaccessible either from the rear or the side. The sight of two yellow flashes from the half frosted windows of the hall stopped her long enough to hear herself breathing loudly. She drew in a long breath and just as slowly let it out. A small flight of four steps was just a step away. The suddenness of her fall into the laurels below gave her no time to utter a sound. From between the struts a hand had snatched at her ankle, toppling her sideways onto the waiting laurels.

She could feel the leaves pulling at her stockings. The dusty ground covered in dead leaves clung to her dress. She shook her head and began to rub her elbow. She attempted to stand, taking her weight on her hands. There by her side was Iris. The pink of her clothes screamed at her.

'Iris!' The word fell from her mouth in less than a whisper of a gasp. Vera began to shiver. She put her arm under Iris's lolling head. 'Iris,' she whispered.

'So,' came a voice from the darkness, 'you just had to come. Didn't'ya? Course, I knowed yer would!' Vera sat upright cradling Iris in her arms.

The voice continued, mocking in its tone. ''Cause you only drops your drawers for the Yanks? Ain't that right?'

Vera stayed silent. She pulled Iris closer to her. Iris was moaning softly.

'What you done to her?' Vera demanded. She began to feel dizzy. 'So, 'elp me if you've laid one finger on her . . . '

'Oh shut up, you stupid cow. So what you gonna do about it then? Come to think about it, always fancied a bit of a threesome, like.' Ronnie gave a coarse, hard chuckle and rubbed his hand thoughtfully across his chin.

Vera watched as a red glow was pinched out between his fingers and thrown into the shrubbery. As he stood up Vera spotted the glinting bottle cap that hung from his jacket pocket.

Iris began to moan louder. Vera pushed away the hair from her face to get a better look at her.

'You bastard!' she yelled at him, 'she's drunk.'

Ronnie laughed again. 'She di'n't kick up no fuss . . . not when I tells 'er it's ginger beer.' He pulled the half bottle from his jacket and gave it a wave of triumph, snorted and began walking towards them. 'Anyways it ain't 'er I wanted . . . '

In the briefest glimpse of moonlight she saw his face leering down at her. She felt sick. Protectively she pulled Iris even closer to her. Defiantly she held his gaze. 'You're a pig, a filthy dirty 'orrible pig. Someone will come.'

He sneered. 'Oh yeah, like what? The cavalry?'

Vera's heart was thumping. Then suddenly, Iris broke the silence with an uncontrollable giggle.

'See,' he said, squatting down on his haunches. Cupping Iris's chin in his large hand he started to shake her head roughly to and fro. 'She's enjoyed herself. Ain't yer?'

Iris let go a ripple of giggling that finally exhausted itself.

'Bastard, eh? Well, you'd know all about that, then, wouldn't yer?' His fingers began climbing up Vera's leg.

His jacket draped over her as he leaned menacingly into her.

'You'd know all about bastards, you've got one of yer own ain't 'cha?' He was moving over her. 'You comes to a place like this, dressed like that. If that ain't askin' for it . . . ' He broke off. He lunged at her. Vera raised her knee and caught him firmly on the jaw. He fell back. Quickly Vera snatched at Iris, pulling her clear of his immediate grasp. Seconds later his hands were high on her leg. She struggled free, kicking at him wildly. His filth ingrained fingers were still groping her neck and shoulders.

His hand was now hard on her thigh. She kicked out once again. Iris gave another moan. Looking down, she saw the serene untroubled look on her face. Iris was lying on her back, her hands limp across her middle. Blind panic ceased Vera. She could have run, she could have screamed, but for some strange incomprehensible reason she could do nothing. With her hands flat to the ground she began shifting herself backwards away from Ronnie. The sharp leaves felt like razors against her skin.

Ronnie had leapt to his feet. His frustration and anger, mixed with vast quantities of whisky, made him see only Vera slithering away from him. His jacket flew open. It caught on the bushes as he strode towards her, his arms thrashing at the foliage in his way.

Vera looked up, seeing him almost on top of her. She covered her face with her hands as she felt her body numbed with fear. A single cloud drifted across the moon.

In the hostile darkness that surrounded her, she waited. There was a loud crack that echoed in its solitary connection. 'The girth may have widened and softened, but not this!' Father Brennan's Irish brogue was rough and his silver grey hair had flopped over his forehead as he bent menacingly over Ronnie's sprawled body lying inert on the ground at his feet. He pushed his fist closer to his face, straddling the groaning semi-conscious Ronnie. 'This, me boy, is still the same fist that floored Billy Tonkin, and it took him, a *real* man, not a sniffling wretch like you, four days to get off his backside. You understand me?' He had grabbed the dazed form to its feet by his ill fitting collar. Father Brennan shoved him away. 'You'd better get yourself out of here before I finds a policeman. Be away with you, before I changes me mind!'

Vera scrambled across to Iris and watched and listened in amazement. Iris was sleeping like a baby. Feeling Vera's warmth she curled herself up and snuggled her head into Vera's relieved body.

'Is the girlie all right?' It was more of a demand than a concerned enquiry.

Vera, dumb, just nodded gratefully.

Dusting down his cassock and his hands, Father Brennan added, 'I think that's the last we'll be seeing of that.' He stopped and looked over his shoulder at the figure scaling the wall at the foot of the 'cut'.

'Well, it will be when I've had a word with his Maureen.' He saw the look of shock on Vera's face. 'Well, I declare then, we'll just have to . . . ' He stopped once again, abruptly choosing his words carefully. 'Absence of truth,' he said, smiling.

Vera was horrified: a man of the cloth lying. 'You mean lie?' The colour had returned to her face and Iris was moaning softly in Vera's lap.

'Now, me girl, did I say anything about lying? Now, absence of truth, that's a different matter. Anyway, don't go worrying your head about such things. Let's get you both back into the dance.' Once again Vera looked horrified at the thought.

Father Brennan offering a helping hand, between them they raised Iris to her unsteady feet. He gave a quick look up and down. 'I don't think she's . . . A bit of spit and polish and she'll be right as ninepence.'

Together they moved slowly to the verandah. Iris had regained a slow walking motion. At the top of the wooden flight she opened wide her eyes and, staring into Vera's face, said simply, 'I feels that tired, I think me teeth 'ave gone to sleep.'

Vera's face fell in half with a beaming smile of relief. Father Brennan said, 'That's it, me girl, a good cup of strong tea and you'll be just fine.'

The three slipped back through the fire exit under cover of a waltz. The dimmed lights gave them just enough time to reach the ladies' cloakroom without a soul being any the wiser.

Father Brennan had been right. Two good strong cups of tea and they were fine. Well, Vera felt recovered but she wasn't so sure about Iris. The effect of alcohol had to a greater degree worn off, but she seemed distantly quiet. But Vera put it down to tiredness. Chris had been surprised to see Father Brennan with them, but it was a pleasant surprise. Nothing, Chris had thought, ever happened with a priest around. Neither was she surprised to find Iris so tired. 'Gets herself so strung up, if you know what I mean.' She had babbled nervously on the doorstep 'in the presence of God' then answering Vera's silent question with a shake of her head, 'Sylvie was that tired, just fell asleep, she did, sitting on the floor. I thought she'd be better having a sleep here, so I popped her into Iris's bed. Collect her in the morning about eight, if that's all right. She'll 'ave her breakfast, and you know just how good they get on.' She finished on a high note, looking for Vera's consent. Vera, too tired to argue or explain, not that she wanted to, just nodded.

So, Vera was now walking with Father Brennan along the empty streets. They walked in companionable silence until Vera asked, 'Were you really one of them prize fighters?' She asked, though she wasn't quite sure what she meant.

A boyish reflective grin showing neat square white teeth welcomed her question. Then he laughed. 'Sure was. Bare knuckle.' The he raised his fists and took up a John Sullivan stance. 'Course, I was only a bit of a lad.' He spoke almost apologetically. 'I've not been a man of the cloth all me life.' And like every other person she knew he tapped the side of his nose knowingly, followed by one of his enormous winks. Vera laughed so loudly he put a finger to his lips saying, 'Hush me girl, we'll have all the curtains twitching! Shh,' he urged for silence. Turning the corner he looked at Vera and in a quiet voice filled with concern asked, 'Do you think Iris has . . . ' he struggled to find the words, 'all right?' he finally managed feebly with a vague wave of his hand.

Vera understood the heavily veiled question. It had worried her too. She answered truthfully, 'I don't know.' She gave a heavy shrug of her shoulders, then shook her head slowly and, facing him said, 'I don't know. I think she's . . . well, all right . . .' Her voice trailed away.

They had both stopped walking. Francis Brennan ran a worried hand across his brow. Then, looking directly into Vera's open and honest face, 'You make me a promise. You'll be telling me if you find different. Understand me?'

Vera nodded solemnly, understanding the seriousness of such consequences. She shuddered just at the thought and what she kept in the corners of her memory. She shuddered once again, this time inwardly, thinking how grateful she was to see only the small landing light on in Chris's: no deep explanations. What had Father Brennan said, 'Absence of truth?' She still wasn't quite sure what he meant.

'Oh,' Father Francis uttered quickly as an afterthought. 'I nearly forgot.'

Vera hadn't noticed the brown bag he had been clutching under his arm. 'These are for . . . well, I don't like to see good food going to waste, so I had them popped in this bag for you and Sylvia. Nothing like a bit of a midnight feed!' he said, rubbing his hands together after handing over the goodies. 'Remember it well,' he remarked with relish.

Vera peered into the brown bag. Inside there were bridge rolls and a few curled sandwiches. 'Thank you.' She watched the warmth of his memories showing across his dimpled smile.

'Right, you are. Safely home.' He opened the gate for her and Vera was pleased to be home. And keeping her fingers crossed, she didn't wake 'Big Mabel'.

'Go quietly now, me girl. God bless you, child.' He began walking away, then with a quick glance over his shoulder in a hoarse whisper said, 'You'll not be forgetting now. You know where to find me – anytime!'

Vera gave another nod and mouthed, 'Goodnight.'

Francis Brennan, being a fully paid up member of the 'long goodbye' school of farewells, took himself silently back to the closed gate, then bending low across it whispered at a startled Vera, 'Nice boy, that Harry. Good manners, clean . . . ought to keep in touch. Yes?'

Vera grinned. 'I hope so,' she said, blushing at the thought.

With his hands clasped behind his back, his head bowed in thought, he gave a little skip in turning about, and having the final word murmured to himself, 'Not a bad singer for an Englishman . . . ' Then with another hop to round the corner, he was gone into the night.

As she pulled the key through the letterbox, Vera offered up one of her silent prayers. 'Please don't let Mum wake up.' She added, 'I hope the gin's working.' Once inside she carefully threaded the key back and waited until it had stopped swinging before she took to the stairs. The bag rustled. She held it pinched between two fingers well away from her and trod the stairs, remembering that the fourth one from the top creaked. Safe behind her bedroom door, she let out a sigh of relief.

She stepped out of her dress and hung it on the back of the door. The window was still open. She stood relaxed, her head resting on the palms of her hands, staring blankly into the darkness. Nothing ever happened or was heard in these gardens. She gave a self reflective nod of remembrance of her childhood years in Victoria where all she heard was screaming, shouting and for all she knew murder being committed. But not under this window. She pulled her nightie over her head and instead of getting into bed, sat on the floor, slumped against the wardrobe door 'Crumbs' she remembered, would be found! She got herself comfortable and began digging into the bag. For some reason she was ravenously hungry. She pulled out a very curled up sandwich. Her ankles crossed in their customary long legged fashion, she bit in hungrily. When she ate the now even harder bridge roll, the mustard and cress filling had her tongue reaching around the corner of her mouth to retrieve the lost strands. She wiped her mouth with the back of her hand, and smacked her lips with satisfaction. She stifled a giggle at her unladylike manners. She knew that she had eaten more than enough. Her mind was filled too with memories of the evening. They rolled around in her head like a nightmare roller coaster. Some flashes good, some she had to forget. Would she see Harry again? She pulled her thoughts up short and carefully folded the bag. As she pulled herself lazily to her feet the key of the wardrobe caught on her nightdress. At first she was irritated, then something drew her round to it.

She removed the small but ornate key and held it tightly in the palm of her hand until it hurt her. She had been sure that she had locked it away; why then was the door opening?

She watched as the door swung eerily open. With the faint light behind her she stood, thoughtfully staring into the gloomy wardrobe. 'Mum,' she said under her breath and in a second she had dropped to her knees. Her slim arm searched for the shoe box; her fingers probed every corner. She fell back heavily, sighing out loud. She reached up to the lock, inserted the key and turned it purposefully. She swivelled herself around, drew up her knees, pushed her fist into her mouth and sighed once again. In the darkness she was beginning to wonder doubtfully about this day of sighs, lies and . . . 'absence of truth'.

Chapter 6

The hot July melted into an even hotter August. Even though the weather sizzled and headlines in the newspaper glared out bigger and bolder with each rising degree, there was nothing remotely unusual about the predictable steady tick and tock of each day that passed in the Surridge household. Rose and Tom with the usual scowling and protesting Patricia made for Mrs Harold's guest house in the small back streets of Ramsgate for the umpteenth year, taking the 'factory fortnight', last week in July first in August. All three were neatly ordered into the back bedroom, which boasted 'a garden view' though it overlooked nothing more than a cross between a builders' yard and a rubbish tip, although the name of the house was 'Seaview'. That view was strictly for the gulls, who regularly swooped into the garden for food and who just as regularly 'plopped' on the window. Not a word was ever uttered, except that Rose would declare how wonderful it was to see wild life at such close quarters!

They returned home as they always did with a promise on their lips that 'next year we'll try one of those holiday camps'. And Tom would wistfully hope that one day all guest houses would sell ale. It was only a dream, but it didn't stop him wishing.

Gladys and Arthur stayed, as they always did, stayed put. Gladys would try a little more gardening but even with a large sunhat she found the weather unbearable. Arthur refused to budge; every year he would protest, 'They don't want to see people like me on their holidays. Me, a war veteran, better off stayin' at home.' He would then rub his leg and wince with exaggerated mock pain. Arthur, it has to be recorded, went nowhere. He would then finish his annual speech with, 'Put me feet up now.' Arthur's feet were rarely down, unlike his arse which was always shaping a deckchair. Whilst Gladys toiled and wilted, Arthur's feet would be found neatly angled on a canvas stool, his arms folded across his chest, a neatly knotted handkerchief placed securely on his head. Gladys would prod him occasionally so he didn't burn in the same place twice. When the heat was really too much he'd take himself off to the Dog and Ferret to ease his parched throat. Then on leaving he'd turn around and forget which leg he was limping on that day. But no one ever noticed, as they were all too used to War Wound's ham acting.

Mrs Lownds took her annual holiday with her niece somewhere in Hampshire. She would give Vera a week's money and always wish her 'a very happy holiday'. This really didn't give Vera more free time; it gave Mabel all the more time to dole out more chores for Vera to do. Relining the larder shelves was the first job. Vera thought, 'At least it's cool.' Then followed the scrubbing of the steps at the front, followed with another coat of red Cardinal on the kitchen floor, not forgetting the cooking, shopping and the ever present Iris.

Iris would sit on the front steps without knocking, and wait for Vera to finish. Sometimes, the boys playing on the green would call out to her to come and join in their game of cricket. Unaware of the rules, especially the ones the boys made up to suit their abilities, Iris would just dash around for the ball, whooping with pleasure when she caught it.

One afternoon, Vera was dusting the parlour and seeing Iris clearly enjoying herself on the green, felt in her apron pocket for the postcard Mrs Lownds had sent. 'Must show Iris.' She looked down at the four-picture card. One showed the New Forest, another showed a very old church, another showed a beach and the last was a harbour. She slid it back into her pocket and promised herself that once she'd finished she'd make some tea and would sit with Iris and show her the card. Immersed in her thoughts, Mabel's voice boomed out behind her, almost frightening her to death. 'There's somethin' wrong with that girl, carryin' on like that!' Mabel gave a short nod of her head towards the galloping Iris.

Vera gave a shuddering sigh. 'There's nothing wrong with her, she's just a bit of a child herself. You know that.'

'Huh,' Mabel replied, unconvinced. 'Not from what I've 'eard. Now I must go. Don't go spendin' all the time out there with that one. You hear? Oh, and before I forgets, we'll 'ave the macaroni cheese for tea – not too much cheese, you know how it upsets me if it's too . . . ' Mabel stared back at her daughter's questioning look. 'Macaroni cheese, girl. You know. And remember cheese costs, so grate it fine like.'

Big Mabel lurched through the parlour door, Vera following silently behind. She waited as her mother picked up her handbag from the floor. The catch was open and as Vera waited she watched astonished as the small rustling packet was pushed into the side pocket followed ever so swiftly with the leather saddle-stitched purse. Mabel looked up, her face colouring. 'What now?' she demanded and before Vera could answer she snatched the bag over her flabby arm and said, 'Tomatoes, slice 'em thin. They're salad ones, you know.' Big Mabel lowered her head, brushed down her heavy bosom and pulled at the close fitting hip of the skirt. 'Well? Was there somethin' else?' Then, as if she was answering her own question, pushing past Vera she said in the dimness of the passage, 'That reminds me, get out the greatcoat and them old blankets from the big old wardrobe. A good bashing with the handbrush over the line'll do 'em a treat? 'Ave you got all that, or do I 'ave to do it meself?' Mabel gave her daughter a haughty look of indignation and her head jerked back as she clasped her hands across her straining middle, the large handbag dangling from her arm. 'Well?' she demanded again.

Vera stared down at her. Did she dare ask? Tipping her head back and looking down at her mother she asked, 'What did you mean?'

Once again Mabel flushed, 'What about?' Her tone was irritable and impatient.

'About Iris. What you 'eard.'

Mabel made a huffing, 'Don'cha go talkin' to me, your mother in that tone. That's my business,' and as she turned towards the front door she tapped the side of her nose, adding, 'I knows.'

The evil smile that spread across her mother's face made Vera fell physically sick.

'I'm orf. I think you've got enough just to keep you out of trouble … if you knows what I mean?' Mabel sneered over her shoulder before shutting the door noisily behind her.

For the first time in her life Vera was overcome with faintness. She leaned against the door frame for support. Her heart was racing now as fast as her thoughts. What had her mother meant? That's if she meant anything. And if she had heard anything, who from? Was it about that night? Who would know? The questions came thick and fast, her head swam. She lowered herself into one of the kitchen chairs. The blackness that had crept in on her was now receding, but her head hammered so hard she was sure that anybody around would hear it.

She was standing with the kettle in her hand, filling it from the tap. 'Father Brennan?' No, no, she reproached herself. 'And anyway Mum wouldn't go anywhere near a priest,' she found herself saying out loud. With the kettle singing softly to itself on the high gas, she settled herself down into the chair. She leaned against its high back, stretched languidly and rubbed the back of her neck. 'Oh my God it's hot,' she groaned miserably, waiting for the kettle to boil. Impulsively she willed herself upstairs. Somewhat reluctantly she opened the old wardrobe. She knew what she would find. In fact she knew exactly what she wouldn't find. But she could be wrong. She put one hand on the side of the wardrobe to steady herself. Dropping to her knees, she allowed her fingers to search for the familiar shape of the shoe box. Satisfied it was empty, she sat down heavily on the edge of her bed.

The sun was full on the back of the house. All the windows were open and there was no breeze, not even a hint of one. Her head started to swim. She regained her balance and once again sat down on the edge of her bed and stared thoughtfully through the open window. 'So, I was right,' Vera sighed heavily, 'and I know too.' She gave a slight chuckle.

As she left the bedroom, she had made up her mind. 'This'll be the last time!'

She made a pot of tea and whilst waiting for it to brew she flung open the front door, expecting to find Iris on the step. Instead she found her in high spirits playing rounders with the boys. Vera called to her. Instantly Iris looked up, dropped the narrow plank that served as a bat, and ran towards Vera.

The gate banged, Vera winced and Iris asked breathlessly, ''Ave you finished, then?'

Vera nodded. 'I've made some tea and I think I can find some cake.'

Without waiting to be asked, Iris sat down on the step and waited. Vera looked down at the pink face, breathless like an excited child. Iris looked up and caught Vera's lingering look. 'They're winning,' Iris said enthusiastically.

Vera shook her head sadly and said silently, 'I hope I'm wrong.' Then turning back to Iris she said, 'Shan't be a mo', have a look at this.' She pushed the postcard into Iris's waiting eager hands. Sitting together on the step, welcoming the shade of the house and the cool green of the high privets, Iris wanted to know where the postcard came from. 'I ain't never been to the seaside.'

This wasn't true, Iris had spent months by the sea recovering but like most things, she had forgotten. Or did she really not remember?

Vera patiently went on to explain where Mrs Lownds had gone. She explained what a harbour was and how old the church, in fact a cathedral, was. Iris sat clutching her knees, hanging on to Vera's every word.

Iris had eaten all the cake and had asked for some more. Vera threw the grouts on to the earth under the privets and suggested they have another and with the promise of more cake. Just as she stood up a ginger haired, freckle-face boy was standing at the gate. 'Can we 'ave some cake?'

Vera grinned. 'You don't miss much, do you, Trev? You'll have to share.'

'Cor, thanks!' The boy shouted at his mates, 'We're all right, we've got some.' His voice echoed across the green.

As Vera turned to go in, there came a loud hooting from the end of the road. Instinctively she turned around to see who it was and as she did she became aware of Iris standing rigid beside her. The colour had drained from her face, looking down.

This time Vera followed Iris's fixed gaze. 'Ronnie!' Vera managed at last to think out loud. She grabbed at Iris's arm and dragged her inside.

'Oi, what about me cake?'

Vera shouted back, 'Later!' Then banged the door shut.

In the kitchen, Vera was shaking so much she couldn't put the cups and saucers down on the table. The soft childlike features she had seen in Iris just a few minutes earlier were gone. All Vera could see were her large eyes filled with fear. Quickly, she lighted the gas and without thinking how to ask just said, 'What you frightened of?'

'Can we 'ave our tea in the garden, like a picnic, like Sylvia and Doris does?' Iris replied, ignoring the question and beginning to jump on and off the kitchen steps.

Vera raised her head and sighed yet again.

'Trev,' Iris said.

'Trev?' Vera's voice was raised to the point of incredulity.

'He don't play fair.'

What got into Vera she didn't have time to think over. She snatched at Iris and pulled her into the kitchen.

'Tell me,' she said, her voice rising, 'What 'appened?'

'When?' Iris asked, looking into Vera's harassed face.

Vera started to sway. She put her hand to her head and before she could say another word, Mabel's voice shot across the small kitchen. 'Told ye!' Her voice was as always triumphant in its tone. Vera reared back and reeled around.

'Told yer, didn't I? She ain't so well as you thinks.'

Mabel's bulk pushed through the two women. She dumped her handbag on the table and with a cursory glance over her shoulder, said, 'Well, if you're makin' some, I'll be 'aving some tea. Me feet is fair killing me. Just like this weather. Ol' Tibbs is the same, don't know 'ow she 'anging on so long. Don't miss a trick, that one.' She stopped to draw breath and ease herself into the stout wooden chair. Then, tossing her head at Iris, she said with a smile, 'A bit like 'er, really!' Mabel gave a gravely laugh.

Vera physically pushed Iris into the garden. She had never wanted to kill anyone in her life before. But she clenched her teeth and glared at this vile woman, her mother.

Mabel, unconcerned, continued. 'So where's the greatcoat and the blankets for airin'? I told you not to go wasting yer time with that one.' Mabel gave another shake of her fleshy jowls towards the garden.

The sound that followed could be heard echoing across the gardens on this still afternoon. Vera, consumed with anger, struck out at her mother's face and the feel of her cool hand contacting her mother's sweaty flabby face gave Vera infinite satisfaction. Mabel struggled to her feet, speechless. One look at her daughter's face gave her clear warning. Silently she shuffled to the door. In the safety of the passage she said, 'I'll 'ave me tea in the parlour.'

Vera waited to hear the door shut to. She stared into the garden, watching Iris playing a solitary game of hopscotch on the grass. 'I've 'ad enough,' Vera thought. This decisive thought was interrupted by the lid of the kettle clattering over the boiling water. She turned off the gas tap and dropped exhausted onto the chair.

As Vera collected her thoughts over the next few days, the word 'apology' never crossed her mind. 'Thanks' to whomever gave her the courage of her convictions she felt more inclined towards. It was still the sound of her cool hand connecting with the flabby flesh and the silent stare of astonishment of 'Big Mabel' that became pivotal in her way of thinking. That single action squared her shoulders permanently and gave her the resolve and determination she knew she once lacked. No more! She was now resolved and resolute and she welcomed the barrier that had built up between her and her mother.

Not only did she welcome it, she was grateful for the space it offered. Never had she felt so free in deed and in spirit. Other than the night of the dance. Caught up in her new found confidence, Vera had not noticed the change in Sylvia, nor the conspicuous absence of Iris.

Sylvia had become distant and withdrawn, also reluctant to leave her mother's side. Sylvia had noticed something different about her mother and she missed Iris and wondered why she hadn't been around to visit as often. Neither did she want to be left alone with her Gran. She couldn't find the right words to tell her mother how her Gran had dragged her though the garden into the kitchen and had slapped her hard twice, once on her face and once on the back of her legs. She had seen her Gran's florid face, puffy and angry as she struck out at her, only because she and Doris had laughed out too loud. Sylvia had not cried, neither did she tell anyone. She had thought to tell her Aunt Gladys, but she wasn't sure. Her mother seemed bolder and stronger. It seemed to Sylvia as if her mother had taken over the running of the house.

Mabel was spending more time with Mrs Tibbs. On her return both Vera and Sylvia would watch as she lurched from side to side until falling into her chair.

Tidying up the parlour, Sylvia found a small piece of paper on the floor. Vera was in the kitchen preparing tea. She handed it to her. Vera gave it a brief glance, said nothing and tucked it securely into her apron pocket. After tea Vera asked Sylvia, 'Where did you find this?'

Sylvia, sitting on the side of their double bed, her legs swinging freely over the side, put down her book and stared at the paper pinched between her mother's fingers.

'Found it on the floor, down by the side of Gran's chair, where she puts her bag.'

Vera studied the billet doux. Silently she asked herself the date; satisfied she was correct, she went to the wardrobe. Sylvia watched, fascinated her mother's slow cat-like movements. Putting down her book she slithered across the bed and watched intently, hanging over the edge. As she watched it reminded her of the day her mother showed her the beautiful blue dress and the pretty earrings. 'I wonder.' She too was now asking silent questions. 'What has she got now?'

Sylvia was to be disappointed. Vera had nothing to show her, not even her face; that reflected both pleasure and steely determination. Vera's fingers withdrew from the now familiar corner. She dusted them together and stood straightening her lithesome frame.

Sylvia's disappointment showed clearly in the twinkle reflected in Vera's eye! She picked up her twice abandoned book and left her bare legs swinging.

Vera, her thoughts wandering, still looked down. She put her hand on Sylvia's leg.

'How did you do that?'

Sylvia looked down miserably at the leg her mother had stopped in mid swing.

'I run in some nettles.' She spoke the words clearly, but unconvincingly. Vera took the sun-tanned leg onto her lap. 'That,' Vera declared, 'isn't a nettle rash.'

Vera searched her daughter's face. Sylvia, like her mother, was not given to lying. 'Nettles don't bruise,' Vera's voice was flat.

'Did too,' Sylvia said defiantly.

At that moment the wandering thoughts began to crystallise. Another look at her child's face told her everything Vera needed to know. She let go of her leg and pulled her dress down over her grazed knee. 'You'd better go down and ask your Gran for the witch hazel out of the cupboard.' Vera told her to do this just to judge the child's reaction.

'No. No, it's all right. It's all better. We was fighting, honest . . . ' she wailed looking appealingly at her mother to believe her. Vera didn't. Vera knew that the time was now right. A few home truths and skeletons would be raised and removed once and for all!

'All right. Then, t'morrow we'll make some sandwiches, knock for Iris and we'll 'ave a bit of a picnic in the park. How about that?'

The child nodded gratefully.

Vera stood up. 'You'll be back to school soon.' She looked down at her child's face. It had relaxed and its friendly outgoing features had returned in full. That is how *my* daughter is going to stay always. Vera made a silent vow.

Turning to the door with the small square in her hand, she spoke silently. 'But first things first.' Vera tapped the side of her nose and grinned broadly.

The door clicked to behind her.

It was during one of Mabel's gin induced slumbers that Vera restored the buff coloured ticket to the zipped compartment of the old scratched leather handbag that never left Mabel's side, other than when she was drawn into the arms of morpheus.

The following Monday morning Vera with duster in hand stood back from the large oval table that nestled neatly beneath the diamond shaped leaded lights of the dining room windows to scrutinise her work, and was taken aback when Mrs Lownds offered her a white envelope.

'My, my, what a wonderful job you do make of this table.' Mrs Lownds spoke breathlessly with admiration and delight, enjoying the feeling of her finger gliding over the highly polished surface. Vera understood that Mrs Lownds was not only deaf, she was also rather forgetful.

Vera followed her through the door.

'Mrs Lownds?' she queried, knowing that the contents held her week's money. 'It's Mond'y.'

A little flustered, the tiny woman turned around, looking at Vera somewhat confused. 'Oh yes, it's my niece, you see, I have to visit her once again. Family matter. You understand?'

Vera nodded, although she wasn't quite sure if Mrs Lownds was as certain.

She repeated, 'It's only M'n'dy.'

'Yes, yes, my dear.' The genteel figure turned once again. 'I haven't given you much notice, so I should be pleased if you would accept this.' She underlined her intentions by patting the envelope with her small trembling fingers.

'Oh, there is something, I should like you to do for me.' The diminutive figure, hands clasped loosely across her grey skirt, looked hopefully up at Vera.

Vera nodded expectantly.

Mrs Lownds pointed a finger to the carpeted floor, then just as swiftly raised it to her lips. 'I don't want you-know-who . . . ' she said making stabbing gestures with her finger once again at the oversized moggy that was trailing a figure of eight around her frail legs. 'I wonder, would you be kind enough to visit and do the necessary for . . . ' She ended on a delicate high and whispered tone of confidentiality.

Vera smiled. And before she could answer, Mrs Lownds had continued. 'Mrs Gordon who would, well, do,' she gave a soft embarrassed cough. 'She too has business matters to attend to.'

Vera smiled even more welcomingly at the suggestion.

'Could I bring Sylvia with me?' Vera paused at this point, not wishing to embarrass this very ladylike woman any further. 'You leave it to me.'

Mrs Lownds' hands, firmly clasped, raised in joyous gratitude.

'Thank you, thank you, my dear. You really are so very kind.' With a slight sigh of relief she moved towards the kitchen door, having conducted the conversation unwittingly along the hallway. 'Your daughter is as welcome here as you are, my dear, and I do hope you know that. Thank you,' she added in a final tribute of thanks.

The cat was obviously pleased with the arrangements made, because she sharpened her claws on the basket behind the kitchen door, stretching lazily, searching for the sunniest spot then, with a quick lick of her paw across her chin, she curled up contentedly. Vera looked on at the over-indulged pet and she could have sworn that the feline femme fatale winked at her. 'So,' Vera observed,' when the lady's away you're out to play.'

The cat purred.

'Then,' said Vera, once again in silent planning, 'so shall I.'

In the afternoon in the High Street, from behind, Gladys heard, 'Mrs Bowles.' The female voice was urgent and breathless. Gladys stopped in mid stride and slowly turned around. She thought for a moment she recognised the voice, but she wasn't sure. Gladys' bulk eclipsed the small figure directly in front of her.

'It is Mrs Bowles? Vera's sister?' the voice enquired with a greater urgency.

Gladys looked into the sparkling grey blue eyes staring back at her.

'Ah,' Gladys gave out a sigh of recognition, 'Mrs Lownds?'

The frail voice hurried along, 'I'm so pleased, I do hope I haven't detained you?'

Gladys smiled, waiting patiently for the softly wrinkled face to regain its usual composure.

Mrs Lownds, catching her breath, said, 'I am visiting my niece.' Then, waving an envelope in front of Gladys, she added apologetically, 'I forgot to give this to your sister Vera this morning.' Once again Mrs Lownds caught her breath. 'I hope I can leave this with you in absolute . . . ' she hesitated, then added softly, 'confidence?'

Gladys was surprised at being considered trustworthy and highly flattered. It wasn't until she opened her hand to receive the envelope that she understood this frail figure was most certainly not frail of mind.

'Gladys?' The name was spoken more as a command rather than as a request. 'I do mean in absolute confidence.'

The envelope had been withdrawn.

Mrs Lownds' face coloured a little pinker. 'Gladys,' she repeated, her words falling into silent thoughts. She looked into the full moon shaped face, showing obvious concern and patience. 'I think, Vera has . . . ' Once again, she hesitated. She wanted to say an admirer; instead she lowered her head and drew herself into Gladys's conformable frame, whispering, 'a young man.' Taking confidence from her words, she said a little bolder, 'I think this should be kept to ourselves. Yes?' Wondering now if she had offended, this open faced woman hastily added somewhat breathlessly. 'I am well aware of Vera's circumstances.' She searched the face to gauge the reaction. 'I am extremely fond of her and her daughter, and I wouldn't want to think that I have . . . er . . . ' She began searching her mind for the right words. She gave up that quest and squeezed Gladys's podgy hand that rested across her thick middle.

Gladys placed her free hand on top, saying, 'Don't worry, this,' she took the envelope, 'is safe with me. I'll make sure it goes straight into our Vera's hand. Is that all right?'

Mrs Lownds nodded gravely, taking in every syllable. 'I just don't want to cause her any . . . ' Her mind was searching again . . . 'complications,' she finally managed.

Gladys knew what she meant by 'complications'. Mrs Lownds was well acquainted with 'Big Mabel' and took the necessary steps to avoid her at all costs.

The two women stood for a few seconds in silence and joint understanding.

Gladys broke the silence. 'It'll be just fine, you just leave it to me.' Her tone was reassuring; Mrs Lownds face brightened.

'My dear,' she said giving Gladys's hand another understanding gentle squeeze, 'please forgive me, I really have to go now. I have a train to board. I'm so pleased we have met once again.' She side stepped past Gladys, took a few faltering steps towards the station, turned back and left Gladys with a small regal wave of thanks.

Gladys, not a believer in fate, wondered as she stepped briskly out that perhaps it was just a coincidence she had decided to walk through the park to shop on a Monday. Normally, Monday would be filled with laundry and cleaning. Still, it was a lovely day and if the walk had done her good, then taking into consideration that Arthur was at home, he would be firmly stuck in the deckchair ogling the brassy blonde from next door. Gladys gave a light chuckle and smiled to herself, saying, 'And he thinks I don't know.' She clipped her bag shut, securing her errand, and crossed the road to take the short cut home. 'Men!' she said out loud, her broad beam being the last to disappear around the corner leading into the 'cut'.

Gladys put down her bags on the table. She washed her hands at the sink and stared idly into the garden. There was Arthur sprawled in the striped canvas. Everything in the kitchen was exactly as she had left it two hours earlier. She filled the kettle and called out through the gingham framed window, 'Do you want a cup of tea?' She blew out the match and flicked it into the ash tray that sat on the top of the cooker. The only response she heard when she popped her head out of the kitchen door was snoring.

Smoothing out the neatly embroidered tablecloth she took from her handbag the letter. 'When?' she asked herself, 'when can I give this to her?' She tapped it thoughtfully against her fingertips. 'It'll 'ave to be Friday.' She wasn't altogether happy with that as it meant she would have to keep it from Vera for four days. The kettle gave a shrill scream.

Gladys filled the teapot. Suddenly it came to her. 'Of course, how silly of me, she won't tell Mum about Mrs L. seeing her niece. I'll take it around tomorrow at Mrs L's.' She sat down happily and relieved and sipped her tea contentedly.

'Where's mine then?' Arthur's gravely tones filled the kitchen. Gladys looked up, smiled, and tossed back her head, saying, 'There. The same place I got this one from!'

Arthur grunted, turned away and strode sullenly back to his 'throne'.

Gladys grinned. She felt wonderful.

Chapter 7

Vera was feeling good too. She waited listening for Sylvia to fall asleep, hearing the child's gentle rhythmic breathing. Contentedly Vera sat on the floor, her long legs crossed as usual at the ankles. She stared out through the window, her gaze lingering on the rising full moon that snuggled between the two corner houses. Was it this making her feel nostalgic, thoughtful and reflective? It had been on an evening such as this that she had lied for Rose for the very last time. She leaned back against the bed, clasping her hands together, cradling her head. At fifteen Vera had been taller than Rose, but even then Rose could be overwhelmingly persuasive. At her then regular weekly request Vera had squared up to her and refused, shaking her head violently. 'Oh Vera,' Rose had whined in her adenoidal pitch. 'Oh go on, just once more,' she had said in her sly bleating manner. 'I'll do all the washing up next week. Promise.' Vera had looked at her sister's perfectly manicured fingernails and lily white hands.

'No!' Vera had said and slammed their bedroom door behind her. Vera knew that it wouldn't be Rose's last try. Not that she cared if Rose did the washing up for the rest of eternity! Vera had made up her mind not to lie to that nice Tom ever again. Rose had crept into their bedroom, closing the door silently behind her, then, leaning casually against the chest of drawers, said sweetly, 'Vera, when you, well, get to know about men and things,' softly polishing her fingernails on the bodice of her dress, 'you 'ave to make certain kinds of sacrifices.'

Vera had leapt to her feet, her face an inch away from Rose's, whose breath she could feel on her face coming hot and fast.

'I know what you're up to. How could you do . . . ?'

Rose darted back to the door, 'Shush,' she said, 'Mum'll hear you. You'd better try and keep that temper you'rn under control.' Her tone was thick and authoritative. She didn't finish.

'I'd 'ave no temper if you didn't go around treating 'im,' she tossed her head at the unseen front door. The bedroom door was now vacant of Rose's decorative form, as Rose had swiftly slunk into the corner to escape Vera's dramatic wildly flaying arms.

Rose was now on the defensive. 'You don't know nothin' about these things. I'm not asking you to lie, well, not exactly, well, I won't be 'ere, will I?' she said pleadingly to the towering Vera.

Seeing Vera's flared nostrils, she then decided on a more relaxed approach to the problem in hand. Sitting on their bed, she patted the threadbare, lumpy, wine coloured eiderdown, inviting her sister to sit.

Reluctantly, understanding her sister's manipulative ways, Vera sat down, her arms folded tightly across her. She fell heavily and the springs creaked under her weight and sighed angrily. 'I know exactly what you want me to do,' Vera said hotly, glaring hard at her sister's painted face, 'and,' she added acidly, 'if Mum sees you goin' out like that it won't be the washin' up you'll be scrubbing! And that frock!' Vera continued without drawing breath.

'What's wrong with my frock?' Rose asked angrily, her eyes narrowing. No one but no one criticised her couture, least of all her stupid baby sister.

Vera didn't need to be asked twice. 'It's too short, too low,' she said, staring down at the heaving cleavage made more obvious by the low square neckline. 'And,' she added defiantly, 'it's too bloody tight!'

Rose started, her face purple with indignation. 'How dare you,' her voice low and breathless, 'you dirty mouthed cow.' She spat out the words, forgetting her self importance. 'It won't be me scrubbin', it'll be Mum scrubbin' your mouth out with soap!' She stood up suddenly. 'That, me girl,' her finger wagging under Vera's nose,' is the kind of talk that gets you in trouble.' Realising she had turned the confrontation in her favour, she turned slightly and said in a slow provocative tone, one eyebrow cocked with assurance, 'We'll say no more about this. When Tom knocks, just take the flowers or the chocs.' She hesitated for a second, a thought suddenly striking her, 'Where does he get the chocs from?' She gave a brief shake of her head, none of her business, 'probably,' she concluded, 'from that posh boss of his,' then a worse thought struck her: black market? Turning to Vera, 'You can have the chocolates,' she said, smiling up at Vera, 'that's if he brings me any of course.'

Vera watched, with red faced fury during her sister's icy dismissal. 'Shove yer chocolates. I'll do it just this once more!' she screamed down at Rose's prostrate quivering mass that had fallen backwards on the bed.

Rose took a steadying breath. As she looked up into her sister's face she couldn't remember ever seeing her so angry. She waited for Vera's footsteps to stop at the bottom of the stairs before raising herself on one elbow, gasping for breath. She stood slowly and smoothed out the creases in her dress. Quickly, she wetted the tips of her fingers and smoothed away the few straggling hairs from her hot face. Gathering her thoughts and senses, she knew she had to get downstairs to Vera. She looked quickly at the delicate wristwatch, smiled, and slowly mouthed the words as she once more ran her fingers over her dress. 'Well, *he* likes it . . . '

Ten minutes later there came a knock at the front door. Vera stepped forward to open it. Rose screwed herself up behind the door. 'Go on,' she hissed. 'Open it, and remember what I said. Right!'

When Vera opened the door Tom was standing on the small front at the foot of the steps, his back towards her. When he turned around and saw Vera standing there he smiled broadly and said, ''Ullo, Vera, luv, how are you? That sister of yours ready then?' In his hands were a small bunch of flowers and a large box of chocolates.

Vera smiled back, a warm genuine welcome. 'She's 'ad to go out, Tom.' Her tone was apologetic and reassuring and how she hated herself for it.

Tom's face fell into a crease of disappointment. 'Out?'

Vera nodded slightly. 'Margaret's not well, and wants Rose to go over; what I mean is that she's gone over, just after tea like . . . ' She hated herself even more as she watched the crestfallen Tom push the flowers and chocolates at her. Guiltily Vera took them.

Then brightly Tom said, ''Ere, you 'ave some of them,' his finger pointed at the chocolates, 'and you tell Rose I says so.'

Vera managed a weak smile, remembering the conversation she'd had with Rose earlier. Tom had half turned, then as an afterthought he said, 'I tell you what. I'll come around tomorrow with a couple of bottles about dinner time.'

Vera gasped, 'I don't know 'ow long she'll be. She 'as stayed overnight. You know what it's like, eh?' Even Vera didn't quite know what she meant, but it sounded reasonable.

Tom nodded in agreement. ''Course I do, luv, I'd brought the car tonight, thought a bit of a spin might blow away the cobwebs and do us a bit of good, eh?'

He had half turned his broad stocky body away from her, a hand already on the gate latch ready to open it

'Tom,' she called after him, a tremor in her voice, 'you and Rose gonna get married?' It was lucky for Vera that Tom had his back to her, as a large foot found its way from behind the door and kicked her hard in the ankle. Vera winced. She held a small smile as Tom turned back to face her.

He smiled his generous smile. 'What's this then, Rose got me down the aisle already, then?' Tom was now standing on the red painted bottom step. 'Or 'ave you got designs on me?' he asked light heartedly, tweaking the end of her nose between his fingers and thumb. His voice and actions did not make Vera feel childish, it gave her a warm feeling of belonging. She was uncertain of the feeling but it was there, and it was a feeling she remembered strongly.

Without giving her time to respond, Tom had opened and closed the gate behind him and was stepping out along the pavement, a cheery wave following him. 'Cheerio, remember me to your Mum.' He quickly disappeared around the corner. Vera stood dumb in the doorway, her hand raised in more of a salute than a friendly wave. She found herself being pushed towards the stairs as the door closed on her.

Rose's face was white. 'What'd'ya wan'a go an' say that for?' Her lips were tightly pursed and the words steamed through the slightly open slit.

Vera stumbled back only regaining her balance on the wide stair where she had landed flat on her bottom.

''Ere,' Vera said, just as angrily, 'You 'ave em.'

Rose snatched the flowers and the box from her.

'Oh sod it!' Rose's voice was filled with exasperation, 'You 'ave em.'

Vera felt the guilt thrust into her ribs. It was then she saw 'it'. She couldn't stop herself from laughing. 'What's that?' Her blue eyes widened in disbelief. She heard Rose's body give a shimmy in reply. For Vera that was just too much. She collapsed in a heap in the corner of the stairs.

Unperturbed by this outburst, Rose swaggered into the small passage, at last revealing herself from behind the door.

Vera pointed at Rose's shoulders and asked again, even though she knew what 'it' was, 'What is it?' She bit her lip as she watched her sister throw the unfortunate creature around her generous shoulders.

'It stinks.' Vera held her nose.

Rose had had enough. 'It's dead!' she barked at Vera.

'Well,' said Vera, 'if it ain't he don't look very 'appy.'

'It's the fashion,' Rose's voice was level and informative; she knew about these things.

'Rose, wher'd'ya get it?'

Rose shot her sister a warning look to ask no more. Vera knew without being told. 'If Mum finds out, she'll skin you alive.' The shriek of laughter that followed left Rose frozen; even the fox's head dangling from her raised shoulder gave a knowing glassy stare. Humiliated to speechlessness Rose swept from the passage through the door and into the street, leaving Vera a crumpled giggling heap in the corner.

Her tears of laughter cleared into mistiness. Wiping her nose with the back of her hand, she looked down and saw the large plaid slippered feet standing astride in front of her. Instantly, she stood up. The flowers and box fell from her lap. Quickly she retrieved them. Mabel said, 'I 'eard the door.'

Vera gulped. 'Yes, it was Tom. Rose had to go to the lav, so Tom said he'd start up the car.' She astonished herself at the way she lied so glibly. Seeing Mabel eyeing the flowers and the chocolates, she added, 'Rose didn't want to take 'em with 'er.'

'Very nice,' Mabel observed.

Vera looked at the now wilting bunch of flowers and said, 'They are luvl'y.'

Mabel snorted. 'Not them . . . the sweets!'

Firmly, Vera replied, 'Tom said I could 'ave some.'

'That's right, give us em 'ere.' Mabel loomed across and snatched the box from her. 'A nice cuppa tea go down well, too.' The remark lost its demand as Mabel strode into the parlour with the box rustling open. The warm night filled with the sweet smell of chocolate. Vera looked at the bunch of flowers. 'And,' Mabel's voice boomed, 'they wouldn't say no to a drop of water either!'

Vera sighed and stepped down into the passage, resigned to being teamaker for the rest of the evening.

She took in the tea and as she set it down on the small table Mabel said, 'Nice, that Tom.'

It was then that Vera's curiosity started to get the better of her. Almost as if her mother had read her mind, 'I was 'aving a bit of a nod,' she said quickly.

Vera said nothing but looked at the box that had been swiftly emptied of its contents, then watched the trickling brown melted chocolate coursing through the corners of Mabel's thick lips into the creases of her chin. The longing she had felt earlier, disappeared suddenly. Between mouthfuls Mabel commanded, 'You can cut yerself a bit of cake.' The sloshing stopped enough for her mother to gasp, 'I'll 'ave a bit too, and another cuppa tea to listen to the play with.'

Vera left the room with a wry smile dancing across her lips. 'Funny that, thought it was your ears you listened with.' She made another pot of tea, covered it with its multi coloured cosy and presented it with cake to her mother on a small tray. Without opening her mouth, Mabel made her thoughts clear, 'That'll be all.' Pleased to be on her own Vera sat on the kitchen steps. She didn't realise that she'd fallen asleep until she came to suddenly. She rubbed the side of her face where it had slid down the rough cast wall, and shook herself awake, then looked up into the night sky. There hanging in front of her was an enormous moon resembling an oversized dinner plate glazed in silvery yellow. She shivered, and rubbed her bare arms, stepped back into the kitchen and securely locked the door behind her. Without making another sound she took the stairs and within minutes had slid between the cold sheets.

Sylvia stirred. Vera loosened the snow white sheets framing the child's shoulders. The child moaned softly. Vera watched as her eyelids flickered. Satisfied she was just dreaming, Vera leaned back once more and returned to her thoughts.

It was the moon she vividly recalled. There was something else. Yes, that's it. Vera's mind raced. It was the stillness that brought it all back.

Vera couldn't be sure. The moon had swung over to the far side of the window. Had it been the front door clicking shut, or was it the gate? Or had it been the low voices drifting up from the passage below that had woken her? For the second time that night she shook herself and listened intently. The voices were muffled, but she could make out Rose's voice. 'Rose?' Rose home already? It had made her listen even more closely to the faint voice. She heard Mabel say, 'Well?'

There was no immediate response. What on earth was Rose doing home already?

Vera slipped from the bed and sat close to the bedroom door. She didn't dare open it as it had a habit of squeaking when you least expected it. With her ear close to the door, sitting on her knees she concentrated on every sound that filtered upwards.

'Well?' Mabel growled again.

Rose was whining on about something.

'That's too bloody bad, then. You know what you gotta do.'

Vera could hear Rose sniffing. She was crying and Mum wasn't taking any notice. Then she heard Rose say, 'I can't, I can't . . . '

'Don't seem to me you got much choice.'

'He's so, so,' there was a long pause, 'short,' came the answer.

'Short or not.' There was another long pause. 'You should know by now, you know what they say, they're all the same size in bed!' Mabel had spoken matter of factly. The words were filled with sarcasm; Mabel gave even a deep sardonic gutteral laugh.

Why was her mother still up?

Rose was stifling sobs at the bottom of the stairs. Vera heard the larder door creak open. They goin' to 'ave something to eat, at this time of night? Vera couldn't believe it.

From the darkness she heard her mother's voice. 'Then you'd best 'ave some of this.'

The larder door creaked closed. Rose was sniffing and sobbing even louder.

Mabel's voice bellowed thickly from the kitchen. 'S'no good, that won't 'elp. You knows what you gotta do. So, do it!'

A strangled cry came from the passage. Mabel's voice quickly followed. 'There ain't no runnin' from it. If that don't do the business, you knows what will!' Mabel's voice was cold. Vera sat back on her heels and tried to think.

In seconds she heard Rose coming up the stairs. She quickly slithered back into bed, praying that the springs wouldn't creak. As the door opened a subdued Rose entered slowly and silently. Vera watched as she undressed. The claws of the unfortunate fox scraped over the top of the chest. Sniffing all the while, Vera wanted to reach out to Rose and comfort her, even tell her everything would be all right. But she couldn't and she didn't know what was wrong. Why was life so complicated when you lied? She was certain that had something to do with it. She began to think of the lies she had told that day. Never again would she lie to or for anyone!

Rose slid into bed beside her. Vera, her back to Rose, felt her sister thrashing about, hot and uncomfortable in the heavy night. She twisted around slightly, looking over her shoulder. The moon was low and the sun wouldn't be long rising. There was an eerie glow in the room. There on top of the chest of drawers, glinting in the pinkish glow, was the small silver wristwatch.

The broken night left Vera tired, she'd overslept. The sun was streaming through the window. A sideways glance confirmed that Rose was up but she already knew that, as she couldn't hear any snoring. She stretched lazily even though she knew her mother would issue orders from the kitchen, hearing the bed springs creak their usual alarm.

If the night had been bewildering, this Sunday would prove perplexing. The first thing Vera noticed was the watch missing from the top of the chest. The bedraggled fox fashion accessory still lay sprawled and beady eyed and helpless; then sun stroked its coat, threading through the copper and red tones. Vera began to think 'how pretty' until sleep finally left her. Then she remembered, '... and that is where the smelly thing'll stay, too!' she swore, viewing it with disgust. The bright day encouraged her to clamber out of bed, only the squeaky floorboard would signal her rising.

On the dot, Mabel's voice thundered up the stairs and through the loose floorboard that sprang under her foot. 'If you're up, you get yourself down 'ere. I wants the paper, the potatoes need peeling ...' and the list became indistinct as the voice lost its volume. Or was it just that Vera stopped listening? She quickly slipped on her clothes and went downstairs. In the kitchen she expected to find Rose but Mabel was still talking as if she hadn't stopped. 'Don't go forgetting to wash 'n press yer blue cotton. You know that does for work, an' Mrs Lownds likes things nice and neat, like!' Vera hadn't even stepped into the kitchen. Mabel saw the look on Vera's face. 'What's wrong with you, then?'

Vera lifted the bubbling kettle from the gas. Mabel moaned. 'Ain't I got enough to do? You ain't got no time for that. 'Ere, take this,' and from the deep pocket of her apron she produced a half a crown. ''Ere now, take this; I wants the newspapers, all of them,' she said meaningfully. 'An' some change. Tom'll want something to read after 'is dinner.'

Vera stared into the garden. 'D'you 'ear me?'

Vera squeezed the half crown in her palm.

'Don't just stand there, girl, the shop'll be shut soon.'

Vera heard the clock chime in the parlour. 'Good God,' she thought, 'It can't be that time already?'

She hurried across the green up the hill beside the 'cut'. She was quicker on the way back. Tom comin' to Sunday dinner? Nobody ever came to dinner on Sundays. And where was Rose? Breathlessly she opened the front door, her fingers covered with newspaper print. Carefully she closed the door, making sure she left no fingermarks on the cream paintwork. Once more standing in the kitchen she watched in astonishment as Rose sat sipping tea.

'About time too,' Mabel snatched the papers from Vera's hold. 'Change?' she demanded her hand outstretched. The change trickled into Mabel's red hand. 'Hum.'

Vera stared at Rose. Rose stared up at Vera, her cheeks colouring up slightly.

Mabel turned away to attend to something that might or might not be burning in the oven. Vera mouthed the words, 'What's goin' on?'

Rose flushed crimson, then shrugged, and returned to her tea. Vera gave her a dig in the ribs. Rose spluttered.

'That'll do, 'ere, take these.' She handed Vera the 'good' bone handled knives and forks. What her mother said next floored Vera. 'Take 'em in the parlour, lay the table in there. Just pull the table out a bit, you can squeeze round the back against the wall and Rose'll sit on the corner. Won't you, luv?'

Vera finally found her voice 'Spoons?' she said absently, wondering why all the fuss.

'Yeahh.' Mabel leaned aggressively across the table at Vera, her hands hard on her hips. 'Spoons! Don't suppose you'd say no to a bit'a jam tart and custard, eh?'

Vera swallowed: put like that she'd rather eat rat poison! As she thought this, the jam tart was rescued from the oven and set down on the gas stove. 'There,' Mabel said beaming, 'way to a man's 'eart.'

Vera viewed the volcanic spluttering quickly congealing red dollop, spread over the jam splattered blue ringed enamel plate. Aware that Vera was still standing there Mabel barked, 'Well, go on. Don't just stand there. Tom'll be 'ere soon.'

Vera's mouth sagged. Mabel still wasn't finished. 'An' leave me runner on the table, I don't want me table scratched, an' don't forget the cruet from the sideboard.'

Vera wandered numbly into the parlour. It was as she stretched in the sideboard searching for the cruet, 'That's it!' she cried out. 'That's it!' she repeated, as she straightened. 'Somethin's really got up 'er nose. What?' The word kept going around and around. 'No, it's more than that. What is goin' on? She hasn't stopped moaning all morning!' What had gone on last night? Vera was sure she remembered everything. She knew where Rose had gone. She'd even lied for her. What's Mum gotta do with it? Or had she dreamt it? She shook her head. 'I know what I 'eard.' She finished laying the table; the glass cruet in its silver plated holder took centre place. Stepping back, she remarked, 'It's bare. It needs some flowers, serviettes and things. Mrs Lownds always has flowers on the table, even in the kitchen.' Vera shrugged and as her shoulders dropped, she sighed.

The clock chimed once again. 'Glory! this day's galloping by,' Vera said with exasperation and a hint of ever growing despair. The gloss painted brick walls of the cream and green kitchen glistened with steam. The red tiled floor looked damp too. Her mother was clattering and banging lids over various shaped pots and pans. 'Tea?' Vera asked simply.

Mabel rounded on her. Her face florid, she dived between Vera and the sink and from behind the straggling floral curtain hanging limply from the draining board Mabel grabbed a large enamel pot and shoved it hard into Vera's rumbling stomach, saying, ''Ere.' As she struggled to stand upright a newspaper was slapped on top. 'Now, do something; peel 'em.'

Vera followed her pointing finger. The old enamel bowl that had been repaired with a washer was heaving with potatoes. Her face dropped.

'That's all you been doin', dithering in doorways and hangin' about. So do somethin'. Mabel's flabby arms flapped as the huge earthy mound was piled on top of her already groaning tower. 'Just get out there.' Mabel released the burden and waved one hand to the garden while the other snatched up her apron and wiped away the sweat from her eyes.

Vera watched.

'Go on then!' Mabel urged, turning back to the steaming pots and pans. Vera stepped cautiously into the garden. She unburdened her load, settled herself on the step and spread the newspaper wide across her knees for the peelings.

She grabbed a spud. The knife was ready for action but before she began she looked up and couldn't believe her eyes. Rose was in the garden; Rose was wearing a cotton frock; Rose wasn't wearing any stockings; Rose wasn't wearing any shoes; Rose was sitting on the grass now, her head was nuzzling into Tom's neck. Vera blinked hard, then blinked again. 'Never,' she muttered under her breath, 'Rose never comes in the garden.' Vera felt her mouth gaping wide.

A sudden sound made her jump. She reached down to retrieve the knife which had fallen from her grasp. She stared blankly at the backs of Tom and Rose sitting so close together you'd be lucky to get a fag paper between them, Vera remarked silently. With the knife held firmly in her hand she began tackling the earthy chore. The giggling and whispered words rising from the bottom of the narrow garden made her raise her head. But it was no good, she couldn't grasp what was going on. Where had Tom sprung from? She had been standing at the front door lying last night for Rose. She shook her head, hoping that some kind of sense might fall in place. She finished peeling the potatoes. Standing at the sink washing them clean she then filled the pot. Her eye was still fixed on the carefree pair at the bottom of the garden, sitting just out of the shade of the old apple tree. It made no sense.

Her thoughts were brutally interrupted. 'Giv'us them, then we can 'ave us dinner.' Mabel pulled the pot from Vera and banged it down on the stove behind her. Vera still hadn't moved; her body, inert, watched silently as the figures, hand in hand, stepped towards her.

''Ullo, Vera,' Tom said cheerfully, 'Cat got yer tongue?'

Vera shook her head slowly. Rose's eyes were lowered to avoid Vera's questioning glare

'Now,' Tom said, tapping the side of his nose, 'Listen to this.' He gently pushed past her, giving Rose's trailing hand an encouraging tug to follow him.

Vera, her senses becoming less numb, scowled at Rose. Rose followed Tom demurely into the kitchen where Mabel had put their plated dinners in the oven, ready to serve later. She had sat herself down at the table; her puffy hand wiped away the sweat from her face. Seeing Tom and Rose standing together she looked up, her expression stony; a hint of expectation glimmered darkly at the back of her yellowing bloodshot eyes. She fixed them with a narrow gaze. Catching Mabel's look, politely Tom raised his hand as a conductor would raise his baton to commence a musical masterpiece. 'One moment, if you please.' He left the kitchen and brought in from the cool passage a quart bottle of light ale. He gave a boyish impish grin at Rose, who darted away to the larder and returned with three glasses. Quickly he counted them, then turning to Rose he whispered something in her ear. Scurrying back to the larder, she put down a chipped glass tumbler, giving Vera a quick glance over her shoulder. Vera watched horror struck as she recognised it as the one from the bathroom.

Mabel didn't utter a sound. Vera was rooted to the spot. Rose was as crimson as her namesake. And Tom seemed to have grown to six feet tall, and his grin was just as broad.

Vera heard herself gulp in anticipation.

Tom quickly filled the glasses, offering one to Mabel, one to Vera then finally one to Rose. He cleared his throat, and lifting the last glass he turned directly to Mabel and said soberly and with great dignity, 'Mrs Surridge, Mabel. Mum. No, before you,' he stumbled a little, then with a disarming grin he raised his glass to his lips and said, 'Rose has this afternoon agreed to be my wife! Your Rose will soon be my own "little petal".'

Everything went so quiet, Vera thought she had died. The sun, the room, the afternoon was so still. 'Somebody!' screamed Vera inwardly, 'say somethin'!'

Mabel lifted her glass, drained it swiftly and it was returned to the table, its dull ring seeming to jar everyone into reality. 'Allow me.' Tom took the empty glass and refilled it, handing it to Mabel who accepted the foaming beverage, quaffed it back just as quickly and with a single movement of her elbow returned it once again, as she wiped her mouth with the side of her hand.

No one had moved.

Tom had hesitantly raised his glass to his lips, and just then Mabel spoke.

'Where'ya gonna live?'

Instantly Tom put down his glass. 'Charlie Bates, he 'as this 'ouse in Catford, well his missus di . . . ' he paused, 'passed on, so he's gonna live with his sister. The house needs a bit doin' to it.' Then added, 'It's got four bedrooms and a bathroom.' It was at this juncture that Rose added unnecessarily, 'Four bedrooms.'

Mabel asked, 'When?'

Uncertain how to reply to Mabel's question, he decided to answer honestly. 'Second Saturday in September.'

Mabel's face remained expressionless. 'Where?'

Tom fairly threw his drink down the back of his throat. Erring on the side of caution, Tom decided not to fill Mabel's glass again. It wouldn't seem proper, he thought. 'St John's, in the High Street,' he managed to say.

Vera's hand was hot on the tumbler.

'Well,' Mabel finally said, 'That's settled.'

Tom nearly swallowed his tongue. 'We'd like Vera to be chief bridesmaid, of course.'

At this announcement, Vera's eyes narrowed hard on Rose who had practically disappeared into the corner of the larder. 'That's right, Rose?' he said, asking for confirmation. Then turning to Vera and raising his glass, 'And very fine you'll look too,' then swiftly added, 'Not to outdo the bride though, eh?'

At this point Tom had leaned over the table and said confidentially, 'We've gotta . . . ' He looked about him before continuing, 'a nice bit of silk . . . parachute.' He spoke the words in a hoarse whisper, nodding knowingly.

'Well, that's settled then. We can 'ave our dinner now.'

Rose left the sanctuary of the larder. Tom filled his glass. Mabel swept past them into the parlour, issuing orders to bring in the dinners. Vera was standing very still, her fingers gripped tight around the glass.

'Go on,' Tom said, taking pity on Vera. 'Drink up, it's a special occasion, it'll be your turn soon!'

Vera resignedly opened the oven door, only to hear Mabel shout from the parlour, 'We ain't got the cork place mats. Bring 'em in!'

By the time the clock had struck three they had all given up trying to chip away at the boiled bacon now welded to the plate as was the unusual crispy cabbage. Mabel's plate, however, was perfectly clear. This was down to the large slice of bread Mabel had demanded, and that Vera had pulled out of the bread bin, to clean not only her plate but her knife and fork too. At this tense moment Tom reached into his jacket that hung from the back of the chair and pulled from it, like a rabbit from a magician's top hat, a half bottle of gin. Standing up, he offered it to Mabel, saying, 'Just for you, to drown your sorrows in, if I ain't good enough for Rose.'

Mabel's eyes glistened with eternal pleasure. As she took the bottle she stared up and hard at Tom. Yes, he was too short, and was too old for her Rose. But Gladys was already married and considering all the circumstances. ... She belched loudly, her thoughts still full. Older men, she considered to herself, were steady. Her 'arold had been nearly twenty years older than 'er. So, she concluded, 'He'd just 'ave to do.' The watery eyes showed no sign of emotion. She picked up the plates, saying nothing as she piled them in front of Vera, then with a clatter threw down the knives and forks on top. The clean spoons she put to one side. Perhaps, they'd 'ave the jam tart and custard for tea. Pushing the pile closer to Vera she said, 'Tea!' Then with her hands clasped in front of her, her elbows resting on the table, she said suddenly, 'Why the second Sat'd'y? Bit sudden ain't it?' she goaded.

Tom's eyes nearly popped out of his head, 'Mum, Mother,' he said, emphasizing the word. 'There ain't nothin' sudden, or quick, or hasty about . . . ' He didn't know how to continue. He looked appealingly at Rose for the first time. Rose lowered her head. Vera banged the spare spoons down on the top plate, glared at Rose, then left the room.

Trying to ignore Rose's crimson cheeks and horrified look, he left his chair and stood beside Mabel, who herself hadn't moved a muscle. 'There ain't nothin' funny-like, honest.' His whispered words in Mabel's ear were lost. She was staring at Rose, enjoying her obvious discomfort.

'It's to do with tax, September, getting married, I means.'

Tom heaved an audible sigh of relief and sat down on the chair Vera had vacated. He waited for Mabel to finish picking her teeth with her podgy little finger before answering. 'Well, yes, that does 'ave something to do with it. It is because, and I, we that is,' as he spoke he lowered his head reverently, his fingers interlocked almost in prayer or a barrister about to deliver a vital piece of evidence. 'Rose and me, we 'ad an understanding, I knew Rose was in no 'urry but . . . '

Mabel watched, enjoying every second of the explanation which she knew had no truth in it.

Tom had finished and had stood up. 'So, Mrs Surridge,' he said grimly, 'if you think that of me and Rose, I can only . . . '

Mabel waved her hand. 'Oh, do sit down, you're doin' me 'ead in.'

Tom bobbed down as quickly as a chastised schoolboy.

'I was thinkin' about the frocks.' She laboured the sentence, gaining thinking time. Mabel gave a quick look at Rose, who frankly, through Mabel's eyes, seemed to have wilted. 'Colour?' Mabel demanded.

The door banged open and Vera struggled through with a large tray.

Rose paled to parchment and said breathlessly, 'Soft green, with them long gloves without fingers.'

'Oh God,' Vera thought as she put down the tray, her eyes rolling heavenwards.

Tom stood up and raised his hands, saying, 'This is somethin' I dunno' nothin' about, I'll take me fags and have a quiet smoke in the garden.'

Vera dumped down the large cup and saucer in front of Rose; the saucer was swimming in tea. This escaped Mabel's notice as she had successfully on her third attempt opened the bottle and had already downed a large swig. Taking advantage of this lull in the verbal proceedings, Rose looked up knowingly at Vera whose frame hung menacingly over her, smiled a long slow smile and sipped her tea, the drops plopped loudly into the brimming saucer.

By late afternoon the sun was fierce on the back of the house and Vera felt herself drooping. She had finished doing the washing up and had at last stacked away the final cup and saucer on the shelf. She dragged the curtain across the front of the draining board to hide the saucepans. Sighing heavily, she shook her head in an attempt to shake off her tiredness. She began to fill the kettle, and over the rushing water heard the front door close, followed by the familiar sound of her mother's snoring. She leaned against the cool wall waiting for the kettle to boil. The jam tart was still on the top of the stove, Vera eyed it, her face screwed up in disgust. Standing in the kitchen doorway she stared blankly into space. Folding her arms she rested against the door.

One thing was certain: she was angry. She wasn't a child; she knew what was going on. She wasn't stupid. Tom was such a nice man, how could they? She took her tea upstairs into the bedroom and pushed the window up. There was a faint breeze, and oh how she welcomed it. She'd decided to wait up for Rose and then she'd see!

Vera gave a nod of resolved determination.

Before settling herself on the floor for what she knew would be a long wait, she needed evidence. With the evidence found and safely out of sight, she made herself comfortable on the floor, resigned for a long night. She must have nodded off as her empty cup had slipped from her grasp. Carefully replacing it into its saucer she heard the catch on the front door being released. She pulled herself up, folded her arms and waited for the creak on the fourth from the top. She rubbed her eyes, adjusting to the now dark sky.

The door slowly opened and Rose stepped silently into the small room. Vera moved her long legs, Rose stumbled, gasped and said, 'What you doin' on the floor?' Vera could hear her dress rustling in the dark corner by the window.

Rose was breathing heavily as she gave the curtains a swift pull together. Vera was now on her feet, her slim boyish frame looming menacingly over her sister. 'You're pregnant!' she said in a threatening low voice, daring to be contradicted. She added in slow, heavy emphasised, undulating tones, 'I ain't silly or daft, and I'm not a child!' She took a breath. Rose had become very quiet. Vera took advantage of this lull in her normally garrulous sister. 'There's a name for women like you.'

Vera was sure she heard Rose give a sly laugh before she answered, 'Yes, M . . . r . . . s . . . ' Then the room echoed to the rise of her throaty little chuckle. Vera's hand was raised then rained down hard on her sister's unsuspecting cheek. The blow shocked Rose into wide eyed silence. Vera gave her a shove and Rose fell onto the bed, sobbing in spasms like hiccups. Vera was as determined as ever, even more so. No crocodile tears were going to sway her. From beneath the bed she grabbed at the cumbersome brown wrapped parcel with a narrow sleeve neatly set around its bulging middle. The package landed in Rose's lap. In the darkness Rose's sheer terror at the sight of this parcel halted the sobbing hiccups. 'Well?' Vera watched the white face and waited, her arms firmly folded in front of her.

Rose was still staring at the neatly wrapped, clearly unopened packet of sanitary towels. Rose felt cornered. Gathering all her inner strength she looked up into her sister's unfaltering questioning gaze, held it firmly and answered, even though an overwhelming feeling of embarrassment hung over her, as they didn't talk about those personal things. 'You've been goin' down my personals,' she said accusingly. She stood unsteadily and tottering the two steps to the shared chest of drawers, placed the unforgiving packet beneath her undergarments. Feeling now a little more in control, she added loftily, 'I purchased others.'

Vera glared. 'That right? Why you got another packet in the bottom drawer then?'

Rose ignored her sister's intimidation, tottered back to the bed and dropped on to it. Hardly had she seated herself when a small heavy sparkling object dropped into her lap. Before she had a chance to examine it, Vera had swooped and snatched it back. Rose felt her face flush with anger.

She could hear Vera's voice icily in the warm room saying, 'It's 'is, it's 'is. The oiu polou, the toff down the Palais. It is, isn't it?' Her face was a couple of inches away from Rose's increasingly flushed cheeks. Vera had turned the now clearly visible wristwatch over and with her free hand was stabbing at the reverse of the delicate watch face. 'That's where you was, begging *him* to marry you. 'Im, a toff. Don't you remember what old Aunty Betsy used to say?' She drew herself up, put her long fingers on her lean hips and said, '"Don't go marryin' above your station"'...and you call me silly?' Crouching down over Rose's quivering body: 'So what was it Mum gave you? The old wives' jollop, gin or...?' She paused at this point, then levelled into Rose once again, finishing flatly, 'Or get Tom to marry you.' She picked up the small wristwatch and turned it over, once more looking at the date glinting ominously in the sudden burst of moonlight. 'Strange 'ow that date's the same as the weekend you stayed with Margaret.' Rose felt her sister's breath on her now ashen face and heard her whisper, 'Just two months ago, right?' The room fell heavily silent. 'I've done with lyin' for you, for me, for nobody, never again.' She stretched out her arms wildly. Suddenly she felt exhausted.

Rose stood up so suddenly her head glanced off Vera's chin. Vera steadied herself quickly. Instantly she saw the fight in Rose's face. Glowering up at her sister, Rose growled darkly, 'I've seen your little toy soldier waitin' for you in the park.' She grinned smuttily.

Exhausted or not, Vera put out her arm and gave Rose yet another shove onto the bed, leaned over her and said, 'I'm sixteen next month. And I'm telling you now, Rose, you're never gonna get away with this. You'll pay for it, I'll see you do, you just wait and see!'

Rose was astounded that her revelation had left Vera unruffled. She cowered into the corner of the old bed against the wall, drew up her knees, risking her bulging seams and sobbed quietly and forlornly.

Vera remained unmoved. She stared out of the window listening to Rose's witterings. In a strange way she began to feel sorry for her. But she kept asking herself, 'How could they do this to such a nice man?' Then she heard Rose say firmly, 'I don't even like him.'

Vera turned to her sister and thought that Rose was suffering just a touch of remorse until she heard her say, 'He's too old, too short and he's got ginger hair!' As Vera grabbed at her she wailed, 'I don't even like green.'

Vera hauled her terrified sister to an upright sitting position, narrowed her eyes and said, 'Then you just gonna 'ave to learn, you miserable cow.'

She dropped her sister onto the bed, stood at the door giving her a long lingering warning look and before leaving the room issued the warning. 'You ain't gonna get away with this. You gotta live with it. Remember that!'

The door closed softly, leaving the bedroom veiled in an overwhelming heavy fearful silence.

Rose picked up the pillow, buried her face into it and sobbed.

For all Vera had said, implied, threatened even, she knew she would never betray Rose; neither would she break her promise: never would she lie for anyone ever again. How Rose was going to overcome a 'short' pregnancy wasn't her concern. Rose, she knew, would be more than resourceful in her handling of such a delicate matter. Everybody would talk, but there could be no back of hand whispering. Rose would be married and that would be the end of it.

So on the second Saturday in September, Rose was dressed in parachute silk; Vera was dressed in green lining taffeta from a coat. Gladys made button holes; Arthur got drunk. Mabel wept openly – too openly! Tom, dressed in his smart double breasted demob suit, looked extremely happy. Mr and Mrs Carpenter made nothing more than a flying visit to wish the newly married couple well, and to leave the car for Tom and Rose for their honeymoon in . . . Ramsgate. The weather held. This was good as the reception in the garden demanded fair weather. The small box Brownie cameras snapped enthusiastically at the blushing pair. Vera noticed that the bouquet of mixed flowers seemed a little too large and Vera was sure it was held just a little too low. The couple was showered with rice and confetti. Tin cans were tied to the back bumper. While everybody cheered as they waved goodbye, Vera in the garden was cleaning up. Still in her faded green taffeta she looked down at the ankle length creation and thought, 'I don't think I like green either.' Shaking her head she went back into the kitchen for the final round of washing up.

For the first time since the end of the war, Vera slept alone in the small back bedroom, and the silence now in the house made her increasingly aware of her lack of purpose. Her two brothers were dead, her father whom she never really knew had died when she was four. Gladys had been the first married; now Rose. What, she had asked herself sleepily, lay in store for her? Her aching feet and exhausted mind gave way to welcome sleep.

Chapter 8

Vera uncrossed her ankles stretched and yawned. How vividly the memory stayed; was it really that long ago? She shook her head slowly with disbelief. A wry smile crept across her lips, as she remembered how much stronger and feistier she was in those days. Life changes, not always for the better. She reached across the bed and pulled back the white sheet from the snuffling sleeping child's face, Vera smiled; there were some things worth every moment of mental anguish and physical pain. Sylvia slept on peacefully. 'What goes around, comes around'; with these words spinning she reminded herself out loud, 'It's time!' Although tired she felt mentally stronger; she knew what she had to do and with a week all to herself, she was certainly going to make the most of it!

She slid silently into bed beside Sylvia. For some unaccountable reason she suddenly recalled daring once, when sharing with Rose, asking her mother why she couldn't have the small back bedroom. Her mother had replied icily, 'It's still the boys' room.' Now, with her plan clearly outlined in her mind, she felt her stomach give a sudden lurch. She tenderly kissed Sylvia's cheek and sighed contentedly. The week ahead would prove more than revealing for the dusty corners and lost skeletons.

The following morning dawned, promising yet another warm sunny day. Vera rose at her usual time so as not to arouse her mother's suspicions. In the kitchen she urged Sylvia to eat her toast and jam. They both felt part of a conspiracy and kept their shared laughter low. Vera reached for the kettle to refill the teapot. With it poised over the brown pot, all around her blurred into one. The full kettle made a dull thud as it landed heavily on the table. Vera grabbed at the edge as she felt herself swaying. 'Ooo er,' she moaned softly, daring to raise a hand to her forehead.

'Mum?' Sylvia asked nervously. Then she added brightly, watching as her mother steadied herself, 'You din't half go a funny colour.' Seeing her mother's colour return she continued munching on her toast and strawberry jam. Vera leaned into the sink, turned on the tap and began splashing the cold water around her face and neck. She took a long deep breath, then, lowering her head, let it out slowly.

''Ave some toast, mum.' Sylvia waved a thick slice under Vera's nose.

'No, no, thanks,' she mumbled. Then quickly noticing the child's puzzled expression she said, 'We'll get us some cakes at the baker's.' This brought a bright smile back to the usually cheerful child.

Before leaving for Mrs Lownds, she checked the kitchen and gave a nod of approval, even though she knew Mabel would leave her breakfast cup and saucer in the sink with everything else she'd use in the day. As she lingered in the doorway ready to pull the door shut the calendar hanging below the shelf, its snowy scene so glaringly out of place, locked onto her gaze. 'September,' she whispered to herself, acknowledging the heavy print as she heard the kitchen door click behind her. 'September,' she said once again, ushering Sylvia with a wave of her hand towards the front door.

Gladys Bowles had risen early that Tuesday morning, too. She had given a half glance over her shoulder at the snoring Arthur, his arms folded across him, his head high on the pillows, his fleshy cheeks and chins puffing out and rippling with each juddering snore. His bristly unshaved face filled her with nothing, absolutely nothing! She stood on tiptoes to see into the garden below. His deckchair imprinted with his shape hung forlornly, the striped canvas drifting occasionally with the light warm early morning breeze. Gladys smiled to herself. She gave him another glance, and before she had finished blinking she had left the inert frame, and had sailed regally downstairs. In the kitchen she lighted the gas ring and the grill roared red. Then she flung open the back door. Like a renewed woman she stood and inhaled deeply, her apple cheeks flushed pink with anticipation.

Normally, Gladys would make toast and a pot of tea, and perhaps boil eggs, but today was different. If Arthur wanted breakfast, he could jolly well get it himself! She busied herself, her long dressing gown's cord tightly knotted around her ever spreading middle. She stood leaning against the back door, crunching on a slice of toast, smiling all the while. From next door, she heard a man's gruff laugh, almost leering. It was coming from the small bedroom. 'Mmm,' mused Gladys, listening to the raucous giggles and squeals. 'That,' she said, looking up at the window, 'that is most definitely *not* Daphne's husband!' She thought of Arthur in bed upstairs and was instantly convulsed into giggles. Brushing crumbs from herself, she spread another slice of toast generously with marmalade. From beneath the pink checked gingham covered table she pulled out her large leather handbag. With the toast firmly clenched between her teeth she pulled out some papers. Two envelopes, one open, the other neatly addressed and firmly sealed, she placed carefully into the middle zipped compartment. From the well of the bag she retrieved a tattered magazine she had folded into four. She looked around, the slice still firmly clenched between her teeth. The marmalade began to drip onto her chin; cheerfully she wiped it away, making certain none dripped onto her precious cargo. She took the large tan canvas zipper bag from behind the door and placed the magazine almost reverently onto the bottom. She zipped it up, gave it a gentle pat then placed them both back under the table.

Back in the bedroom, she shimmied herself inch by inch into her navy cotton poplin dress, then holding a deep breath, she quickly pulled up the side zip. One look in the mirror instantly told her that this would be the last summer this dress would see. The matching tailored belt was lashed around her waist and with another struggle she pulled the buckle into the nearest eyelet. 'There,' she said, relieved, smoothing down her hair. Her tiny feet slipped easily into her equally tiny navy sandals. Lifting her skirt just a little she eyed her slender ankles and said, 'Oh well, there's something to be grateful for. As for the rest,' her eyes clung despairingly at the bulging figure reflected in the mirror.

Behind her she heard scratching and with a weary look, she turned around; standing behind her dishevelled in blue striped flannelette pyjamas stood Arthur, yawning. As he yawned noisily, Gladys suddenly thought, 'He's got teeth like a horse, well, maybe not as many!' Bleary eyed he stared at her, puzzled. 'Where you goin'?' he demanded between yawns.

Gladys ignored him and continued to coolly look him slowly up and down. His hair, thin and sparse, had been raked through with his large blunt fingers raising the little into something resembling a question mark. His face was blotchy; red and blue tiny veins stood out on his cheeks. His thin neck, with an obvious absence of adam's apple, hung like curtains draped ready for an afternoon matinee. His pyjama top was crumpled and buttoned up like a child's, missing every other buttonhole. The bottoms hung around his white slack loose skin, the cotton cord dangling miserably from an uncertain waist. His scratching continued both across his hairless chest and his white grey stubble. Gladys's gaze lingered at his feet. They weren't to be seen. The bottoms had slipped, leaving him with flannelette flippers for feet. Gladys sighed. 'Do you know who you remind me of?' Her tone was brisk.

The scratching ceased as he stared emptily at her. She didn't wait for him to reply.

'Sweet Pea!' she declared.

Arthur's face became even more confused. He repeated 'Sweet Pea?'

Gladys, shaking her head, her hands on her hips, was rocking back and forth surveying him closely. 'Yes. Sweet Pea. Olive Oyl? Popeye?' Her voice was raised with each name offering explanation. At last she said, 'Spinach!' as a final clue to her conundrum. Arthur had folded his arms across his chest. 'I don't like spinach.'

A mischievous smile danced over her lips as she unashamedly stared long and hard at the gaping pyjamas. Still rocking back and forth she said with her head cocked to one side considering the sight, 'Obviously.'

Arthur's hands clasped together and dropped instantly in a vain attempt to sever Gladys's withering stare.

Without another word she left the bedroom and picked up the bags she had left at the foot of the stairs. Behind her Arthur came tumbling down, one hand tugging at his now slipping bottoms. As she opened the front door, she stopped and glanced somewhat amused at the rag bag on the stairs. Thinking he had got her attention, he said in a domineering tone, 'And what about me dinner, then?'

With the door now open, Gladys looked up once again and with a generous laugh said, 'Don't worry about your dinner.' Then as she stepped onto the path she shouted over her shoulder, 'It's in the same place as your breakfast. It's called the larder!'

As the door closed, Arthur raised his fists to his eyes and rubbed at them furiously in an act of frustration. His pyjama bottoms fell silently and unceremoniously to his ankles.

It was then that Gladys on impulse lifted the letterbox and called through it, 'Don't forget, Arthur, it's Tuesday: you limp on the left!'

The gate clicked to behind her; the sun was shining, the birds were singing and all looked rosy in Gladys Bowle's world.

As Gladys left the memorial gardens, where she had lingered longer than usual, admiring the manicured lawns and flower beds, she heard, 'Oi! Glad, you've left them larks coughin' this mornin'!'

Smiling, she walked towards the familiar voice.

'Hello, Tom.'

Tom returned her warm smile, saying, 'Or 'ave you got ants in your pants?'

Instantly Gladys remembered the reflection she'd seen earlier that morning and had looked at so despairingly. Without thinking, she said, 'My bloomers are big enough to house two enormous colonies of ants!'

Tom blinked in astonishment at this. Gladys was a good sort, well, she had to be. She was married to Arthur after all. He sat tapping the steering wheel in an attempt to distract himself and beat the belly laugh that was rising in him. The belly laugh won! His broad features fell in creases of laughter and as he looked up through the open window he saw Gladys rocking in gales of laughter. Another look and Tom could see that Gladys was positively glowing. Recovering slowly, he said, 'What you up to then, girl?'

Gladys had taken her handkerchief and was dabbing at her eyes. Shaking her head slowly, she said between gulps, 'Oh Tom,' still laughing, 'sorry, I don't know what came over me.'

Tom spied the canvas holdall. 'Leavin' "War Wound" then?'

Once again Gladys surprised him. Regaining her composure, she leaned against the gleaming vehicle in a confidential manner.

'Haven't seen you at Mum's, lately.'

Tom sniffed loudly. ''Ow is her majesty, then?' That was how he always referred to 'Big Mabel', out of her earshot of course.

She paused before answering, 'Much the same. Another day off,' she added knowingly.

Tom looked sideways into the soft reassuring eyes, fringed with long dark lashes. He sighed heavily, then, shaking his head asked, 'You won't say . . . '

Gladys's lips formed a warm understanding and gentle smile.

'Yeah, you're right. What them Carpenters is up to is beyond me. I think it's the missus and her . . . ' He raised his hand in the shape of a glass to his lips and nodded briefly to Gladys. She returned a sympathetic nod of understanding. 'Course,' Tom continued, 'Rose don't know.' He had been staring into space, then looking at her again he found her still smiling at him.

She squeezed his arm, saying, 'Your secret's safe with me. On the subject of secrets.' At this Tom's eyes widened with interest. 'I'm just on my way to see Vera. I have,' she hesitated.

Tom hadn't listened; he was rubbing his hands together. ''Ere, the ol' girl wouldn't mind if I popped in through the back alley to the kitchen for a quick cuppa later. I'll be gasping by 11 o'clock.'

'I'm sure Mrs Lownds wouldn't mind in the least, because,' she paused teasingly, 'she's gone to stay with her niece for a few days.'

'Oh,' Tom said, puzzled. 'Why's Vera round there then?' he added, shaking his head.

She shrugged nonchalantly. 'Having a holiday.' She pouted her lips and put her finger to them. 'Mum's the word, eh?'

Instantly understanding, Tom tapped his nose as he said, 'Gotcha!'

Gladys thought for a moment before continuing, 'Mrs Lownds gave me a letter for Vera before she left, and as she's looking after her cat, well, I thought . . . ' She wanted to say more but thought better of it and her voice trailed away.

She stood back from the car. 'Right you are,' Tom said enthusiastically. He started up the engine and the gleaming limousine purred softly into life. The indicator clicked out. Gladys took another step back. With his head thrust through the window, he called out as he pulled away, 'Still don't explain why you're out and about this early, though!' As he drove away he flicked her a courtesy salute. Then she heard him shout, 'I'll be round for me cuppa later!'

The first thing Vera did on arriving was to open the kitchen door for Bessie. The overfed moggy was languishing in its cushioned basket. It looked up at her, just mildly inquisitively. It stretched a long leg, lowered its head and with eyes still firmly fixed on Vera set about grooming a paw. Vera stared down at the indulged creature. 'Are you goin' out, or what?' The cat turned sideways, stretched out, and with a quick movement curled itself up, closed its eyes and began purring contentedly.

'Can I go out in the garden, Mum? I won't make a noise, honest. Please?' Sylvia was hopping from one foot to the other.

'All right, but don't let your ball go on the flowers. Okay?'

Before she'd finished speaking the child had skipped out into the long beautifully cared for garden. Apple and pear trees set off the shaded area at the rear which was a haven for bluebells in the spring. Their fragrance always filled the kitchen. From her bag she took her apron. Vera felt oddly awkward. It wasn't as though Mrs Lownds told her what to do or followed her around; the fact she wasn't there made her feel uneasy. 'So, it's some work I must do.'

Vera found the cat's food, then, eyeing the spoilt feline now snoring, decided not to feed it just yet. Looking around her, she could see there was really nothing that needed attention. She had cleaned and polished yesterday. Standing in the panelled hall, her hand resting on the polished bannister, she decided that the bathroom paintwork had been neglected. With this in mind she returned to the kitchen. From the household cupboard she armed herself with a bucket, and into it she poured some washing soda and household liquid soap. Vera loved the bathroom; it was decorated in a pinky lilac wall covering that had a sheen which she couldn't resist smoothing her fingers over. She stopped to look through the arched landing window. The top was stained glass and even on a dull day gave a rosy glow to the landing and the hall. She had scarcely taken a step into the bathroom when she stopped dead. Putting down her bucket she viewed the muddy paw prints on the bottom of the bath. 'Humm,' she said, leaning over to examine the evidence further. 'And I thought cats didn't like water.' She leaned across and closed the window that had been left open. The dimpled glass with the sun behind threw hundreds of tiny images of Sylvia playing in the garden. 'No wonder it's tired. It's been out on the tiles!' The cat had obviously, in Vera's opinion, taken advantage of this escape down onto the outhouse and with a single agile leap had found the ledge. 'Crafty things,' Vera muttered under her breath. With the paintwork washed, she wrung out her cloth and bounced off her heels onto her feet. She hadn't been standing for more than a few seconds when her knees buckled beneath her. She grabbed at the handbasin to save herself before all went black about her. She raised her head and looked at the face in the mirror. The face was ashen; the blue eyes appeared larger and prominent. Beads of sweat had broken out across her forehead and her short hair now clung to her face. She turned on the cold tap and splashed her face and neck for the second time that morning. 'September,' was all she managed to gasp before she was sick.

She emptied the bucket into the drain outside the kitchen. Sylvia was playing with the fat cat on the neat lawn. The cat was on its back, its paws toying with a scrap of paper she had tied to a piece of garden twine. 'Look Mum!'

Vera smiled briefly and stepped back into the kitchen to rescue the singing kettle. Having made tea, she trawled in her bag for the fruit buns. Opening the bag released the spicy sweetness. Vera heaved. Putting her hand to her mouth and breathing deeply, she allowed herself to fall onto the chair. Her raised open palms waited for the weary heavy head to fall. Once there, Vera sobbed gently, her body swaying. Only her hands heard her. 'What'll I do now...'

She felt all her new found strength, determination and resolve ebbing away with each spluttered syllable.

The shrill sound of the ringing doorbell brought her up suddenly. She wiped her eyes with her apron, and looking over her shoulder at Sylvia still in the garden, sniffed purposefully as she brushed down her apron. She ran her tongue over her dry lips before opening the door. 'Gladys!' Her arms dropped to her sides as she took in the stocky form.

Gladys, standing in the porch, ignored her sister's look of incredulity and smiled warmly, hoping that her feelings of similar surprise at the white-faced, red-eyed, tear-stained individual standing in front of her hadn't been noticed. 'Vera?'

'Gladys,' Vera repeated softly.

'Well, my dear, am I to stand here?'

Vera pulled at her sister's arm. 'What'you doin' here?'

Gladys took Vera's elbow and guided the silent open-mouthed Vera along the hall slowly but surely towards the kitchen. The two women remained silent until Vera was seated at the table. Gladys peered into the large breakfast cup. 'Empty, I'll make some more. Ooo, fruit buns, lovely.' She left her bags under the table and was bustling at the sink. She gave a quick sideways glance at her sister. Her pale drawn face worried Gladys but also . . . She allowed her thoughts to drift as she said, 'Mrs Lownds gave me a letter for you, yesterday.'

Vera raised her head. 'Yesterday?' Her voice was trembling, although her genuine surprise was clearly evident. 'Yesterday was Monday, you always do the washing on Mondays.'

She heard her sister give a hollow laugh. The unusual hollow laugh brought Vera to her senses. 'But I've just made tea!' she protested weakly.

Gladys shook her head, placed a hand around the small teapot then, shaking her head again, poured on the boiling water. 'There,' Gladys said easily, 'why don't we take this in the sitting room?' It was more of a direction than a request.

Vera looked up horrified and shook her head.

'Here, you take this.' Vera took the tray and watched mutely as Gladys waved at Sylvia who was running up to the door.

'Auntie Gladys,' the child exclaimed cheerily and breathlessly. Gladys handed Sylvia a plate with a bun and a small cup filled with milky tea. 'Here you are, my dear, have a breakfast picnic. 'And,' Gladys bribed, 'There might be another bun, later on.'

Sylvia ran back to the cat, who had lost interest in the game and had found a sunny spot in which to bask in peace.

Gladys turned around to find that Vera hadn't moved. It seemed as though she was rooted to the spot. Gladys removed, with unusual deftness, the reason for her visit from her bags. She popped it onto the tray that the unseeing Vera was holding at arm's length. Quickly Gladys said, 'Let me take that.' Then with her free hand she turned her sister full about and watching her anxiously led her into the cool sitting room.

Setting down the tray Gladys, on straightening up, looked around the room. She had visited a few Christmases ago, when Mrs Lownds had flu. It was a genteel room. There was a small suite, its cared-for oak frame decorated with pleasing bright chintz covers. The matching curtains and low, round, cross-legged, heavily engraved brass topped table, although continents apart, complimented one another. The lady's writing desk that sat daintily in the corner was Glady's favourite piece of furniture. She felt herself beginning to sigh. On the small sofa Vera sat hunched in the corner, her head lowered and her face just as pale; her hands were clasped and the fingers twitched nervously. To the right of Vera was a dark wood rocking chair. Gladys poured out the tea and pressed it into the twitching fingers.

Gladys's weight set the rocking chair in motion. She struggled to set her feet down so as to reach her tea. Safely settled back, she cast another anxious glance over Vera. She nodded confirmation of her observations but said nothing. Another lunge to the table secured Gladys her spicy bun. Leaning back she ate quietly and waited.

Vera started rocking. Gladys shot her a worried glance. Vera seemed to gather momentum. Gladys slid from the shiny seat onto the floor and grabbed the cup and saucer from her. Quietly she put them down on the table. The rocking form started to moan softly from behind her trembling fingers.

Gladys felt helpless. Then suddenly, like a volcanic eruption, Vera jumped up, threw her arms open and cried out in pain, 'I hit her! I hit her! I slapped her. I wanted to!'

The suddenness of this revelation and its torrent of spewing words left Gladys wide eyed and shocked; this wasn't what she was waiting to hear. She took Vera's hands, put them together and gently but firmly set her back down on the sofa.

Vera fell into silent body wracking sobs.

From the open door she head, 'Here you are, Auntie Gladys, I've made you . . . '

In the doorway stood Sylvia. In her hands were daisy chains. Gladys found her voice after a nervous cough. She said, 'My dear,' and put out her hand.

'Oh no,' cried the child, laughing. 'It's for your head, it's a crown, see?'

Obligingly, Gladys lowered her head and waited to be crowned. The child continued, 'This is your bracelet.' The daisy chain was wound around her wrist. 'And this is Mum's.'

'Thank you, dear. I'll take it.' Quickly changing the subject as she watched the child's eyes roam the room, she placed a firm hand on her arm urging her into the hall. 'Did you want another bun?'

Sylvia nodded and smiled.

'Very well, you'll find it on the kitchen table. I'll be out shortly to make more tea.'

She had gained the child's attention who then in her usual way skipped happily into the kitchen. Gladys watched and waited, hovering in the doorway before stepping back into the room and closing the heavy door behind her. She lowered herself into an armchair, staring blankly at the empty fireplace, the grate filled with an arrangement of soot dusted dried flowers. Its summer embroidered tapestry fire-screen was set to one side. She kept asking herself silently, 'Vera hit Sylvia?' Her head wagged slowly in disbelief. 'It isn't possible. She just wouldn't . . . ' Her silent thoughts and fears spilled over into tears. She had never seen her sister like this. What had happened? When? And Why? She tugged at the hanky she kept in her belt and began to dab at her eyes.

Vera was moaning louder, Gladys made out what she was saying. 'What'll I do now?'

Wiping her nose quickly, she stuffed the hanky up her sleeve, watched anxiously and waited in the vain hope that she could make some sense of what Vera was trying to tell her.

Gladys took the safest route to explanations and from the table pressed the cup into Vera's trembling hands. Vera slipped. Gladys made out the word, 'September.'

'September?' Gladys mouthed the word. Then asked herself, 'What's the significance of September?' She thought hard and said to herself, 'September. There's nothing special about September. There's Rose and Tom's wedding anniversary, and that was about all . . . ' What was once doubt now loomed like a dark raincloud over her. Presently she said aloud having reasoned out its significance, 'September.' It came through her lips like a small gas escape. She too then repeated dully, 'September.'

It was the silence that drew her to look at Vera. 'Vera, please tell me. I don't know what's wrong,' she lied with confidence, 'but I know I can do something. Just tell me, dear.'

She found herself catching her breath, waiting for Vera to speak. A strange look came over Vera's pale face. It was as though she had just noticed Gladys. It held a mixture of surprise, relief and a degree of uncertainty about where she was. Her enormous blue eyes darted and flickered around the room. They finally settled on Gladys's grey face.

Gladys heard herself saying, 'Vera, my dear, you're not well.'

Vera's huge blue eyes locked onto hers, pleadingly. Ashamed of what she was about to say, she lowered her head and, speaking softly, said, 'I hit Mum. I slapped her.' She gave a sniff then added matter of factly, 'Hard.'

The silence which surrounded her was pole-axing. Between her fingers she twisted the hem of her apron, waiting for Gladys to say something.

From beside her she heard a gutteral noise. Alarmed that her sister's anger had been roused, she turned her head. Raising her eyes she blinked disbelieving at the vision in front of her. Gladys's legs were apart. Her elbows were on her knees; her head was in her hands. She was wiping away tears with the back of her hand. The noise Vera had heard was Gladys whooping with laughter. Gladys struggled to sit upright. The back of her hands were still wiping away tears coursing down her face. Vera's mouth dropped open. Never having seen her sister in such a state, she found the laughter contagious and she too began to laugh uncontrollably. The two women caught sight of each other; it rendered them both into even louder raptures of helpless laughter. At length Gladys, still insensible, unbuckled her belt and threw it to the floor. Finally, she leaned back into the chair, gasping for breath. Her tiny feet were left suspended in mid air, dancing with sheer delight. They both had their arms clutched around their middles, gasping for relief.

Vera wiped her face with her apron. Taking a deep breath she stared at her sister's red shiny face. They exchanged knowing looks. Gladys struggled to her feet and, smoothing down her dress, she said, 'I'll make some more tea. What's the time?' Having glanced already at the clock, Vera said, 'It's half past nine. Why?'

Gladys had reached for the tray. From it she took the envelope and gave it to Vera. 'I won't be long.' She touched her sister's shoulder in a show of understanding and affection. 'I wish I'd been there . . . ' With another reassuring touch to Vera's shoulder she said, 'Read your letter first; we'll talk again later.' Still sniffing and holding back more laughter Gladys left the sitting room.

Vera reached down and rolled up the abandoned belt. Putting it on the table it sprang open. Vera ripped open the envelope but before removing its contents she looked closely at the postmark. It meant nothing to her. Leaning back, with the sheets spread over her knees, she began to read. Leaning forward, smiling to herself, she said, 'Harry, it's from Harry.' Putting the sheets back in order, she began at the beginning. By the time she had finished Gladys had returned with more tea.

She answered her sister's enquiring nod with, 'It's from Harry, he's working in a place.' She squinted at the writing and held the sheet closer to her face here. 'You read it.'

Gladys felt affronted. 'Oh no, it's private. Mrs Lownds is sure you have a young man.'

Vera shook her head. 'Oh no, not this one. He is,' she hesitated, 'just a friend. Here, you 'ave a read.'

Taking the letter, Gladys lifted the pages to the light behind her. 'My, my.'

Vera gave a look of interest as if she might have missed something. Then recounting the day's events, she asked, 'What did you come round for then, Gladys?'

Gladys had folded the letter in half and was passing it back to her sister. 'This,' she said, adding another nod for effect.

''Course,' Vera said shyly, 'I'd forgot.'

'He sounds a very interesting young man. He's singing at the Grand Hotel in Le Touquet next week.'

Unimpressed, Vera replied, 'That's in Devon?'

Gladys shook her head. 'No, it's in France.'

Still unimpressed, Vera felt more pressing things closing in on her. She took the letter and slid it into her apron pocket.

The tension had eased, but still Vera sat picking at the hem of her apron. Gladys didn't know much about this man, Harry, but if Vera said he was just a friend, that was good enough for her. She'd heard some talk about the evening of the dance, but had dismissed it as just talk, spread about by that dreadful Mrs Timms. Mum and her were as bad as each other!, Gladys said to herself. There were so many questions in her mind. Sipping her tea, she saw how wretched her sister was feeling. She took a deep breath and asked gently, 'Why did you . . . ' she paused, waiting for a look of acknowledgement. She said at last, 'Slap Mum?'

All Vera did was to shake her head slowly. Then spreading wide her hands she stood up. Looking intently into the fireplace she said weakly, 'I shouldn't 'ave, even though she hit Sylvia.'

Gladys gasped audibly. She repeated her sister's words. 'Mum hit Sylvia?' On the tray went her cup and saucer; she shuffled forward, perched on the edge of her chair and looked up waiting for Vera to carry on. Vera said almost apologetically, 'She was . . . ' She couldn't look at Gladys. 'Well, you know what I mean?'

Gladys nodded gravely. 'Yes,' she answered honestly. 'You mean she was drunk.' She watched Vera swallow hard. 'That's no excuse or reason to hit a child.'

Vera's face twitched with embarrassment.

Trying to help her, Gladys, now in control, asked, 'Why did Mum hit Sylvia? And where?' Her tone was flat and direct.

Vera had paced the room and returned to the sofa. 'She . . . ' Vera felt a little flustered, not sure what to tell her first. Then as Vera spoke, her body sagged wearily into her chair, with her head lowered, her hands and palms together resting between her knees. Before speaking she shook her head.

She started again, 'Chris got us the tickets.' She stole a sideways look at Gladys. 'Bit of a break, like, for her and Iris of course.' She allowed her body to relax into the sofa. Crossing her legs at the ankles and folding her arms around her she continued, 'I spent me 'ousekeepin'. Didn't mean to.' Another quick glance at Gladys. 'I wanted a new dress. I 'aven't been anywhere posh,' she said miserably. She threw a long look at Gladys. 'Went to Mrs Chapman's . . . to cut a long story short. Iris . . . well, she never 'ad nothin' nice to wear either; then she saw one of them birds in a glass box, you know what I mean?'

Gladys couldn't be sure, but gave Vera a nod of encouragement.

Vera said wistfully 'I wondered,' her tone was more thoughtful, "ow Mum knew me frock was there? I do now.' Her hand disappeared under her apron, and from her dress pocket she produced a small shiny object. She put it on her palm and stared at it hard as if it was some kind of curio. 'See?' she said as she handed it to Gladys.

'So,' Gladys's voice was filled with recognition of the gaudy trinket, 'you found this in the dark oak wardrobe?'

Vera nodded, puzzled at her sister's knowledge.

Gladys turned it over. She too stared at it. 'Novelty value,' and she gave a dry laugh. 'It's still there; the silver plate hasn't worn off then?' A warm earthy chuckle filled the room. Gladys's playful teasing showed in her eyes as they met Vera's wrinkled brow. She laughed again. Gladys added enigmatically, 'The love token.' More interested in Vera's tale, she left the small wristwatch on the arm of her chair; with another quick nod she once again urged Vera along with a wave of her hand, adding, 'I'll tell you more about this, later.'

Vera blinked at her sister's dismissive air. Completely bemused, she had forgotten how far she had got, She stared enquiringly at Gladys for help.

There came another wave of Gladys's hand as she said, 'Never mind about this,' and gave the gleaming timepiece a cursory glance. 'Tell me more about your dress.'

It has to be recorded that Gladys's figure was not designed for fashion, but anything that happened behind the door of Sybil Chapman's with her cronies was always worth listening to. Obligingly Vera opened her mouth, gulped and gave serious consideration to what she was about to tell. Relaxed back, realising that Gladys was not going to criticise, assuming her usual pose she began again.

'Iris was real taken with this bird, an owl it was; she was, . . . well, knew quite a lot about 'em. Umm, 'ow did it go?' She began humming the ditty: 'A wise old owl, lived in a oak.' She interrupted herself. 'It was you that reminded me, when you said about the old oak.' She heard Gladys give a sniff at the finger Vera had jabbed in her direction. She read that as a sign of impatience. Apologising for her rudeness she resumed her lounging pose, wrapped her arms about herself and began in earnest. Just before she spoke Sylvia appeared, draping an arm around her mother's shoulders. This time Gladys sighed good humouredly, wondering if she would ever hear the end of this story. She dug deep into her hip pocket and produced a thru'penny bit. 'Here you are, my dear,' she said, offering it to her niece. 'Take this.'

Sylvia looked at her mother for approval, Vera smiled, nodded, then added, 'Straight there and back. No talkin' to no one unless you know them.'

Sylvia shyly took the coin, kissed her Auntie Gladys thanks, and dashed away, leaving Gladys flushed with pleasure. Then Vera assumed her parental tone: 'Use the back door; mind them dogs in the alley.' The silence was shattered as the back door banged shut.

Gladys had settled herself back into her chair and removed the 'love token' to the table in front of them.

Vera answered the silence with, 'Put me dress in the big old wardrobe hidden behind the greatcoat we puts over the bed in the winter. It took me ages to press it, it looked a treat. When I got back Saturday afternoon all it needed was a quick rub over with the iron, just to freshen it up.' Another sigh. 'I should have known that somethin' was wrong.' She reflected for a moment on that afternoon. 'It was too quiet.' She waited for a knowing nod from Gladys. 'She was behind the door. I swear she was waitin'. Me frock was a heap on the floor at the bottom of the stairs.'

Gladys shifted.

'I thought she'd cut it up, you know 'ow she is when she's . . . '

'Drunk,' Gladys said the word for the loyal Vera. 'Drunk!' Gladys said it once more.

'What with that and everythin' else . . . ' Vera shrugged helplessly. 'I just kept out of her way, and I 'ad to wait until she fell asleep.' Vera's voice was getting just a little stronger. 'I sneaked out with Sylvia.' She slapped her hands hard on her knees. She gave Gladys a wistful look. 'I can't go back. What am I gonna do?'

Gladys ruffled like a mother hen; that was enough for Vera to carry on.

'She said some really 'orrible things, about what she 'eard about Iris.'

Gladys said to herself, 'I bet I know where she got that from,' without being formally asked. 'That old Mrs Timms and that guttersnipe "nephew" of hers.'

Vera was astounded. She knew that there was talk about them being related, but no one seemed to know how.

'It wasn't true what Mum said. I was with her all night. I took me eyes off her for a minute, or two,' Vera had stood up.

'Vera,' began Gladys, assuming her matronly tone, 'Iris is a young woman and very pretty, too.' She slipped awkwardly from her chair onto the sofa beside Vera, taking her hand. Gladys said, 'We can't be in two places at the same time.'

A crestfallen Vera looked down. She turned to Gladys. 'I made a promise, I've made a lot of promises just lately, not to everybody, just for me, and I can't even keep them now!' The tears started to fall.

Taking Vera's hand, Gladys gently pulled her sister down onto the sofa beside her and said soothingly, 'There, there.' This made Vera sniff even louder. Gladys snatched the ever present lavender fragranced handkerchief from her sleeve and dropped it into Vera's wavering hand.

'Why not?' Gladys asked firmly, even though she was becoming more and more convinced of the answer.

Then, quite unexpectedly, Vera threw her arms around Glady's neck and sobbed.

Vera's lashes, laden with tears, slowly lifted. The late summer sun filtered through the stained glass leaded window, a dancing kaleidoscope of creamy yellow, in front of the water film. It magnified her memory of another September day hazy with age. Clinging to Gladys she closed her eyes and allowed the drifting patterns gradually to settle once more . . .

*   *   *

139

That Friday morning she had got up earlier than usual. First, she had had to collect the smoked haddock from James's wet fish shop. She had raced home so's she could iron her dress before going to work. Today was her first pay day. Her first real money. Mrs Lownds was a widow and she'd advertised for 'help' around the house. Vera had spotted her card in the confectioner's window on the top road. Vera hadn't minded in the least that the old lady wanted her to clean, it was a real job with real money, working for a real lady. Today she wanted to look really nice. Mrs Lownds had trusted her to do the shopping too.

As Vera crossed the green she made a face at the bulky ponging newspaper-wrapped fish. Once in the kitchen, she rinsed the yellow pieces under the tap, plonked them on an enamel plate, covered it with a damp tea cloth and found a place on the marble slab in the larder. After quickly closing the door she shuddered: how she hated the smell and feel of it. Climbing the stairs in twos she missed the fourth from the top because it creaked and tiptoed past her mother's bedroom. Vera groaned silently when she heard, 'I 'ope it's a nice little bit of fish!' Standing in front of the closed door Vera made another face. She answered brightly, 'Luv'ly.' She shuddered again then set about ironing her plain blue dress.

By eight o'clock she had left the house, having given her mother tea in bed, tidied up in the parlour and kitchen and peeled the potatoes ready for tea later that day. With her shopping bag gripped tightly in her hand, the church clock struck eight as she turned the corner into the Avenue. She was feeling very good about herself. The September sun hung low and watery, and there was a distinct chill in the air. Vera swung open the black painted wrought iron gate. Her fair hair bounced as she shut it securely behind her. She gave her dress a quick brush down with her hand and rang the bell.

Mrs Lownds, tiny, genteel, and sprightly for her years, opened the door. In her hand a set of keys jingled. 'Here,' she said, handing them over to Vera. She added, 'I'm not getting any younger. I want you to have your own set of house keys.' Then with a darting smile at the beaming young face, she said with a shake of her finger, 'You won't lose them, will you, my dear?'

Vera beamed even more broadly as she took them. She bobbed down to get the milk. With the milk safe in her arms, her foot hooked around the door to close it. She stood for a second in the hall feeling taller than her already above average height of her sixteen years. She positively swelled with pride. 'And this,' she reminded herself, 'is just the morning!'

Shortly after three Mrs Lownds arrived back from the library with her selection of books for the weekend. Vera had finished the washing up, left from lunch. She had washed the kitchen floor over and just stepped back into the kitchen, having emptied the bucket into the drain outside. Spotting the tiny frame in the open door, Vera asked, 'Shall I make some tea?'

With a smile, Mrs Lownds waved a dismissive hand at her. She put her books down on the table. 'Oh, how pretty!' she exclaimed, admiring the neatly laid tea tray complete with a posy of flowers in a miniature vase. 'You're such a thoughtful chi . . . ' She stopped herself, turned towards the pretty girl standing smiling from ear to ear in front of her and said kindly, 'What a very thoughtful young woman you are.' If it was at all possible, Vera returned an even wider grin. And if the ever so slightly dimmed with age eyes weren't mistaken, she saw her young friend's eyes well up with tears.

The kettle whistled softly to itself, taking Vera's attention. She filled the waiting china tea pot. Mrs Lownds left her books on the table and in the sitting room she unlocked her writing desk drawer. From it she took a white envelope. She called to Vera in the kitchen. The door was ajar and Vera hesitated before entering. Timidly she knocked on the door.

'Yes, my dear, come in, please.'

Vera wiped her hands on her apron and put them behind her.

Mrs Lownds smiled and gave Vera the envelope. 'Now, you take this, and run along. I'm sure you have lots to do at the weekend. Dances perhaps?' The elderly lady's eyes shone with girlish memories.

Vera wanted to shake her head and tell her that it meant smelly smoked haddock, ironing and cleaning and that she would have the shopping and washing up and . . . Even though her thoughts raced, she smiled, tucked the envelope into her apron pocket, bobbed an unnecessary 'thank you', and waited to be dismissed.

'My dear,' Mrs Lownds urged once more. 'Run along, you're only young once.' Then she added unnecessarily, regretting it instantly, 'Prompt on Monday, now.'

Vera, halfway through the door, stopped mid stride, turned and gave a dazzling smile.

'Goodness me,' the gentle voice reprimanded herself. 'All those years in India, servants, and you still cannot get it right, my my.'

Vera appeared once more in the open door. 'I've made your tea and put some biscuits out and oh, just thank you ever so much.' She rushed from the hall out onto the porch, forgetting herself until she heard the gate clank to. She pulled herself up short, closed her eyes and didn't open them until she had turned around. On opening them, all she saw was a smiling Mrs Lownds, waving goodbye, her high necked blouse complete with its distinctive cameo brooch catching the late afternoon sun. Vera waved back and danced to the corner of the Avenue.

Racing across the green as she had done in the morning, she waved to the boys absorbed in their game of football, their discarded jumpers for goal posts. They called cheerfully after her.

Vera jumped up onto the top step. Her fingers thrust searchingly into the letterbox for the key, but the string had become caught up. She leaned lightly against the door. To her surprise it slowly opened. Her fingers stuck in the letterbox; she wrenched free and peered around the door. Putting her bag on the bottom stair she looked into the small parlour, expecting to see her mother, but the passage was cold, dim and empty. She sniffed. 'Cigarettes?' She opened the kitchen door and there leaning against the opposite wall stood Tom, cigarette in hand. He said nothing as she took the kettle to the sink saying, 'Tom, you did give me a turn. I'll make some tea, then, eh?' The sound of the water rushing into the empty kettle covered her sigh of relief.

She had filled the kettle and lit the gas ring and still Tom was silent. Vera stepped forward to open the kitchen door. As her hand reached the key, Tom said thickly, 'Where's Rose?'

Vera turned around once more with relief on hearing his voice. Half turning, he grabbed her shoulder and pinned her against the larder door. She winced as the catch dug into her back. He repeated his words. 'Where's Rose?'

Vera looked straight into his eyes. It was then she smelt it. 'Whisky,' she said silently, her face showing no sign of recognition. Her shoulders were flat against the door.

'I don't know,' she answered honestly.

Tom's face was inches from hers. 'Where's Rose?'

Vera shook her head, remembering her promises. 'I don't know, I've just got 'ome from work. It's me first pay day. I left 'ere just before eight. I 'aven't seen Rose, honest.'

She felt panic rising and swallowed hard.

'She came over this mornin' with Patricia.'

Vera shook her head. 'I 'aven't seen em.'

''Course,' said Tom, his voice hoarse with anger. 'You always tell the truth, that right?' He didn't wait for an answer. 'Just like you stood on them steps, with 'er behind the door, lyin'?' His voice was hard and filled with sarcasm.

She watched his eyes narrow into hers. He was hard against her, his breath hot on her face.

Vera swallowed again, to ease her dry mouth. She managed to say evenly, 'I didn't see the car.'

He growled, 'No, I walked from the pub! Bloody liars, the lot of you women.'

She cried out, 'No Tom, No! You don't understand . . . it's not . . . it ain't what you think.'

He snarled back, 'I don't think, I bloody well know!' His lips lifted into a cruel fixed smile.

Vera watched the raised hand, fingers twitching. Closing her eyes she waited resignedly for its contact. Her back was numb, her fingers grabbed at the door panels. She had walked into a nightmare. Never had she seen Tom like he was now. She wanted to scream out loud. She wanted to tell him, the neighbours, the entire estate, just what Rose and her mother had done in 'that' September so deeply engraved in her memory forever. But she couldn't. Still, she waited. The silence in the kitchen was deafening, then she heard a whimpering. Her thoughts instantly fell on baby Patricia and Rose. She dared herself to open her eyes. Tom was standing in front of her, his hands covering his face wet with tears. 'Why, why, why?' he repeated over and over again. 'What've I done? What am I doing?'

His face was contorted with shame and the realisation of the silent presence of Vera. He reached out for her, taking her about the waist, and drew her slowly to him. His arms went around her and she felt his body shudder with every sob. Instinctively, she put her arms around him. He drew her closer. His mouth parted as if he was about to speak. His eyes were warm and tender, then his lips came down hard on hers. Vera felt no surprise, no fear. She just wanted to make him and everything better. She spoke softly. 'Tom,' she whispered soothingly.

Vera didn't resist as he unbuttoned the front of her dress. His breathing came in hard hot bursts. Her dress was off her shoulders, He licked and bit gently into them; his hands lifted her firm round breasts to his lips. His tongue flicked hungrily, his teeth nipped at the neat, pointed, hard, baby pink nipple. Vera leant against the door, her back arched. The pulse in her neck quickened; her heart raced. Her skirt was high above her waist. Tom eased her gently onto the table then, his hands firm against her soft buttocks, scooped her up and pulled her hard down onto him. Her arms were around his neck. She wrapped her arms and legs around his hard stocky body. She felt the sweat from him wet against the inside of her thighs. She felt his body give a jerk out and up. She heard him let out a low gutteral groan as she felt herself explode inside. Bright lights danced drunkenly in her head, as her body ceased for a second before quivering uncontrollably. After a few seconds he straightened up, only to allow his head to fall onto her throat. Vera moaned with the sheer pleasure of completeness, and freedom from herself. Releasing her fingers, she let herself be lowered onto the floor. Her arms were still around his shoulders.

Vera opened her eyes to find an open mouthed Gladys staring at her in silence.

'See,' Vera blurted out.

Gladys looked on at her sister's dazed expression. Vera leaned away, adding, 'I can't say nothin'.'

Gladys snatched at Vera's shoulder, her tone stern. 'There never was a GI or any other soldier for that matter, was there?'

Vera, head in her hands, shook it miserably.

Gladys, the wristwatch held between her fingers, prised it from between Vera's hands. 'This, what do you know about this?' With it cupped in her hands she stared at it long and hard.

'They made it up, all of it. They tricked 'im. I knew what they were doin'. Mum told her old wives' jollop,' she hesitated, 'or Rose had to get Tom to marry 'er, and she did.' She twisted the watch around her fingers giving a sideways glance at Gladys. She asked simply, 'How could they?'

Gladys found herself breathing harder with anger, not because of Vera but for herself. She knew Vera was pregnant. Vera didn't need to tell her. Rose got what she wanted; now Gladys hoped Rose would get what she deserved. Vera had broken from her crying 'Mum'. She sighed the word heavily and nodded at the watch. 'Pawns it every Monday and Friday, I think . . . Mond'ys definitely.'

From behind them they heard, 'Me Mum's not well. She went all of a funny colour before we come out this morning.' Sylvia stepped towards Gladys and offered the large open bag. 'Wann 'ave a look at me gobstoppers, they changes colour too,' she said enthusiastically.

Gladys looked into the child's face and thought, 'The image of Tom. I wonder how many others can't see the wood for the trees?'

'Can I go out and play with the cat again?'

Gladys nodded. Once more the happy child was heard scampering across the kitchen to find the now much exhausted feline. Gladys sat with her thoughts, allowing them time to fall into place. How right she had been, and how she had judged. How now, she wished, she had turned her thoughts around. Catching Vera's forlorn and weary look, she took advantage of her vulnerability and asked, 'It is Tom's?' Her voice was soft and understanding; inside she was feeling flustered. She added, 'I mean, as well, too.' She waited for Vera to reply.

Gladys cast a worried glance at the mantle clock. Vera appeared calmer and Gladys sensed she felt easier. She had stopped crying. Uncertain how to begin, she wondered if her news would be met with tears, disbelief or hostility. She began, 'Vera, I saw Tom this morning; he was outside the memorial gardens.' She paused, waiting for a response. Gathering confidence from the silence, she continued, 'He said he'd pop in for some tea about eleven.' She gave another look at the clock; Vera did also. 'Apart from your letter, I did have another reason for coming here today, dear.'

Vera snatched at her sister's wrist. 'Oh no, Gladys, you can't go and leave me 'ere on me own.' Her eyes were wide, childlike, and once again brimming with tears.

Undeterred Gladys spoke on, softly but earnestly: 'Dear, I have to go.'

It was the way she said 'go' that pulled Vera together. 'What d'you mean, go?' she questioned equally softly. 'Go? Go where?'

Gladys took Vera's hands in hers. 'Vera, dear, I am going away,' She hesitated, seeing the fear creep back into Vera's wide eyed gaze.

Patiently, Gladys continued. She placed both of Vera's cold still hands into one of hers as she stretched in her awkward manner, sliding the folded magazine from the chair. 'I would like you to read this.'

Vera sniffed noisily and wiped her nose with the back of her hand. Somewhat distressed by the sight, Gladys searched for her handkerchief. She watched Vera absorbed in the print. Her head nodded with each word she read. The small passage had been clearly defined with oblongs of thick black ink. Vera's sniffing ceased. White faced, she stared blankly at her sister and asked, 'What's a lady's companion?' She had read the advertisement but hadn't understood it. She thought it was something to do with luggage.

'I have taken this situation as a lady's companion. Mrs Boughton Smythe. She is a lady just like Mrs Lownds. She lives alone in a large detached house with a chauffeur cum gardener cum handyman.' Nothing flickered across Vera's face. Gladys took a deep breath. 'She lives in Arundel.'

Before she could finish Vera said, 'Oh, I know where that is, it's that place where that cake comes from that we 'ave at Christmas.' This threw Gladys's train of thought for a second. Smiling understandingly she said, 'That's Dundee. Arundel is in Sussex, not far from the sea.'

Vera said, 'Oh', almost to herself. Then quick as a flash she squared up to Gladys and gasped, 'You got a job?'

'At last.' Gladys sighed with relief.

'But you can't, you're married.' Vera's voice was shrill with horror.

Time was getting short; another quick look at the clock confirmed this. Gladys, in easy measured tones, painstakingly began to explain. 'I've left Arthur. I am not going back today or tomorrow or ever.' Gladys found herself smiling. It was the first time her plans had been aired and she felt comfortable and confident with her decision. A warm glow came over her. She continued, regardless of the comical horrorstruck look on Vera's face. She knew what she was about to say would upset her sister, but as she sat reviewing her life an idea began to form in her mind, something for Vera, something for their future. She would say nothing now. On this morning, which was rapidly disappearing, she would tell Vera all about Mrs Amelia Broughton Smythe.

Vera sat straight backed, hanging on every word, wide eyed, open mouthed, spellbound as a child might listen to a fairy tale.

Mrs Amelia Broughton Smythe, Gladys explained patiently, was used to travelling, but since her husband's death she had became something of a recluse. She had a housekeeper who took care of the general running of the household. She made the occasional visit to town, usually at Christmas. Recently, however, she felt strong enough to resume her travels, but only for the winter season. She was a little arthritic and felt that a personal maid would not be her choice, even if one could be found. She then decided on a companion, who could be relied upon in a personal emergency, and who would be both presentable and personable especially at the Captain's table and the like. So she placed the advertisement in *The Lady* and after many interviews decided that Gladys would suit her lifestyle for, as she had said haughtily, 'any woman of middle years who is prepared to take charge of the reins. Even though I do not subscribe to divorce or separation I do admire a woman of spirit and you will suit just fine!'

Then as if adding weight to her words, Gladys handed Vera a letter she struggled free from her hip pocket. 'This is her letter offering me the post.'

Vera took the envelope and read the neat regular copperplate hand. Slowly, she folded the single sheet, put it back in the envelope and returned it to Gladys's waiting hand.

146

For a second Gladys felt lost for words. She searched her sister's downcast expression. She was just about to speak when Vera asked, 'Don't you love Arthur, then?'

Vera soon heard her sister's reply, Gladys gave a girlish peal of laughter. She repeated, 'Love Arthur? Would you?' As she spoke she had a mental picture of Arthur dressed in pyjamas looking every inch like an overgrown 'Sweet Pea'.

Vera was astonished. She always thought people married because they loved each other. 'Why'd you get married?'

It was Gladys's turn to sniff heartily. 'He flattered me!' Her answer was straightforward and honest.

Vera looked up. 'What'd he say?'

Delicately dabbing at her nose, Gladys said, 'He told me I looked like Melanie.'

Vera tipped her head sideways and screwed up her face. 'Melanie? Melanie who?'

Gladys gave a hoot of laughter. 'Melanie!' She prodded a finger into her sister's curved body. 'You remember. Melanie, *Gone with the Wind*!'

Vera surveyed her from a lowered eye level. Melanie, she remembered, was a short rather curvaceous woman, played by Olivia de Havilland. Again she stared hard at her sister. Gladys patted her bulging middle. 'Not quite the same now,' she acknowledged, looking down at her tightly corseted figure. Vera began to laugh with Gladys at the self deprecating joke. It was true Gladys did bear a resemblance to 'Melanie' even though her waist had gained inches over the years. Each forgot their imminent problems and fell into howls of laughter.

Gladys, seizing the opportunity, said, 'If I can change my life, you can change yours too.' Her voice was emphatic. She raised a hand saying, 'Listen, life is different now. It's changing all around us even as we sit here. Women won't be satisfied being ushered silent into the kitchen; they will want to be heard, and their voices acknowledged. Even votes were just the beginning. Women of all ages fought too, in the front line and at home. Men's memories are blinkered and short-sighted. Women won't tolerate being second class, second best to anything or anyone.' Her voice swelled with passion. 'Women will make decisions for themselves, they won't have to ask permission. Oh, this won't happen overnight, but it will happen, and sooner than you think. No more barefoot and pregnant behind the kitchen sink for the modern woman!' She stopped suddenly, realising her ill chosen words. She paused. Vera was sitting staring again into the grate, listening impassively.

Gladys gathered her conscience. 'Don't you see, Mum has used you; she has done nothing for herself for years. You will tell me how tragic it was when Harold and Wilfred were killed in action. It happened to hundreds of thousands of mothers. Please don't tell me that Mum is grieving still.' Gladys took a breath. 'What Rose did was evil and despicable.' She picked up the cheap wristwatch and thrust it under Vera's nose. 'Her life is as cheap as this; she made it that way. Mum's got Rose exactly where she wants her. Don't you see?' Gladys was becoming just a little impatient at Vera's lack of enthusiasm. Vera's silence was threefold. Sighing, Gladys continued, 'You don't have to stay with her, in fact not having you to run around after her twenty-four hours a day might just do her some good,' Gladys finished acidly.

Vera stared absently at her sister and asked gently, 'Then where?'

Gladys sidestepped a direct answer, saying, 'It's your life, it's your choice, it's your future.' Even as she spoke, Gladys knew how empty her words must sound. There were of course two others to consider. Still, she ploughed on.

Vera heard Gladys's voice in the distance, like a shallow echo. Fear gripped her. Grim faced, she turned once more to her sister.

'You said today – you said . . . you're not goin' back today. That means,' Vera gasped, 'You're goin', today?'

Gladys felt her head fall as she said softly, 'Yes.' Gathering the spirit of the moment she said, 'You have to tell Tom, today.'

Vera shook her head. 'I can't, how can I? I never told him about Sylvia.' She looked at her sister for help. Without waiting, she said, 'How can I tell him about this?' She turned her hand flat against her firm belly. Then she raised her hand as if to ask a question. Gladys felt helpless.

Gathering courage, Gladys turned to Vera. 'Vera, I know that everybody thinks I'm a bit of a fuddy duddy, and don't know anything and am not worldly wise.' She spread her hands palms upwards. 'I know you have courage, in fact greater courage than all of us put together.' As she spoke she could feel her lips begin to tremble. Biting her bottom lip, she said firmly, 'Rose is the coward, Mum's a coward. It's women like us who can and will eventually change everybody's thinking. I know that I will be looked on as something of a scarlet woman.' She paused and gave a slight chuckle, thinking of Scarlett O'Hara: I don't think I'll ever fall into that category, she cautioned herself. 'But I do know what goes on around me. Like you, I read.' She waited for an interested glance from Vera. 'Like you I read the tuppenny novelettes. I like a good romance.' She grinned. 'Mind you,

I've never had one! Oh Vera,' she implored, 'if I didn't have an ounce of romance in me and I don't mean love, sex and all that.'

At this revelation Vera looked up, more interested in what her sister had to say. She always believed Gladys's view of life was very conservative. This was a Gladys she had never seen or heard before.

'Romance, that's right, my dear sister, romance! I wouldn't be reading love stories in magazines, neither would I have looked in the situations vacant column, if I wasn't looking for some kind of romantic adventure.'

Vera began to feel a little disturbed. 'You ain't one of them communist women, are you?' She wasn't altogether sure of what she was asking but it seemed the right time to ask.

'Good gracious, Vera, absolutely not,' Gladys confirmed, understanding exactly what Vera was driving at.

They burst into hapless laughter leaning shoulder to shoulder.

'Oh right, so that's what you women get up to in the morning when there's no one about?'

The familiar tones drew Gladys to her feet. Her fist clenched hard as she stuffed the small wristwatch into her pocket. 'Hello Tom. My word,' her voice was light, 'you are a little early,' as she gave a quick look over her shoulder at the clock. Vera had frozen into the sofa.

Tom said as Vera rose stiffly, ''Ello, Vera, luv.'

Vera smiled weakly, her face drained of its flushed laughter.

'Tom,' she managed, finishing with a forced smile.

''Ere, now, don't you go runnin' around on my account, I can't stop. Ol' Charlie Gibbons caught up with me, the missus wants to go shopping up west. I'll get me coppers and cards if I don't get a bit of a move on.'

Vera began to feel the colour returning. She also felt Gladys's hand around her waist.

'Oh come on now, Tom, you've always got time for a cuppa,' Vera said encouragingly.

'No, I really musn't . . . ' He stopped mid sentence, stared at Gladys, then as a broad grin spread across his face he said, pointing a finger at her, 'Very fetching.'

Gladys stared blankly at Vera for an explanation, Vera stared back, shaking her head.

The sound of padding footsteps echoed in the hall. 'Hello, Poppet,' Tom said warmly, catching the child in his open arms and lifting her up to his shoulder. He whispered something to her.

Sylvia leaned over her uncle's head, pointing a small grubby finger at her aunt and giggled. 'Your crown, Auntie Gladys.' Sylvia tucked the finger behind her front teeth and bit on it, hard trying not to laugh even louder. Once again stared at Vera, who herself was now laughing. She too was jabbing a finger at her head. Gladys raised her eyebrows and rolled, her eyes as her lips lifted into a generous smile as she said simply, 'Oh.'

'New fashion then, is it?' Tom asked.

Gladys said solemnly, 'And that's where it's staying.' And that's exactly where the daisy crown stayed.

Tom lowered Sylvia to the floor. 'I really 'ave to go.' He gave a cheery wave and with a single stride into the hall he called back, 'Oh, by the way, if anybody asks you 'aven't seen me, all right?'

Vera and Gladys exchanged knowing glances. 'Rose,' they mouthed together.

Later, in the kitchen, they stared in silence over their empty coffee cups. Conversation was stilled with thoughts neither could mouth. Vera took their cups and put them in the sink. As she listened to the roar of the water it dulled her senses, rather like a spoonful of icecream. She felt numb.

Her thoughts started to race. There was so much she wanted to say. She wanted to thank Gladys for understanding. She rounded into the centre of the room only to see Gladys with her head lowered over her open handbag.

'Don't they 'ave daisies in Dundee, then?'

Vera looked on in silence as Gladys removed the daisy chain, gently wound it around her fingers and pressed it carefully between two pages of her leather bound diary.

Gladys smiled, 'Arundel,' she corrected gently. 'Yes, but these are special, and they always will be.' Her eyes misted as she watched Vera swallowing hard to choke back the rising tide of tears.

Sylvia bounded noisily into the kitchen clutching the cat under her arm, its overfed bulging belly hanging low and exposed. Its glazed expression showed its indignation at having its belly scratched so publicly. Sylvia dropped suddenly cross legged onto the floor. Vera watched, torn between her sister and her daughter, as the cat kneaded the plump legs, curled itself comfortably and fell asleep, purring contentedly.

Vera was unsure of where to begin. Her voice began to shake as she asked, 'D' you 'ave to go today?'

Gladys scooped her white cardigan from the back of the chair. Lifting her face, her eyes filled with tears, her red rimmed dark eyes stinging with the onslaught of unchecked saltiness. The doe like eyes scanned the gentle Vera's features. How she wanted to tell her everything would be all right. How she wanted to hug her, cradle her in her arms and love her as she would have loved her own children had she had any. Vera's hands were tightly gripped on the sink, the slender fingers showing white knuckles. 'You 'aven't got no things with you.' She released one of her hands, sweeping her arm over the kitchen.

Gladys caught the trembling hand in hers. It fluttered so alarmingly Gladys thought this must be how a butterfly must feel when free of its chrysalis. She drew Vera to her and brushed her cheek with the lightest of kisses, her lips stemming the stream of tears.

'You goin' away, Auntie Gladys?'

The two women drew themselves up. Vera lifted her apron and used it as an improvised hanky. Gladys's hand flew to her belt for the ever present clean laundered handkerchief which had been long discarded to the sitting room floor. She raised one of her little stubby hands to her eyes and brushed away a newly emerged tear. She found herself sniffing as she said, 'Yes, and I want you to take good care of your Mummy.' Then Gladys said what everybody always said, 'And I want it to be just our secret.' She raised her finger to her lips and gave a slight nod.

The child smiled up at her, saying in a hoarse whisper, 'You mean, not to tell Gran.' Her eyes glistened with conspiratorial glee.

Gladys bent down to retrieve her cardigan that had fallen to the floor. On rising she turned to her sister. 'That's why I brought the canvas bag with me.'

Vera eyed the bag doubtfully. 'But it's empty.'

Gladys gave a silent nod. 'All I need is two white blouses and two black skirts, a sort of uniform,' she said. 'This,' she said, flapping a hand up and down her navy dress, 'will do until I get myself settled.'

Vera dug a fist into her apron pocket.

Gladys continued, 'That's why I have to leave now, my dear. First to the shops and then the five minutes past four from Waterloo.'

At this Vera burst into tears. Gladys steadied her to the chair and urged her to sit. Vera obeyed dumbly.

Between muffled sobs and gasps Vera said, 'It's really 'appening. You're really going. Oh Gladys, what am I goin' to do?'

Gladys had clung to her idea but this was not the time to make promises she might not be able to keep. She soothed and cooed at the trembling Vera.

Sylvia abandoned the cat and went over to her mother and sat by her side. Gladys acknowledged the child's concern with a warm smile of encouragement. Vera put an arm around her daughter's shoulder. Then, as if finding some inner strength, she patted her and ruffled the still and quiet child's hair. Straightening her shoulders, she looked up into Gladys's face. With her free hand she wiped her now grimy face, sniffed loudly and smiled. At length she said, 'You're right. It's my,' she looked down at Sylvia sitting on the floor beside her, 'our future.' Then she dropped her gaze meaningfully to her middle. At this Gladys gave a slow smile of approval. 'I don't know what we're goin' to do, but it won't include . . . ' Her voice trailed away. Gladys wasn't sure what Vera meant, but she was certain it would be for herself, her and her own family.

Uncharacteristically, Gladys tore a page from the back of her diary. Her face solemn, she handed it to Vera. 'This is my new address and telephone number. I want you to know that you can call me any time you want.' She paused. 'I'm sure Mrs Lownds wouldn't mind if I telephoned you here.'

Vera blanched visibly at the thought.

From her pocket, Gladys produced the wristwatch. Carefully, she put it into Vera's still hands. 'This,' she said, 'Rose's ruin, Mum's first class return ticket to Easy Street. For you, Vera, it's your passport to a new life, a beginning for you all. Make sure you use it!'

Uncertain of what Gladys meant, Vera took the watch, turned it around a few times, then looked up at Gladys and asked in a low voice, 'How? When?'

Gladys waved a finger at her sister. 'You'll know. The chance will come to you, it will show itself.' Seeing the face pinched with unasked questions, she paused, leaned on the table, bent over Vera and persisted with a passion rising in her voice again. 'You will know when, you will feel it here.' She put her fist into her full bosom. 'You'll know, I promise you, you'll know.' And Gladys added, raising a hand, 'When you do, you will be free; free for the first time. Free, Vera, you understand, Vera? FREE! Freedom! To have your own life.' Gladys's breathing had become rapid. She coughed to calm herself. Her sister's eyes looked just like windows in need of polishing, thought Gladys. 'They'll soon open and shine once again.'

Gladys bustled around the kitchen and was surprised to find that Vera was deeply absorbed, her fingers tracing over the engraved initials on the back of the watch. Without looking up, Vera said almost to herself, 'I thought it was expensive. Rose said it was.' She spoke as if she believed Rose's words to be gospel. 'I suppose it looks cheap now,' she added, giving it another twirl around her fingers.

'It's cheap, all right,' Gladys's voice was brusque. 'Typical of the so called gentry, give themselves away. The watch, him, as cheap as each other. Why Rose thought for a minute he would marry her is beyond me.' Her tone was now matter of fact. 'It's the sort of present a Right Honourable would give to a servant, a female servant of course. All shiny and glittering. Huh, he probably told her it shone like her eyes. He married Lord Middleton's daughter in the October,' Gladys finished cynically and equally matter of fact.

'Servant?' Vera queried, 'I though they met at the Palais?'

Gladys nodded in agreement. 'They probably did, wholly engineered by him, I should think,' getting into her vocal stride, remembering the occasion well and saying nothing, and certainly not in defence of Rose. 'Rose worked as a parlour maid. It was difficult to get domestics, let alone proper servants, after the war, but it was the only work Rose knew, so back into service she went.'

Vera looked up, interested.

'Stanley was and probably is one of those hooray henry types, beaten by father and idolised by his mother. The family lived over Beckenham Bickley way. Usual thing: large house, plenty of money and much too much time on his hands. That's where Rose comes in.' Gladys took a breath and clicked her tongue. 'Why Rose thought he was in love with her astonishes me!'

'Was he?' Vera's tone was soft.

''Course not! Once he'd taken an interest in her, well, the rest is of course history,' Gladys concluded with a rough wave of her hand.

It all came back to Vera once again, just as vividly, that night in September when she had stood and lied for the last time to Tom. What was it Father Brennan had said: 'absence of truth', that meant if you don't tell you can't lie. Absently, she handed the watch to Gladys.

'No, no!' Gladys pressed the watch back into her hand. 'Use it. The sooner the better!' she urged in her familiar voice.

Vera put it in her pocket and saw that Gladys, standing in front of her, was waiting, her cardigan over her arm, the large canvas bag with her handbag gripped firmly in her hand. Vera stood up. 'I'd best be off, my dear.' Vera watched gulping as Gladys went into the hall, opened the front door and stood waiting. Vera, with Sylvia clutching at her hand, exchanged looks of tenderness. Gladys tipped her tubby frame onto her toes, kissed her sister and said, 'Goodbye, my dear.' Slightly overbalancing, she bent down to Sylvia and kissed her gently. 'Don't forget, young lady, you made me a promise, remember?' Sylvia nodded, two large tears rolling slowly down her cheeks. As mother and daughter blinked Gladys had reached the gate. Without turning around she pulled the gate shut. Its familiar clunk raised another tear. Vera and Sylvia hand in hand stood on the step watching the short tubby frame stepping stolidly away from them. Vera watched until the recognizable figure had changed into a dot, then a dark speck until it finally vanished from sight at the bottom of the road. Neither waved.

Chapter 9

Vera felt troubled. That night she tossed and turned. Sylvia was restless too. Vera made a point of steering clear of Mabel, not that they exchanged more than half a dozen words in any one week; now, Vera didn't want to be drawn into conversation. With Sylvia back at school soon she spent the evening repairing and pressing her school clothes. She kept the watch in her pocket, often taking it out and looking at it. How obvious it was to her, how much she had changed. A few years ago she had a voice and a temper, an opinion, although never taken seriously. She'd had dreams, desires. They had long since deserted her and been replaced by the treadmill of housework. It followed her like the dull throb of cogs turning, each tooth slicing away another second of her life. Vera knew now they were grinding away at her too. Everything Gladys had said was true. She knew that somewhere inside she should feel guilty, some kind of remorse, sorrow even, if it was not for Sylvia. She felt nothing, only suffocation. Now how could she stop the wheels turning, how could she step off the treadmill without falling on her face? Her longing she had kept faithful to but it could no longer be the part of her life she had once dreamed of. It was too late now. In the darkness she whispered softly, 'Tom.' She gave the lumpy pillow a hard punch, pulled it into her and hugged it tight.

The early morning was misty, Vera rose feeling fighting fit and full of beans. She didn't feel sick either. A look in the small mirror showed her eyes bright, her skin glowing. 'You,' she said smiling back at the face, 'need a waggy tail and a wet nose.' She poked out her tongue and pulled at her ears. A drowsy voice from the bed laughed and asked, 'What'you doin?'

'Just being silly.' Vera pulled back the covers saying, 'Come on, rise and shine, I'm goin to 'ave a bit of a spring clean.'

Sylvia laughed, she was happy just to see her mother happy again.

Vera started at the top of the house, occasionally giving a worried look into the garden to see how the long suffering cat was faring. 'Work,' she declared, 'Is the best medicine.' With bedrooms finished, she trundled the cylinder vacuum cleaner down the stairs, the heavy lead wrapped over her shoulder like a mountaineer. Safely back in the hall she called to Sylvia, 'Fill the kettle, luv; we'll 'ave some tea.'

Over tea and sticky buns Sylvia said, 'It's not spring.'

Vera shook her head, saying, 'Don't matter, a good clean never did any 'arm.' Licking her fingers she added, 'Any'ow, it's good exercise, madam!' Playfully, she snatched her daughter's nose between her two fingers, popped her thumb between them and laughed as she said, 'Gotcha!'

'Ouch!' Sylvia laughed, rubbing her nose, and said, 'That's what Uncle Tom does, he doesn't hurt. Like that!' Giggling, she slid from her chair. Vera stopped chewing and threw down her bun. 'Here, you have this, then go and pester that poor creature again. If it 'ad any sense, it would sit on a roof somewhere.' She took the cups and plates to the sink. The child ran past, leaving Vera staring blankly at the wall. Sighing heavily, she told herself, 'No more thinking like that, me girl.'

Dragging the noisy cleaner behind her, she dipped, dived, dragged and generally pulled the siting room into a jigsaw state. She stood marooned, encircled like a wagon train under siege. She viewed her hard work. Deep in thought a voice from behind made her jump with fright. The tiny sparrow-like Mrs Lownds stood as ever neatly framed by the oak open doorway. 'That machine makes the most unholy sound, you can hear it half way down the Avenue.'

Vera gasped. Speaking slowly and deliberately, she said, 'Oooh, Mrs Lownds, you nearly scared me half to death.' She drew in a breath. Looking at the tiny figure she began to smile as she thought, 'How can such a tiny woman sound so terrifying?' She stamped on the innocent grey button and the machine whirred into silence.

The two women stood in silent observation of each other, Vera's face drained of colour, her hand firmly clapped to her chest. Mrs Lownds' eyes twinkled with amusement.

Vera snatched at the carrying handle. Once upright, she pointed a finger. 'You. Why you back now, here so soon?'

Mischievously, Mrs Lownds bent her finger towards Vera and said, 'I didn't say which day I would return.' Smoothing down her skirt, her light coat hanging over her arm, with a glint in her eye she suggested, 'Tea?'

Quickly Vera from across the room said, 'I'll get the kettle goin'.'

'There's no need to rush.' From the small understairs cloakroom she took a hanger and hung up her coat. With a definite glint in her eye as she watched Vera in the kitchen, she called after her, 'Bring it into the sitting room, I would like a word with you.'

As she settled herself at her desk she wasn't in the least surprised to hear a saucer or was it a cup that crashed to the floor. The twinkle was now dancing on her lips. Vera's face peered around the door. 'In 'ere?'

Beatrice Lownds gave a slow nod by way of answer.

The spluttered 'Oh!' stammered back into the kitchen. On her return, Vera anxiously placed the tray on the table. Wiping her hands down her apron and moistening her dry lips she said, 'Sylvia's in the garden torment . . . ' She stopped. 'Playing with the cat.'

'Good.' Mrs Lownds folded her hands on her lap and inclined her head towards Vera, indicating to her to sit down. Nervously, Vera sat on the edge of the sofa looking directly at her employer. Knowing her so well, she knew something was afoot. But what? Beatrice Lownds was now tapping her thumbs together. Once again she inclined her head and studied Vera's worried face. They both spoke at the same time. Vera just ahead. 'Where's your bags then?'

Beatrice smiled easily. Raising a delicate finger she pointed to the hall. 'Just the carpet bag. I would like to speak to you, but first I have something I must ask you.' Her hands were folded and composed in her lap.

Vera gave a heavy sigh and waited.

Beatrice Lownds then inclined her head the other way as if viewing her at a distance. She was now sitting with her back erect, her hands flat on her knees. Without taking a breath, she asked simply, her words filling the room, 'Vera, my dear, you are going to have another child, are you not?'

Vera froze. The words crashed around her head. The room swam. She leaned forward, her arms wrapped around her. 'You ain't goin' to sack me. Would you?' Her voice was muffled as if she'd been chewing cotton wool. 'How'd you know?' Having asked the unspeakable she fell back into the sofa. The tears rolled slowly down her face and dripped miserably off her chin. She made no attempted to wipe them away.

Gently, Beatrice touched Vera's knee. Her voice was soft; her genteel tones roused Vera to hear, 'Good, then I'm right. My visit was not in vain.'

Mrs Lownds turned to her desk and from the drawer she slid out a sheet of lavender fragrant writing paper. Silently she put it on Vera's shaking knees. She shuffled herself back into her chair to wait, sitting straight backed once again. Finally, Vera's eyes opened wide in astonishment, worried. Beatrice cast a penetrating look over the taut features. Satisfied that all was well, despite the surprised Vera's open mouth, she felt warmth returning to the room. Feeling safe to continue, she took the small key that hung from her neck on a fine ribbon of velvet and passing it over her head she secured it into the desk and quietly rolled up the top. Then with a flourish of achievement she slipped out the small writing leaf and a sheaf of papers. To her pleasure she noted that the sniffing had eased considerably.

Vera, still open mouthed, waved the paper at Mrs Lownds. 'I don't think I understand.'

'In good time, my dear, in good time. Indulge an old lady.' Beatrice was smiling broadly as she sifted through the papers on her lap. With her head lowered, intent on her search, she asked softly, 'How is that young man of yours?'

Without thinking Vera put her hand into her apron pocket. 'Oh, he's not my young man. You mean the letter.'

The elderly lady gave a single nod. Confused, Vera said nothing, as she knew Mrs Lownds was about to speak. A delicate hand was raised in a warm dismissal as she said, 'Oh no, the young man, a chauffeur, I think.'

Vera's mouth gaped. Spluttering once again she said in reply, 'Oh, Tom. He's my brother in law.'

Without looking up, Beatrice said with a smile, 'Really. A very nice young man. I think you really ought to tell him, don't you?'

'What?' Vera's tone was flat.

'About the increase in his family. By the by, does your mother know of your confinement?'

Vera's shoulders sagged. A dullness came over her. It showed on her face. Sullenness was overcome as her anger began to rise. How did everybody know her secrets? She'd really only put two and two together herself just the other day. How could they possibly know that she was going to have a baby; she hadn't told a soul! Even Gladys had guessed right. Resentment began to rise until she remembered what she had read, the sheet she still clutched tightly in her hand.

Mrs Lownds, as if reading her thoughts having found the papers, gave a sigh of satisfaction and said in her gentle modulated tones, 'I may be old but I do believe it is wise to keep in touch.' Her half-moon shaped spectacles sat high on the bridge of her nose. Above them her eyes twinkled brightly in anticipation of what she was about to tell Vera. 'There now, that is what I have been looking for.' She leaned towards Vera, her face relaxed, and said, 'I am an old lady, a little deaf but you will find that can be something of an advantage at times.' Then to Vera's amusement Mrs Lownds raised a small finger to her nose and tapped it lightly. 'You understand?' Her tone was girlish. Vera giggled momentarily, forgetting her woes. 'Good,' Mrs Lownds confirmed. Taking a breath then, just as Gladys had done, while Vera sat open mouthed listening to every word, her soft voice spoke.

Mrs Lownds, her hands nestled in her lap, began, 'My niece Frances has a son. Like you, he was born out of wedlock. I know that must sound so very old fashioned, but it is nonetheless true. You are wondering,' she gave a brief wave of her hand, 'No, no, that is incorrect. There are many women in your situation, in fact more now. I feel it was the war. Most were deserted, some perhaps left only with a feeble promise of marriage.'

The younger woman's mouth opened to speak.

Mrs Lownds raised a hand saying, 'No, just one moment. Allow me to finish. No, I am most certainly not going to dismiss you, and secondly, yes, I have known for some little while of your pregnancy. You forget I remember your first confinement. My dear, you have forgotten, I did not dismiss you then . . . ' she broke off. 'Vera, my dear, I would not have kept you in my employ had I not trusted in you and your obvious capabilities. I may be old, and Mr Lownds and I were never blessed with children, but you and Sylvia I think of as my family. You are a caring mother, loving.' She spread her hand across the window, indicating to those unseen outside. 'There are many children with two parents who can only dream of the love you have for Sylvia. She is a delightful child, well mannered, and gentle like her mother and . . . ' she peered over her spectacles and a little smile danced over her lips as she added, 'and as impish as her father, would you not agree?'

At such praise Vera lowered her eyes and bowed her head. She felt confused though; shouldn't she be feeling shame at being found out? Tom was the father, and he was married to her sister.

'This,' Mrs Lownds raised aloft the lavender paper, catching Vera's attention, 'is a situation I want you to seriously consider. Whatever you decide, I want you to know that your work here is as secure as you feel comfortable to continue, and will indeed be waiting when you wish to return. And I should think that the spring would be an ideal time to place a bassinet in the garden; but there, I don't know very much about babies. Frances was our only remaining relative and when Ralph passed away, Mr Lownds left Frances a considerable sum in his will. When two years later Frances found herself alone and pregnant, naturally I suggested she stay here with me. Frances is a strong, if not single minded individual,' the thoughtful voice reflected. 'She agreed to stay until the child was born, but forever restless waiting for his arrival, George – he's nearly twelve, now. She agreed on the understanding that with the money her uncle had left her she would find a suitable property she could use as a home for mothers and babies. Sadly, no such property could be found in this area. I fear it was not the lack of property, it was the nature of what the property would be used for and people need to sweep these forgotten women, some of them no more than children themselves, under a carpet. Eventually, she found a suitable property in a small village in Hampshire, not far from the coast. She spent the first year almost rebuilding it practically singlehanded. It is now a beautiful house which stands in private grounds, almost secluded you might say.' She took a breath and smoothed down her skirt before returning the papers to her lap.

'She runs it with invaluable help of the local understanding general practitioner, and a retired nursing sister. All the ladies at the time of their confinement are attended by one or both as the case may determine. The ladies are encouraged to be independent and self sufficient soonest after the child's birth. She also runs an agency for single woman with children for whom she finds situations suitable for their needs. Sometimes, of course, her ladies do return to their families; it is however rare even in this day and age.' Her voice trailed away sadly. 'Ah, this. I know you have really only glanced at it. Following my visit, Frances would like you to consider a situation with her as "housemother". She has of course included Sylvia and . . . '

Vera, stammering, broke in. 'Housemother? What's that? What'll I 'ave to do?' she asked finally finding her tongue.

Calmly, Mrs Lownds explained, 'As a housemother you will help the younger women, some of them not yet sixteen. You will be invited to help out with light chores, mending, linen, cooking, taking the children for walks, in fact anything that Frances feels you are capable of. Your work will be conducive to your condition. Sylvia could attend the village school, and perhaps now that she is a little older could help out in the kitchen like George does?' Another hand was raised to stop the fair head from shaking. 'Also, to ensure your financial security should you not wish to stay, I have had this drawn up by my solicitors.'

The sheaf of papers that had been resting on her lap she handed to the quickly blinking Vera. She watched as the fair head bobbed intently, attempting to grasp the legal phrasing. Eventually, Vera raised her head, sighed, and said, 'It's all double dutch to me, what does it mean?'

'Quite simply it states that I will give you an allowance of five hundred pounds per annum – a year,' she quickly corrected herself.

'For you to use in any way you want. It will allow you to stand on your own two feet. It will also mean that you will have independence and a freedom of choice. Raising two children is a very expensive business. Frances will of course pay you wages which will include your room and board for you both.'

Vera fell silent, her hand to her throat as she tried to take it all in.

'I agree, it is a great deal to take in. I do not want you to feel threatened. If you would prefer to stay here I will completely understand. Your mother, does she know of . . . ' The elderly lady jerked her head to the side and waited.

Vera just shook her head.

'Go home now, my dear, and think it over. If you choose to accept I will contact Frances on your behalf. I do know, however, that she is keen for you to have this situation and it would mean that you will have to travel down at the latest, this weekend.'

She had hardly finished speaking when Vera said, 'I accept. Is there things for me to sign an' that?'

Mrs Lownds shook her head. 'No, none at all. If you decide you don't like the work or that you feel homesick even, or even if Sylvia finds the move difficult, your job will be here waiting for you.'

'Why you doin' all this?' Vera asked uncharitably.

'You and Frances are so very alike in oh so many ways. Above all you have the courage, where so many others fail. That's all. For my part, I want to be a useful cog in this changing world, and this is the only way I know.' She finished speaking and a wide smile of relief filled her pinched anxious face.

'Cog' was the word which registered with Vera. She had up to that moment believed cogs worked against you; now perhaps they could work for you. Once again she nodded her head enthusiastically, saying firmly, 'I accept.'

Regally Mrs Lownds rose; saying, 'I'm pleased. I want you to go home now, pack a few cases and . . . ' She was interrupted by a small voice coming from the open door. 'Hello Sylvia, my dear. Come in, I'm sure your Mummy has much to tell you on the way home.'

Nervously Vera looked over her shoulder to find Sylvia almost swathed in a beam of bright sunlight. The child was beaming too.

'Right now!' the standing figure ordered. 'Shoo, off with you both.' Turning to Vera, she said quietly, 'I will call Frances this evening; you are sure, quite sure?'

Vera was beaming like her daughter. 'Yes,' she confirmed as she began to load the tray.

'No, no, off you go – now. Shoo!' The voice urged them, melting away with emotion.

As usual mother and daughter walked hand in hand, only this time each was immersed in her own thoughts. Suddenly, Sylvia turned her face up to her mother and said, 'I don't tell Gran, right?'

Vera looked down at the laughing face, and laughed herself as she said, 'Right,' as she tapped the side of her nose. The afternoon sun was warm, and if Vera could grasp everything that had been said and agreed, perhaps the future looked rosier than she could have ever dreamed of last night, or any night for that matter. Together they hummed out of tune and skipped out of step.

That evening before putting the key in the lock Vera stopped and raised a silencing finger to her lips at her daughter. 'Not a word,' she whispered as the key on its new, clean piece of string knocked loudly behind the slowly opening door. Vera winced and her eyes rolled heavenwards with horror as she held her breath; this wasn't the time to be confronted by Mabel. On the way home she'd decided to say nothing, and do as Gladys had done, simply disappear. Sylvia, at her side, went very quiet and still. She too was holding her breath. To their relief no booming, 'That you, Vera?' met them in the dim passage. The pair felt thoroughly relieved, but they tiptoed to the kitchen, just to make sure. It was just as Vera thought: on the table lay a lop sided half loaf which had staled in the high afternoon sun; uneven wedges and crumbs were strewn over the tea cup stained and scratched oil cloth. The sink was filled with used crockery. At the sight of all this, though expected, Vera felt her heart sink and her high spirits dashed. Reluctantly, she threw her bag down on the chair and filled the larger kettle for washing up.

She quickly tidied up and cleared away. She flung open the kitchen door and there in front of her was framed the old apple tree. The early evening sun dappled lazily over its long past fertile life, looking every inch an old master on rough canvas in the making. Just a few more hours and it would be finished. Thoughtfully, she folded her arms and leaped from the top step into the fresh air. Childishly, she zig zagged across the coarse tufts of grass then, breathlessly leaning against its gnarled trunk, under its thin finger-like branches, she plucked absently a handful of prematurely dried up leaves.

Then, with the burnt brown scraps between her palms she ground them into dust. She quickly blew the remains away, scattering them into a slow, low and warm passing breeze. It was symbolic. Vera understood that if she stayed she would be dried up before her time and Sylvia would swiftly follow. That was the way of things, or the way they used to be? Gladys had said that women's lives would soon change. She felt change all around her and knew Gladys was right. But would it have changed if she stayed? Not only would she be old before her time but as gnarled as the tree. Now, with a regular income, she knew she must plan. Her mind was becoming clouded not with doubt, but excitement.

As usual she shook her head. There was a great deal to do, an even greater responsibility; she patted her middle knowingly. There was still so much to take in. Out loud she teased herself, 'Sometimes, those tu'penny novelettes come true and I don't even wear glasses!' She laughed to herself. 'Life can change overnight.' Even saying it out loud didn't make it seem any more real. 'All that matters,' she concluded, 'is that by Saturday we'll be by the seaside.' She spun around; her head swam, leaving her feeling giddy, but at last once again light hearted. She paused at her make-do rockery. 'If they can survive after being dragged up by their roots and dumped in a few bricks and a dollop of concrete and a handful of dirt, then so can I.' It all seemed so simple. But there was still a nagging doubt in the back of her mind. Standing on the top step Sylvia shouted, 'This do, Mum?' The large zipper bag gaped hungrily. Vera took a long stride, her finger raised. 'Ssshhh!' she hissed, and waved the excited child indoors with a quick flick of her fingers.

The slowly setting sun drifted over the grey slated horizon leaving a trail of red and orange tinged roofs, before dropping out of sight, except for a few of the flame-like tendrils clinging to the old corner house wall. Vera stopped to watch for a moment. Resting her chin on her hands, she couldn't remember ever seeing anything quite so startling. She made a mental note: the very next sunset she saw would be high on a cliff overlooking the sea. She gave the stubborn drawer an irritated shove and from the bed Sylvia said in a low thoughtful voice as she bundled her white underclothes into the tan bag, 'I know I'm not to tell, about . . . ' The child shifted uneasily. 'But can I tell Doris?'

Vera turned to her daughter and saw the anguished look on the child's face. She gave a half smile of understanding, parted her lips to explain, then just slowly shook her head. The child's legs dangled awkwardly over the bed and were swinging rhythmically, her sun tanned nut brown knees shining in the glow of the half light. 'Well, if I can't,' she sighed with an acceptance far beyond her years. 'What will Gran do without us and no Auntie Gladys?'

From the bottom of the stairs the front door banged and Mabel's voice cut through the still of the evening. Immediately, Sylvia drew up her knees, slid backwards over the bed and hunched herself into the corner. Vera had yearned to run everywhere to tell everyone who would listen to their news, her good fortune, their new life; hearing the voice she stiffened: no one must know and if we don't tell, they can't either. 'Absence of truth,' she muttered under her breath. Then she added as a warning, as if the frightened child need one, 'Nobody must know, no one, you understand me?' Sylvia gave a weak smile of understanding. Once more the voice: 'Veeeeraaaa'r!' She snatched at the open bag and hurled it under the bed with a quick stab of her foot; she felt it catch on the split floor covering. 'Don't move, I won't be long. All right?' She pinched the top of the upturned nose in the centre of the small round face and smiled reassuringly.

Mabel was waiting for her daughter in the kitchen, one accusing finger tapping the blue-rimmed enamel plate covering the plated dinner steaming gently over a large saucepan. 'What's this?' A yellowing thumb nail flicked off the plate, sending it clattering over the stove before coming to rest upside down on an unused ring. Vera's eyes were fixed open; Mabel narrowed hers in reply. 'Well?'

Vera glanced at the anaemic sausages, mashed potatoes and tinned peas. 'We've 'ad ours,' she stated firmly, without losing her mother's glazed, locked suspicious gaze.

'I don't eat processed peas.' Another couple of yellow fingernails poked around the green vegetable. 'They gives me the wind.' She stumbled slightly and gripped the back of the chair. Calmly Vera relaxed her face and said, 'I'll put it on a tray and you can 'ave it on your lap in the parlour, all right?'

Mabel eyed her daughter even more suspiciously.

'It's getting late, and I know you like to listen to yer evenin' play on the wireless,' she found herself saying alarmingly convincingly.

She watched as her mother struggled with her bag, then in astonished amusement looked on as Mabel threw down the bag in a confused fury. Vera quickly bobbed to retrieve it and dropped it into the crook of her arm, walked steadily from the kitchen into the parlour and laid it in her chair, scarcely daring to breathe for fear her motives would be easily seen through. Vera had never been good at hiding excitement or fear. She felt both, and decided to try and not react to either.

'Come and 'ave a sit, it'll only take a minute.' With every word aired she could hardly believe how sincere she sounded and was quite enjoying this accomplishment.

Mabel stood swaying in the doorway, watching her daughter through dark narrow slits. As she shook her head in disbelief, her chins waggled in slow motion in the opposite direction. 'An' make sure you're not long neither, and make us some tea.'

As Vera swept past she felt an unmistakable feeling of smugness consume her, to the point where a pinched smile pressed into her lips. She was really beginning to enjoy this renewed confidence.

Mabel was sitting propped up in her chair, the tray balanced on a cushion unsteadily across her thick fleshy thighs. Vera tuned in the wireless to the Light Programme, and as the play had already begun she turned up the volume. She set a smaller tray down on the side table, with a full teapot, cup and saucer, a small milk jug and, just for her mother's further gluttonous entertainment, a plate of biscuits. Judging from the weight and bulkiness of the handbag Vera had laid to rest in the high backed chair, it was clear that a full bottle of gin was its sole occupant. Vera, having considered this, hoped that her mother would, after her dinner, tea and biscuits, decide on a liquid refreshment, which meant of course that Vera and Sylvia could continue their packing undisturbed. She stood at the foot of the stairs, one hand patiently resting on the bannister, her back to the door, her ears finely honed to the sound she was waiting for. There it was! an epiglottal roar loud enough to wake the dead! Vera smiled with incalculable satisfaction. She jumped up the first three steps, then instead of stepping over the 'fourth from the top' she took great delight on landing on it until it creaked and moaned so loudly, it brought a round eyed worried faced Sylvia peering around the door.

By eight o'clock on Friday morning Vera and Sylvia had left the house, taking with them the tan canvas bag filled with their belongings, including the blue and red rusty bucket and spade which Sylvia insisted on taking with her, despite her mother's pleading and a sure promise of a new one. It had been an exasperated Vera but an understanding mother who had finally given in. Vera had, as usual, left her mother in bed with her cup of tea at the correct time so no suspicion could be aroused or attention drawn to her. As quietly as they could, they managed between them to drag the reluctant holdall from under the bed, as its brass 'feet' caught on the split floor covering.

They walked wordlessly, dreamlike from the house. On reaching the corner Vera had an overwhelming desire to turn around. She couldn't think why, so resumed her long leisurely stride. She wondered also if, besides all the cheery waves from the boys going about their usual errands and the familiar tap on a window as they passed by, this larger bag had drawn any comments. Turning the corner, she found her shoulder relaxing. 'Perhaps,' she thought to herself, 'we've done it.'

Sylvia was unusually quiet. The child, although mature for her tender years, understood she would be leaving everything and everyone she had ever known. Vera slowed her pace and looked down tenderly at the child. She slipped a comforting arm around her shoulders, and gave her a squeeze. Hearing the child sigh and feeling her lean contentedly against her, they fell into step and headed straight for the park to feed the ducks, and idle away time. Vera would have usually taken the short cut through the Memorial Gardens, but today with time on their hands, and to make certain they didn't see anyone they might know, the park was the far safer choice. In her handbag, Vera had a brown paper bag stuffed with stale wedges of bread.

The larger park had a children's swing park; for the first time Vera had to say 'No' for fear of them being spotted. If that happened Vera knew for sure questions would be asked. At least the 'parkside poshies' kept themselves to themselves. Yes, Vera reassured herself, this park was by far the safer, and it was only for a couple of hours until they could meet Mrs Lownds as arranged.

Soon they were in the park, strolling across the chestnut fenced off cricket and football pitches to the pond. Before it came into view the 'Quack, quack!' of the ducks could be heard. Vera reached into her handbag and gave the brown creased and crumpled bag with its equally crumbled contents to Sylvia. Her daughter's face creased into one huge grin and she began to run towards the quacking. Vera was quietly relieved to see her child acting as a child; there would be a long hard haul before they could really be settled once and for all, and Vera was more acutely aware than most of what it was like to lose a childhood. It was altogether too short, and far too precious to rush. So it was with a slow lingering smile that she watched as Sylvia stood by the low green painted railing, excitedly throwing clumps of bread into the water at the ever dipping shiny heads of the ducks. Vera lowered herself into the bench to oversee the scene. The holdall had hung heavily on her arm. She gave it a shove with the sole of her sandal under the seat of the rough wooden planked bench. Sighing gratefully for the peacefulness, she watched as the hungry fowl dared to venture close to the source of food. She stretched out her legs, crossed them at the ankles and felt content under the ever present warm rays of the sun. Vera gave a lazy yawn. Her curled long eyelashes fringing her lowered lids quivered as her head fell down on the back of the bench, as she listened to the quacking, squealing, flapping of wings, plopping of bread onto water.

Behind her Vera could hear the distant drone of cars chugging painfully up the long exhausting hill. Her arms settled comfortably onto her lap. She must have dozed off. The warmth of the sun and her rediscovered confidence, the feeling of complete freedom had lulled her. Suddenly, she sat up, startled to realise she had just literally closed her eyes.

Sylvia was now throwing bread 'at' the ducks, Vera saw with a wry smile. She smoothed down her dress, her head stopped abruptly, then hovered trembling over its side seam pocket. Lifting her skirt, she cautiously slid in a hand. There in a second, lying in the folds of her skirt draped over her knees, lay her past. The wristwatch glinted brazenly under the morning sun. Its gawdiness struck her as ugly. It belonged in the dark, away from their future. Her stomach tied itself into a palpitating knot. Vera went cold, a shiver ran across her shoulders. When sickness began to rise, she took a deep breath. Silent tears replaced the feeling of nausea. She stared numbly at her lap, her arms folded around her waist. She looked up briefly to see Sylvia waving, at her. She lifted her arm mechanically and a brief smile stretched her pale lips.

'We'll 'ave to go back,' Vera told herself. This tainted piece of fakery represented all that was dirty and deceitful, and belonged in the past. Vera knew there was only one place for it: back in the dark corner of the dark wardrobe ready and waiting to be clutched and abused by Mabel! 'Yes, they'd 'ave to go back, but they weren't staying.' Vera's eyes narrowed darkly. An idea flashed across her mind. Quickly she stabbed fingers into her other pocket. 'Oh, no keys,' she groaned despairingly. 'The keys, I left 'em at Mrs Lownds.' She abandoned her thoughts. With keys she could have taken Sylvia to the Avenue, and left her there while she shot back and put this trinket back into the bowels of the oak wardrobe. Sighing heavily, she was now resigned to returning and keeping her fingers crossed that 'Big Mabel' would be out.

Vera dropped the obnoxious reminder of the past into her bag; the clasp cracked shut. With the bag at her feet she crossed her legs, folded her arms, drew in a deep breath and waited for time to pass. She felt somehow pleased she didn't have a watch. 'Lies, lies, I've lived lies, I told lies. I've been part of lies.' She shook her head. 'No more.' This was really the beginning, it was something she knew was right, something she had been waiting for. She uncrossed her legs. 'Lies, absence of truth? Wasn't it all the same?' No matter how she looked at it, no matter how . . . she was part of it. But that was it, 'part'. She thought hard. 'Part, part of life. Then it came to her; a flickering smile. 'The part that's me is love. I love Tom, and that's why I'm not ashamed or guilty.' She spoke the words softly and slowly with new understanding. Her elbows dug hard into her knees, her head still, her eyes searching this small man-made oasis.

Vera looked on as Sylvia ran to and from the pond edge, squealing with sheer delight; the inner glow of pride and deep contentment moved her once more to tears – tears of thanks for being given a real beginning.

It was the distant sound of the church clock striking that made her aware of time. A quick glance at the sun told her they should be getting along to Mrs Lownds. On the way, the pair dawdled, enjoyed an impromptu game of hopscotch. The heavy clumsy bag stretched between them, each clutching tightly a sweaty handle. Soon they were standing on the path, the gate shut behind them. Vera pressed the bell; its sharp shrill could be heard from the pavement. Waiting, Vera began to feel a pang of loss. Unless they came to visit they might never tread this neat path with its neat garden again. If Beatrice Lownds thought there was something odd about the burden carried between them, she said nothing. Her genteel manner, together with a welcoming wave of her hand, guided them inside, hid her curiosity. A puzzled frown may have betrayed her, and her lack of verbal questioning told Vera that nothing would be asked. Happily, they accepted the offer of tea as the elderly lady, with colour stinging her cheeks, went from room to room, every step bringing forth a flurry of apologies including, 'Sorry, I won't be long,' and even 'Ooops!' was heard from the kitchen.

At last Beatrice Lownds had to hand everything she needed to illustrate her words. She began . . .

Vera felt awkward sipping tea from the bone china cup she had become so used to washing up. She shot a warning glance at Sylvia which said 'best behaviour'. The child smiled knowingly, and nodded slightly.

'Now, where was I?' Mrs Lownds had, over her knees as she sat perched flushed with excitement and enthusiasm for them both, a large map. 'There!' she said, as excitedly as a child discovering Christmas. 'There, just there, my dear – can you see?' Obliging, still with her finger pinned to the map, she swivelled it around to face Vera. Vera, put down her cup and saucer and stared at the yellow, blue, black and red lines. She recognized the blue as sea and the larger black dots, they had to be towns or something important. She nodded uncertainly.

'That is Littlecombe Sands, and just above here is the village where my niece lives, Sedge Mill,' and with a final breath of triumph she pointed at one of the big black dots and said 'and that's Havant, with the station just here.' She screwed up her eyes and peered over the half moon shaped lenses 'Ah, see? You'll be able to get a cab from outside the railway station straight to Sedge Mill, it's about . . . ' she wrinkled her nose. Then with a flap of her hand in a good humoured gesture of impatience she added, 'That doesn't matter.'

Vera had been thinking. Littlecombe Sands. She didn't know why but it sounded flat. Without thinking she asked, 'Ain't there no cliffs then, at Littlecombe Sands, I mean?'

Not in the least surprised at her question the patient Beatrice said, 'Plenty, my dear. You will have splendid views.' She paused and inclined her head as if to ask if there were any more questions before she continued.

Sylvia slurped. Vera frowned.

'That's clear, I think.' The map was neatly folded into a pre-folded oblong and handed to Vera. From her desk, she took two white envelopes.

Vera noticed the distinctive yellow 'AA' badge on the front of the map. It reminded her of Tom; he had a badge just the same on the radiator grille of the car.

The question that had been gnawing away at her got the better of her. Unexpectedly, and in a tone she hardly recognised, she heard herself asking, 'Why didn't you ever tell me about Frances? I mean your niece, not bein' married and that . . . ' It was then, hearing her accusing tone, that her question trailed away unfinished.

Beatrice Lownds leaned back in her chair and studied the pale fine features. The neat short bobbed hair framed the accusing face. Taking a deep breath, Beatrice leaned forward, took Vera's hand, and said, 'I fear you think I failed you.' Vera didn't answer, as she wasn't sure of what she meant. 'Vera, my dear, I am just like everyone else. It is sometimes simpler to say nothing, allow to assume . . . ' she gave an airy flap of her hand. 'Frances put such hard work into making her Home a success. I, that is when asked, would . . . ' She stopped. She watched as Vera's face broke its taut features into the slightest of smiles. Vera was thinking to herself, 'It's this absence of . . . ' Her mind went blank and she returned a puzzled look at the elderly lady.

Mrs Lownds read her expression as one of doubt. Spontaneously, she slipped from her chair, put an arm around the wide broad shoulders, then gently lifted her chin and said softly to Vera, 'I am so very very sorry, Vera my dear, I should have told you; will you forgive me?' Her trembling fingers felt for the lace edged handkerchief she kept at her wrist. Vera watched spellbound; she'd never seen Mrs Lownds cry.

Vera stood up and towered over the diminutive figure. 'I'm ever so sorry; I didn't mean to upset you. 'Ere, 'ave a sit, I'll make us some tea. All right, I'm sorry, it's none of me business. Really I am.' And she meant it. In the kitchen Sylvia whispered, 'Is Mrs Lownds ill?' Vera only shook her head, she couldn't answer; she was crying too. Sylvia gave one of her 'I don't understand' shrugs and went into the garden to torment the unsuspecting moggie.

With dried eyes they drank tea, stirred tea in the delicate bone china cups and even topped up tea. They sat side by side, united in their now equal friendship. Relaxed, they joked, gossiped and each talked of the future now with a clearer vision.

'Ah!' said Mrs Lownds lightly, remembering the envelopes. Taking them from the writing leaf, she dropped them into Vera's lap. Vera looked up, surprised and puzzled. 'But you gave me me wages on M'nday.' She gave a gasp, saying to herself, 'What a lot as 'appened since M'nday.'

Beatrice resumed a seated position at her writing desk. From it she took a large sheet. The top line was printed in heavy black ink. This also Mrs Lownds dropped onto Vera's lap, smiling as it fluttered to a halt. Please to see the quizzical frown creased across Vera's brow, she gave a girlish laugh. 'My, my, there's nothing to be alarmed about.' She crossed her legs at the knees, smoothed her skirt with her fingertips, settled her hands in her lap and said, 'One envelope contains your railway tickets, the other is, I hope,' she blushed at this point, 'sufficient funds to help you both settle in comfortably; changing one's home and occupation is such a worry.' Her face showed that she had been just a little excessive in her explanation. She hurried on, 'You might consider opening a banking account.'

At this Vera gulped loudly. 'The thought!' she exclaimed silently, inwardly terrified at the prospect. She could feel a nervous belch trying to find its way out; she sat perfectly still, staring at the pink faced woman.

'It would be wise if you did. The large sheet is a legal document I want you to keep. You see, my dear, it would be less complicated if I put your . . .' she stumbled, 'your allowance in annually. You see?'

Vera had got the gist, and nodded slowly, for fear of releasing the belch that was becoming increasingly close to expelling itself.

Mrs Lownds was continuing, 'I don't expect you to read all that now, but do read it in your own time and if there is anything, anything at all you're not sure of, please do tell me. Promise?' Vera gave an even tighter nod of agreement.

Just as Vera's body heaved with a resounding belch, it was swiftly followed with a hiccup. Before she had clapped her hand to her mouth and turned almost purple in colour, Beatrice Lownds was standing at her side offering her a small glass containing a clear liquid. 'Peppermint cordial,' she informed her gently. 'The simple answer to dyspepsia.' She added in a low understanding tone. 'I understand it is common for a lady in your condition.'

Vera drank gratefully. Setting the glass down on the brass table, she looked up from beneath her long lashes to find Beatrice, hand to her throat, smiling broadly. 'Better?' she enquired.

The two women laughed in unison.

It was Vera now who was standing in the porch, her back to the panelled hall. Sylvia slipped silently to her side and put her hand into her mother's.

'Take very good care of yourselves and telephone me on your arrival.' Vera heard from behind. She couldn't leave without turning. How she wanted to tell this lady about the watch and how she had to go back, but she couldn't. She dropped the canvas burden to the tiled porch step, turned and hugged the sparrow form to her. Quickly she deposited a kiss on the small, slightly shaking forehead. 'Thank you,' she whispered. She gripped Sylvia's hand, pulled her slightly forward and stepped from the porch. Mrs Lownds had stooped down to the child. She lifted her open face at the chin with a trembling finger and kissed the child tenderly on the top of her nose. She said softly to stop her voice from cracking, 'My, my, it's not the Boer War, now . . . ' she broke off. 'Off you go now, God speed.' Oh why oh why had she said that? Vera stopped in mid step, turned once more, looked directly into the watering eyes and said, 'Me sister Gladys. She might call.'

Mrs Beatrice Lownds nodded sympathetically. Vera knew she didn't understand, she hadn't told her.

With a sweeping, almost majestic gesture, the frail arm raised gave the slightest of waves from the wrist. The door closed. Mrs Beatrice Lownds fell against the back of the door and wept into the waiting lace trimmed lawn handkerchief.

Chapter 10

It was the privets that caught Vera's attention for the first time ever. She slowed her step, and stood staring long and hard at them. It was the only privet hedge that was overgrown and wilfully untidy. From where she stood they looked dusty, no, grubby. The leaves of yellow privet should be bright and shiny.

A few boys were having a kick about on the green. From behind her she could hear a row raging. Across the green on the corner, a group of girls were skipping to 'Salt, mustard, vinegar, pepper...' The remainder of the rhyme was drowned out by 'Goal!' In those few moments Vera had listened to her past. The sooner this guilt-ridden tainted trinket which lay in her handbag was dropped back into the black abyss of its tawdry past the better. The small cool hand in hers tightened nervously. Vera gave it a reassuring squeeze.

Leading the quivering hand, she opened the gate. Inside she bent over her daughter and said, as she pushed her gently but firmly into the corner of the dusty shrub, 'Stand there, I won't be long.' Vera looked down warmly at the huge eyes staring back at her. She repeated in a whisper, 'I promise I won't be long.' She gave the canvas bag a hefty kick into the straggly hedge, took the watch from her bag and slipped it into her pocket. 'Don't move.' She gave Sylvia a gentle hug and said again, having pulled the key through the letterbox, 'Don't move.' The child remained motionless and from her expression Vera knew she was frightened. This made her even more determined to get this over and done with quickly. She was longing to see a different sunset, or, as the door clicked shut, she thought a sunrise would be better. She stood holding her breath at the bottom of the stairs. The heavy pounding of her heart against her chest brought her out into a cold sweat. Panic seized her. For a second it sounded like her mother's heavy footsteps in the narrow passage. She began to breathe normally, or tried to. She still hadn't moved a muscle. She listened hard, her eyes concentrated on the bottom stair. The brass stair rod gleamed forlornly from a chink of light from the slightly open parlour door. Vera wanted to heave an enormous sigh. She didn't. She crossed her arms in front of her and stood on the bottom stair, still listening. She had to be sure. No, she comforted herself, there was no one in. She hesitated, but it was Friday. No 'fish Friday' afternoon. It was still morning, just. Oh, how she wanted to be certain. Her mind began to wander: what if somebody comes in when I'm upstairs? She heard her neck crack loudly like a dry twig as she turned her head to make sure the key was still hanging on its string knotted to the nail hammered into the back of the door. She had a compulsion to snatch it off its tiny nail, just to be sure. She silently shook off this idea.

Falteringly, she lifted a sandalled foot onto the next tread. Still no sound. She found a little more confidence in this slight move. Still with her arms folded in front of her she climbed the stairs stealthily. She counted to herself, one, two, three. Reaching the fourth from the top she paused. She began to feel her heart flutter again. She let out a short breath. Her skirt rustled as she lengthened her step to avoid this creaking tread. Now she stood on the small landing. Three doors stood shut. Their brass knobs reflected the paleness of her dress. The one to her left was her mother's. The one immediately in front running the full length of the house was the boys'. The last one to her right was hers. She angled herself to the door. Lowering her arms, her hand reached out for the knob. When her hand made contact, its coldness felt like an electric charge. She let out a surprised gasp. How was it so when she was so used to the house, in fact every square inch of it? She had after all scrubbed it for years. Why? Why then, did she feel so unsure of where she was? Her eyes still hadn't become accustomed to the darkness. Her eyes ached from concentration. Her fingers curled around the brass knob. She steeled herself. Sylvia was waiting, she told herself, she had to move and move now and get out! Quickly and quietly and unseen, she turned the knob. The door to her relief snapped softly open. She felt her shoulders relax slightly for the first time. Her free hand slid into her pocket, as if to remind her what she was there for. Her eyes were fixed on the bottom of the door.

The door opened slowly and the room opened into a huge spotlight of sun that fell on her. She blinked furiously, trying to clear the watery mist that prevented her from focusing. Still standing on the landing, the yellow of the sun gushed into the dully furnished room. She resisted the temptation to rub her eyes. Still she concentrated. At last the mist cleared and there in the middle of the floor on the cracked and faded floor covering was a pile of clothes. It was built as big as a bonfire just waiting for lighting. Vera blinked and shook her head simultaneously. She felt her stomach twist into a knot of despair. She'd been discovered. Her first thought was to flee. Then, as her eyes began to adjust, she watched in complete amazement as the heap began to move. She felt a cold hand at her throat. It was hers, still cold from the brass door knob. One hand on her throat, the other wrapped around her waist, she looked on dumbfounded as the mass appeared to heave towards her, or was it away from her?

Standing stock still, Vera flinched as the wardrobe door swung wide. The stop runner, broken years before, screeched before the heavy door jarred to a halt. From inside a dull thud came. Vera was holding her breath. The moving mass inched its way towards her feet. Then from inside the wardrobe, Mabel's florid flabby face emerged. A grin of yellow stained teeth lined the open mouthed gape, her eyes as yellow and watery as the stabbing sunlight. They fluttered slowly open, looking drunkenly up at her. Mabel was now on all fours. The heap of clothes Vera had seen was 'ironing' itself into definite garments. An expanse of pink stopped short above a purple threaded red calf; thick stockings rolled down circled her water filled puffy ankles. She was wearing one slipper. Her wrap-around green faded apron, its toes not long enough to make into a neat bow, hung listlessly around her drooping belly that hung to the floor merging with the faced split floor covering. The rag rug, the only sign of carpet in the room, was pushed against the skirting board to the side of the door.

Vera took a step into the room. Instinctively, her hand reached out; even more quickly, she withdrew the offer and tightly stuffed both hands into her pockets. She waited, catching her breath as she watched impassively as a thick arm hooked itself around the end of the bed. The bed moved and creaked under the strain.

As Mabel peered over her shoulder in an attempt to rise, she spotted Vera. She had managed to drag one knee under her undulating belly. Seeing Vera surprised her; the purchase she'd gained drained from her and she fell sideways from the bed onto her back giving a shout of 'Whoooooops.'

Vera still hadn't budged and nor did she intend to until she had finished what she had come back for.

'Ain't it funny,' Mabel said, her words slurred together as she struggled once more to lean her back against the wardrobe. After the third attempt and a fit of throaty gurgles, she succeeded in hauling herself upright from the waist. Her head lolled from side to side. Her face was covered in sweat and a few strands of hair clung to the perspiration. Her apron had parted, showing the full volume of her undulating belly. Mabel sniffed and gave a sight of satisfaction to find herself upright. Beside her just out of reach stood a bottle of gin. She threw herself sideways to grab it, put it to her lips and filled her mouth. With the back of her hand she wiped her shiny thick lips as the overspill trickled into the hairy folds of her chin. By her side lay something Vera couldn't quite make out. She made no attempt to move nearer. The bottle cap rolled away; Mabel cursed under her breath.

Vera opened her mouth to speak. A floppy wave of her mother's hand silenced her.

'It's funny what yer finds when you ain't lookin' for 'em, ain't it?' She looked up at Vera for confirmation of her discovery. On her lap were, Vera couldn't be sure, but they looked like photos. In her pocket Vera's fingers traced the shape of the watch. Vera wasn't sure what she was feeling. But she waited.

Mabel said, 'You ain't the only one to get knocked up, you knows.'

Vera drew in a breath and stiffened visibly, even through Mabel's bleary eyes. She couldn't know, Vera told herself, and still she waited.

Vera took the watch and threw it on the bed. 'That's what you've been lookin' for!' Her voice was steady, strong and filled with revulsion for the mass of . . . Her thoughts didn't have time to develop. Mabel was holding aloft a photograph. A very old sepia coloured one.

Mabel ignored her daughter, and eyed the watch using the bridge of her nose as a fixing point. 'Ah, her too, silly cow,' Mabel said with a laugh. 'And she never could get nothin' right. You's all the bloody same.' She took another swig from the bottle. Her eyes wandered and drifted around the room and over Vera.

Vera turned to leave. Over her shoulder she said firmly, 'I'm goin', leaving. We won't be comin' back.'

Behind her Vera heard a blood curdling laugh of disbelief. 'You, go? Goin' where? There ain't no places for women like you to go. You stupid bitch. Why'd you think . . . ' there was a pause, 'I'm still 'ere?'

Vera stood in the doorway; there was something in the voice that made her turn around. Her tall figure loomed ominously over the fat floundering woman. Mabel was rambling on still. Once more Vera held her ground, and her tongue. What was her mother telling her? Vera shook her head slowly and thoughtfully. Anger flooded her, she didn't know why. There was something; she felt like a puppet; she felt as if she was being used. Drunk, sober or indifferent, her mother was capable of the most disgusting things. The photo was still held high, but Mabel was unaware of its whereabouts.

Vera said, 'If you've got somethin' to say, then say it. I 'ave a job . . . ' She stopped abruptly, hoping her mother hadn't heard.

'Job?' Mabel echoed. 'Job? You gotta job? What about yer

'ousekeeping, it's Friday. And,' Mabel said slowly and meaningfully, 'Where's yer pig?'

Vera ignored the question and stared back at the bleary eyes. Almost as if nothing had been said Mabel once again waved the small sepia photo. 'Don'tcha know who this is, then?' She laughed derisively at Vera. 'You're such a soppy cow, you wouldn't know yer brother unless he fell on yer.' These words had for Mabel quite obviously a double meaning, Mabel rocked from side to side laughing coarsely until the fit concluded with a throaty roll of phlegm rolling around the back of her throat. Vera snatched the photo from the sausage fingers. She looked deep into it. 'Who is it?' she demanded. 'Who is it?' she asked again. She bent over her mother. 'Who is it?' Vera's voice was hard and angry.

Mabel rolled from side to side. She gave a pursed smile, and through the lips came the words, 'Yer brother.'

Vera threw the photo down on the whale like body. She knew the word 'brother' should have quelled her now rising anxiety but it didn't. Vera's uncertainty showed on her face and Mabel made great sport of the unspoken and a long hollow laugh filled the small room. Her face grew even redder.

Vera stepped away, her hands dug hard and tight into her pockets, and waited.

Mabel's hand found the picture, and swiped it out of the valley which divided her enormous breasts. Her white fleshy arm was raised aloft like Excalibur; her heavy fingers grasped at the photo of titanic information. Sneering, breathing hard, she raised herself and thrust the cream and brown picture into Vera's face. 'Yer brother.' Enjoying the moment, Mabel said, 'You don' know nuthin' about friends, you girls, these days . . . take ol' Timms. Wasn't for 'er, for 'er, I'd be dead, but there again, there's worse.'

At this, Vera straightened up and stepped back. She allowed herself to overcome the revulsion she felt for this animal, letting her gaze fall thoughtfully on its bloated features. Brother? No name had been said. What had Mrs Timms to do with . . . ? Her face clouded into a frown. What'd she meant by 'I'm still 'ere'? Her thoughts freed her to look around the room. No longer would she sleep in it, no longer would she stand on the loose floorboard. The sun was high; it was going to be a hot and stuffy afternoon. She unclenched her fists and allowed her now warm hands to fall naturally to her sides. Mabel groaned, a sound of pain; Vera hoped her arse had gone numb.

The photograph had settled itself on Mabel's quickly rising and falling stomach. Mabel huffed as she retrieved the cream and brown photo from the gaping front of her dirty dress. She pressed it against her sloping pyramid shaped breast and began, ''E weren't bad, not really.' She let out a heavy sigh. Vera watched closely; the truth, she felt, was close.

Mabel wriggled a little. 'Berwick Market, 'ad a veg stall. Mavis 'ad been dead years. Big Ron. That's what they called 'im. Ev'rybody called him Big Ron.' For a moment Vera thought the ugly face looked wistful. 'Fair nigh on killed yer ol' dad.' Mabel looked up suddenly as if she had just remembered Vera. 'That's w'at I mean, you don't know nuffin!' she shouted.

Vera smelt the gin and the foul breath. She watched the curled lips sneering at her, slipping quickly into a leer. She backed away, to the door. Her slight body weight pushed it to, gratefully she leaned against it. She lifted her head and crossed her slim tanned legs, making an effort to give an air of indifference, and to suppress the fear creeping over her. She looked down on her mother, fixing her with an even steady gaze. The drumming in her head was the painful dawning of the nagging doubts which she'd kept in the cobwebs of her mind. They were now being illuminated, each strong thread holding a necklace of beaded answers. All she had to do was listen, and wait.

'Gotta get yer meat and two veg from somewhere. We all of us does it. You.' She pointed a wavering arm at her. 'Rose, even, bet that was only a bit of scrag of lamb.' Mabel gave a belly laugh and slapped the lino. 'And,' she added breathlessly, 'Look what she got. Hah!'

Vera bit her lip; she knew she meant Tom.

Mabel had lost her balance and, still laughing, clapped a heavy hand on her thigh saying, 'Huh, should've gone in for the crochet!' She slapped both her thighs. She steadied herself with one hand and wiped her eyes with the other.

'As for Glad,' she fell into convulsions of strangulated giggles then regained her 'dignity' with a further mouthwash of gin, 'it ain't no wonder . . . ' She didn't finish. Her hand slapped at her chest in an effort to ease the bout of coughing that had overcome her. Finally, she belched loudly. Recovered enough, the photo once again took her attention.

Mabel lingered over the photo. When she lifted her head her face was contorted into a quizzical frown. Her eyes ran up and down Vera's tall lean body. Vera gave a shiver. It was a dirty look. But she didn't move. Mabel flipped the small picture onto the lino like a cigarette card. 'See that?' A grimy finger pointed vaguely in its direction. 'That's why yer 'ere.'

The sallow waxy face had a sudden determined satisfaction about it. Vera didn't move.

"E's 'im,' she flapped a hand. "'e's yer bruvver, yer 'alf brother if it was legal an' that. Yer don't get it . . . ' She slapped her thighs in a hearty manner, part amusement, part evil satisfaction.

Vera shuddered inwardly as Mabel's mouth opened, the saliva dripping over her chin. Her paroxisms of laughing had left the corners of her mouth filled with a creamy froth.

Vera wasn't thinking; she was feeling a high tide of sickness in her. She swallowed, fluttered her eyelids shut for a second. All she could feel was a heavy, hand, forested with thick unyielding black hairy knuckles; a mud-ingrained calloused palm, the fingers climbing steadily along her thigh. She opened her eyes violently, narrowed her gaze intently, daring Mabel not to finish.

Mabel read the challenge and settled her massive bloated body, legs splayed for balance. Another swig, a short knowing sneer, a raised eyebrow, one more throat clearing then with her hands resting on her knees, she began rambling incoherently at the floor. She knew Vera was listening. Mabel could never have believed the sheer feeling of joy in such perverted pleasure. A further slap to her thigh gee'd her into speech. There followed a loud sniff. 'Yer Dad was a doddery ol' bugger, twenty years older 'n me.'

Vera's lean, tanned frame melted into the door. She knew now that what she was going to hear would somehow affect her future. She gave a tight shake of her head. Nothing, now, surely could? She allowed a weary sigh to escape.

Mabel was looking up and out of the window. Vera resisted the urge to fling it open wide and fill her lungs with fresh air. 'No,' she told herself, 'whatever she says stays in this room.' Resolutely, she stared back at her mother, and waited.

Mabel was mumbling loudly, her face mobile and agitated. She cackled as if remembering something long past. The almost forgotten photograph found its way on to her legs. Looking down she said, 'Bit of a twist of a crochet hook, and bob's yer uncle.' A sharp short laugh cut into the silence. 'Well,' she continued, 'more yer bruvver.' Another slap sounded on her leg. 'Ol' Timms must've lost 'er magic that day; gin and 'ot baths didn't work neither. Bleedin' 'ard to get rid of, even 'arder bein' born. A bastard all round, like. Wouldn't yer say?'

Vera shuddered. The sickness was rising once more. Behind her back Vera's finger nails dug into her palms.

'Blimey, Vera, I think you've gorn white under that sunburn of yur'n, you looks sort of dusty like.' There was no hint of concern, just self amusement. 'Sensitive then, are we? Goin', leaving; never 'eard the like, still, you always was the one for them flights of fancy. Where's that bastard of yourn, then?' Mabel looked around. 'Out there, I shouldn't wonder, with that bleedin' Doris girl.'

Vera was standing very still; it took all her strength of mind not to turn around and run. She stifled an involuntary groan and clenched her teeth.

Mabel shifted noisily, puffing with the exertion. 'Still don't know if yer Dad knew.' She poked a finger at the picture. 'Can't tell wiv men, can yer? No point in askin' you, Yanks don't count.' She roared with laughter.

Vera's eyes opened wide. She didn't know. She's never known. Vera allowed herself a quick smile of satisfaction. She would never know.

Mabel turned violently on Vera, leaning towards her. She was jabbing a finger, saying, 'Yer father would've turned in 'is grave. Just as well 'e's dead,' she added wildly. 'Think on, 'e would've turfed you out wiv all yer goin's on.' Their eyes met briefly. Vera wanted to kill her.

Then, just as suddenly Mabel picked up the photo as if nothing had happened, or even passed between them. Shaking her head, Mabel said, 'Stayed wiv ol' Timms till this bastard was born. She'd moved over 'ere by then, one of the first she was on this estate. Nobody asked questions then. 'E never knew me. That's what I means about friends; ol' Timms never told. Never said she was 'is Mum neither. 'E called 'er Timms too. Big Ronnie kept 'is trap shut too. 'Ad to really, s'pose,' she said with a touch of reflection. 'When "Big Ron" died Ronnie took over the fruit and veg round. ''E'd been 'elping out as a kid for years. No one took no notice when he closed down the stall and took to this delivery lark.' She laughed hoarsely. 'So, that's why yer 'ere.'

She looked up at Vera. Vera remained motionless. She couldn't believe what was running through her mind. Mabel didn't wait for a reply.

She ran on, 'What I means,' she laboured the point, 'is that, well, the ol' bugger got it up one night.' She laughed, both hands punctuating the moment with a resounding slap to her legs. 'Poor ol' sod,' she said without looking up. She rested her hulk evenly against the wardrobe. She shot Vera a sideways glance, one eyebrow raised questioningly. 'See?'

Vera could no longer contain her feelings of revulsion. In a single stride she was looming over Mabel. Shaking with violence in mind,

Vera steadied herself, her hands on her hips. 'Dyin's too good for you, too quick. When you die I 'ope you die in agony, alone.'

A slow grin began to spread across Mabel's face.

'You're evil, a hypocrite. You've used us all for years. Poor Mrs Surridge,' Vera said, nodding her head aggressively. 'Poor Mrs Surridge, lost 'er two sons, a widow... sad,' Vera mocked beginning to enjoy herself. 'Is that what you think people say?' She wagged her head. 'You'd be surpri...' She didn't finish. 'No, you wouldn't be surprised to find out what people say about you behind your back. Big Mabel? There ain't nothin' big about you. You stink!' Mabel began to slide down the wardrobe. Vera reached out and grabbed her by the chin. 'You're nothing but a violent old cow.' With each word she banged her head on the wardrobe. Her swollen features bounced like a deflating football. Vera's eyes narrowed; intent on revenge, she grabbed her by the ears and crashed her skull even more violently against the wood. The sound rolled emptily around in the wardrobe. Mabel let out a gasp. Vera let go and watched with morbid satisfaction as her mother slumped sideways. Vera leaned across her, picked up the bottle and emptied the remainder of its contents over Mabel's head. She watched a few drips fall from the red bulbous nose.

'Now,' she declared, 'You're well and truly pickled inside and out. Not much left for the embalmers.' She lobbed the bottle onto the bed and smoothed her hands slowly together.

'We're leavin', that's goin' away forever. I broke me pig, and if you can find any money on the floor, you can bloody well 'ave it; you've 'ad everythin' else off us.' As she reached the door, she turned slowly, looking at the silent bulk, and said, 'I 'ope you rot in hell!' The words came slowly from deep within her, words she believed she would never be able to say out loud. She closed the door gently behind her and stepped purposefully down the stairs, lingering on 'the fourth from the top' for the pleasure of hearing it creak for the very last time.

Standing on the last stair, Vera reached out and snatched the key from the nail. Standing on the bottom step before pulling the door closed, she hurled the key into the barricade of privets. Behind her the door closed.

Sylvia stood pale and nervous, looking up at her mother's granite-hard fixed expression. She had ducked quite unnecessarily, moving more from surprise than fear, to avoid the key.

Finding Vera's hand, Sylvia pulled at it. 'Mum.' Her tone was soft but urgent. 'Mum,' she said again, then even more urgently she said, 'Mum!'

Vera looked down. 'Sorry,' was all she managed, as she removed her hand.

'But Mum,' Sylvia persisted as Vera dug into the privets for the canvas bag.

'But Mum, look!' Her voice was soft, her meaning urgent. This was something Vera hadn't wanted. She just wanted to leave and leave now. Still in the privets she heard, "Ullo, Vera, you goin' to the park?'

Vera straightened up, recognising the voice instantly. 'Iris,' she said as if she had just remembered her name.

Iris grinned at Vera over the privets. Vera noticed the red tones of her beech coloured hair dancing as she hopped up and down the kerb of the narrow road. She was nearly at the corner and shouting to the boys still on the green, offering to play goalie. Vera felt herself beginning to shake. Her stomach turned as well. She extricated the bag and dumped it on the bottom step. She felt her eyelids slowly closing, or was that familiar darkness going to prevent her from going ahead with her plan? There was a numbness around her, as though she was in isolation. Her heart started suddenly to pound. She turned to Sylvia and without an explanation, ordered the child to sit and wait on the step. Immediately, Sylvia obeyed.

Vera shouted over the privets, 'Iris!'

Iris turned about, changed feet and bobbed back.

Vera studied the fresh face. 'What did you want, Iris?' Her voice was calm, her face smiling.

Iris looked sideways, thinking hard. Vera sidled to the gate, waiting. When Vera heard her say, 'Auntie Chrissie said . . . ' Vera felt her heart sink. She was now listening ashen faced and tight lipped.

Iris continued in her childish sing-song voice, 'Auntie Chrissie says that I'm goin' to 'ave a baby, just like you. And she said that I 'ad to come and tell you 'cos you know what to do.'

Vera watched dumbly as the radiant face glowed happily at her. Iris said, 'Auntie Chrissie says that if I stays, then I'll get took away.' She looked at Vera for an explanation. Vera offered none.

Iris suddenly disappeared from over the privets. Vera opened the gate and saw that Iris was sitting on the kerb, digging out an ant hill that had homed in a clump of weeds between the paving slabs.

Vera sat down beside her. Iris grinned.

Vera asked gently, 'What else did Chris say?'

Iris shrugged. 'She cried, but you do that when you're 'appy, that's right, ain't it?'

Vera smiled, accompanied with a slow nod. This, she told herself, was the 'something at the back of her mind'. Well, it wasn't there now. She roused herself to face the situation. Before she could ask any more Iris said, 'Auntie Chrissie said that I 'ad to tell you 'cos you'd know what to do. What's it like 'aving a baby, Auntie Chrissie won't say,' she said brightly.

Vera found herself sighing heavily. 'Hard work, hard work,' she said, putting an arm around Iris's shoulders.

'Oh go on, Vera, that's what you always says,' and Iris gave her a playful shove.

Vera knew that Chris was right. Iris would be removed, taken away from her, put in an institution. The baby would be taken away for adoption. Vera shook her head sadly. She knew of only one sound sure alternative. 'How would you like to go to the seaside?' The question was simple.

Iris nodded enthusiastically, 'What, now?'

Vera nodded slowly. Iris's enthusiasm was beginning to rub off on Vera. 'Yes,' Vera said positively, 'today.' Then leaning towards her, she added, 'But you musn't tell anybody.'

How Iris loved a secret. She raised a finger to her lips, saying, 'Cross me 'eart an' 'ope to die.'

Vera eased herself to her feet. She stepped back onto the pavement. Her vision was drawn to a large brown paper wrapped parcel. 'This yours, Iris?' Vera asked, a little puzzled. There were a number of smaller items identically wrapped.

'Yeah!' Iris said, leaping to her feet almost in defence of the parcels. 'Auntie Chrissie said I should take things I want, so I done just that.' She scooped the larger brown parcel into her arms and ripped away the brown paper wrapping. 'See,' Iris said, looking at Vera.

Vera's large blue eyes misted. There in front of her was the large glass case housing a very dead and stuffed owl.

Iris's eyes gleam with anticipation. ''E's dead,' she added helpfully. 'Don't need no feedin'.'

Vera opened the gate, took Sylvia's hand and gently raised her to her feet. Her eyes were misted too. Vera watched a large pear-shaped teardrop roll down her daughter's cheek. 'It's all right, everythin' will be fine. I promise.'

'Is Iris comin' with us?' Sylvia's voice was slight.

Vera nodded.

The weight that once hung around Vera's shoulders draped across her back. Her worst fears were founded. She opened the gate wide and dragged through the canvas holdall.

Iris was looking at her. 'We all goin' together then?'

Vera ushered Iris along the narrow pavement until they reached the corner. With her feathered companion clutched in her arms, she resumed her game of kerb hopscotch.

'Not now, Iris. We've got a train to catch. You'll get tired.'

Iris stopped. Her gleaming beech curls ceased bouncing as she turned silently around the corner, ready to climb the hill. Reaching the top, Vera had the canvas bag in one hand, Sylvia clutching tightly at the other; Iris stood, arms wrapped around the now naked owl.

'This one?' Iris asked excitedly.

'No,' Vera replied simply, 'the one behind.'

The red bus came to a halt. They climbed onto the platform. Vera put the tan holdall into the compartment under the stairs.

'What's this then, girls?' the bus conductor asked. 'On yer 'olidays? A bit late, if I might say so, ladies.'

They stayed silent, finding a seat. The conductor looked on; his hand knocked back his cap from his forehead. 'What'll be then? Three for the *Skylark*?'

Vera took a half crown from her purse. 'Two and a half to Bromley South.'

'Right you are.'

Vera heard the machine give a muffled ding. She took the tickets and stuffed them into her pocket.

As the bus lurched forward, behind them on the red doorstep a pair of eyes were peering through the letterbox. Fingers wriggled in a vain attempt to find the key. The short stocky frame stepped off the cardinal red step. His greying sandy head of hair stood firm against the breeze.

'C'mon, Mabel,' he shouted at the house. 'C'mon, open the door. I got a nice little bit of fish for you.'

'Mabel!' his cry echoed around the empty green.

At the foot of the bed lay Mabel, her eyes open and fixed, her mouth still and parted. The red and swollen tongue hung from the corner; its tip touched the floor.

'Mabel!' Tom's voice echoed once more.

Chugging up the hill, beside Vera, Iris pulled from under the seat the encased owl and began to sing:

> 'A wise old owl lived in an oak,
> The more he saw the less he spoke;
> The less he spoke,
> The more he heard.
> Why can't we be like that wise old bird?'